HUNGRY PLANTS

These seeds were unlike any she'd ever worked with. They were light, with a leaf-like wing attached to the seed pod. The shape reminded her of a maple seed, but the color was as white as death. Despite the hard pods protecting the seeds, the new plants inside seemed to sense her magic. She didn't even have to focus on the seeds before they germinated. Each new plant drew upon its pod and wing so fiercely for nourishment they crumbled to dust. These plants were hungry, hungry as animals, and just as willing to seek out their food.

Jenna didn't like that at all.

There's something not right about these plants. I shouldn't encourage them to grow....

"Hold, two of them!" a man shouted. "Two of the harpies who attacked the most talented, most wondrous Sal-thaath!"

Further shouts answered him. Jenna didn't speak Selathen, but she did know their word for "Avatar," and that was the only word she could pick out. They had to be talking about her and Kay. Even if they were here for Ysabel, they wouldn't mind giving Jenna and Kay to Sal-thaath, the boy who'd attacked Gwen, as well. Jenna had no other plants she could use as weapons, and she couldn't count on Kay to defend them. It was up to her and the strange plants to stop the Selathens.

Chaos Season

Book Three of the Season Avatars

Sandra Ulbrich Almazan

Solar Unicorn Publishing

Sandra Ulbrich Almazan/Solar Unicorn Publishing
www.sandraulbrichalmazan.com

Publisher's Note: This is a work of fiction. Names, characters, places, and incidents are a product of the author's imagination. Any resemblance to actual people, living or dead, or to businesses, companies, events, institutions, or locales is completely coincidental.

Book Layout © 2014 BookDesignTemplates.com

Chaos Season/Sandra Ulbrich Almazan—1st edition
ISBN 978-1-944437-00-8

Dedication

This book is dedicated to the men and women of the Midwest Garrison, part of the 501st Legion. To learn more about our mission and our charity work, please visit www.midwestgarrison.com.

Table of Contents

Grandmother of Stories

Grandmother of Stories, Goddess of the Island People, called Her Avatars together. From the youngest child to the oldest matriarch, they sat cross-legged in front of Her, ears and minds trained to catch and hold every syllable She uttered. They would need them. As more and more mortals developed faster and easier ways to travel, they would come across the Hidden Archipelago where the Island People lived. If the Island People were to remain Her people, they would need knowledge of what they faced, both at home and abroad.

Fortunately, as a Goddess, She could see across space and time to find the patterns which would one day affect the Island People.

"Far across the Salt Water," She began, "is a land much bigger than the Hidden Archipelago. One side is full of life, while nothing lives in the other half. Are you wondering how this came to be? Ages ago, before Gods and Goddesses controlled magic, two powerful magicians lived there. One, an artifact-maker named Kron Evenhanded, wanted to live in peace with ordinary people, while the other, Salth, saw humans as a source of more magic she could collect.

"As part of her studies, Salth conceived a son using pure magic. This child, named Sal-thaath, encountered Kron, and the two of them entered into an unlikely friendship. But Sal-thaath, like his mother, disdained people, and no one, not even Kron, could convince him otherwise. Finally, in an attempt to discipline Sal-thaath, Kron created an artifact to take away the boy's magic. This, however, proved deadly for

the child. The grieving mother found a way to give Sal-thaath life again, but only by draining it from other creatures.

"In the meantime, Kron wooed and won a lovely young woman named Bella, who was kind to everyone and everything, especially animals. This brought her to the attention of a new goddess named Fall."

"Where did the goddess come from?" a child asked.

As his parents shushed him, the Grandmother of Stories smiled. She had Ascended at the same time as all the other deities, but like Them, She wouldn't reveal Her origin to Her worshippers.

"Fall, of course, is one of the Four Gods and Goddesses of Challen," She said. "In Their country, unlike ours, the weather changes with the time of year. They call these changes 'seasons,' and the Four Gods and Goddesses each named Themselves after a season and claimed a unique domain for Their magic. Spring heals people, Summer takes care of plants, Fall tends to animals, and Winter controls both weather and death. Each of them chose three Avatars to serve Them life after life. Together, They planned to give Their worshippers a fertile and prosperous country.

"Unfortunately, Salth had other plans. She still sought revenge on Kron—and now, his new wife—for killing her son. However, Kron's wife was protected by her Goddess. So Salth, who had mastered some of the magic of Time, crafted an evil spell called a Chaos Season. She twisted all the seasons together so that they would occur at the wrong times, then she sent this spell from her Dead Land into Challen, hoping to use the lives she took for her son's survival.

"The Avatars cleaned up the damage Salth's Chaos Season caused, then, despite Kron's warnings, decided to challenge Salth in her own country. They believed their numbers would be enough to overcome an experienced magician, but they were wrong. To save them, Kron created a portal to send them back to their own country, then offered himself to Salth. Before she could drain his magic, he trapped her son in a giant pot with him. Together, Kron and the undead Sal-thaath traveled forward in time about eight hundred years, to the present day."

Grandmother paused for effect and studied Her audience. Most of them were rapt under the spell of Her words, but a few—She marked these—seemed to be thinking about what She had told them. A youth stood, bowed before Her, and signaled a request to speak. She nodded Her head at him.

"Grandmother," he said respectfully, "what do these faraway gods and magicians have to do with our Hidden Archipelago?"

"You may find out soon enough," She replied. "Kron has been searching for his bride, who died many years ago but was reborn into another life as a Fall Avatar named Ysabel. Sal-thaath found Ysabel first, but Kron and three other Avatars named Gwen, Jenna, and Kay rescued her. Now they must decide if they will attempt to attack Salth and Sal-thaath again and end Chaos Season for good. Oh yes, My children, that magic still rages. It must be stopped before any of you can travel to the Dead Land and bring My stories with you."

Grandmother gestured at a pool of water. "The Avatars work closely together in groups of four, one from each season. Gwen, Jenna, Ysabel, and Kay are the youngest group, but their quartet is the only one still intact. Watch now, and we will see if they can tame a Chaos Season on their own. If they fail, their country perishes with them."

CHAPTER ONE

A Flight of Seeds

Jenna Dorshay t'Reve, the next Ava Summer, pressed her arms against her milk-soaked dress and wondered when she would be able to nurse her son. When they'd set off to rescue Ysabel, the next Ava Fall, from the Selathens, she hadn't expected to travel so far so quickly. Now she was stuck in a hole in the ground—literally—while some ancient Avatar mooned over Ysabel. While it was romantic that they be reunited after so many lives apart, she'd prefer it if they courted someplace more civilized.

"Kron! Kron Evenhanded!" The dirt seemed to absorb her voice. Maybe that was why she had to call the artificer's name a few more times before he looked at her. "By All Four Gods and Goddesses, how do we get back to Tradetown? And how long will it take? I don't want Robbie to be weaned before I return."

Beside her, Gwen, the next Ava Spring, grimaced. Jenna didn't have to be linked with her to know what she was thinking. Some strange boy with unknown magic had forced Gwen to stretch her healing magic to its limits. She needed a banquet's worth of food to restore herself. But despite her weariness, she was probably shocked Jenna would mention she was nursing a child in mixed company. *Let her be shocked. Just don't let her remember what happened in our last life together.*

Ysabel drew away from Kron, who turned toward Jenna and gave her a dark look. She hoped he wasn't going to make her dress fall apart in revenge.

"I can portal us back to Ysabel's house," he said. "But not from here. I've never created a portal belowground, and I don't want to risk Ysabel's safety now that I've found her again."

Jenna wondered if he was willing to risk their own safety instead. If he knew as much about the Season Avatars as he claimed, he should know they always worked as a quartet. She and Gwen had traveled from one end of Challen to the other searching for Ysabel and Kay. Now that all of the Avatars from the same year were reunited, they couldn't risk being separated. If something happened to one of them, Challen would be defenseless against Chaos Season for a generation.

"Then what are we waiting for, the summer solstice?"

Gwen spoke so quietly Jenna had to lean over to hear her. "The men…"

"What men?" Jenna asked.

"Three of them were waiting for us when we arrived," Kron said.

Jenna shrugged. "All I saw were bones."

Gwen and Kron looked at each other in concern. Finally, he said, "Let me go up first and make sure it's safe. I can come down and assist you if necessary."

Ysabel glanced at the black-and-white cat that had accompanied them on their mission to rescue her. It had to be her anilink, the special animal that helped Fall Avatars work their animal magic. Anilinks were smart enough to communicate with their Avatars. The cat bounded to the ladder and climbed up, leaving scratches in the wood. A few heartbeats later, Ysabel said, "No one's around, thank the Four."

Jenna bit back her envy. Fall Avatars got anilinks that could go with them anywhere, but Summer Avatars had to force-grow an acorn into an oak tree. The tree would help her connect with the vegetation of Challen, but it kept her rooted to the One Oak, the Avatars' home, most of the time. This trip would be the last time she would be free to travel throughout Challen. She wished she could prolong it, even if she knew she had to be responsible and protect Challen from Chaos Season. When the seasons got so mixed up they all happened at once, only the Season Avatars could straighten them out and make sure no one got hurt or starved.

Since Ysabel was closest to the ladder, she followed her cat. A mourning pendant on a necklace bobbed as she climbed. Kron held the ladder for her. He didn't look like he was trying to peep under her skirts, but Jenna would have bet he wanted to. Supposedly he and Ysabel had been married before, in Ysabel's first life as an Avatar. But while she and the other Avatars had died and been reborn multiple times, Kron had remained alive, traveling forward in time inside an ancient water clock. He had to be eager to resume their relationship, even if Ysabel didn't remember it.

Once Ysabel was no longer visible, Kron scrambled up after her. He should have let them all go first to be polite, but Jenna assumed he couldn't stand to let Ysabel out of his sight. Kay glanced back at Jenna and Gwen. "Is he always like this?" she whispered. "Is he going to stay with us?"

"That's up to Ysabel," Gwen said. "Maybe I was wrong about him planting pottery shards to hurt us, but I hope he doesn't think he's in charge of our quartet." Determination shone in her blue eyes, contrasting with the paleness of her complexion. "That's my job."

"But he's had contact with the Four Gods and Goddesses, more than we've had in lifetimes." Kay drooped. "Maybe I don't deserve to hear directly from Them after neglecting my magic for so long."

"The important thing is that you use it now," Gwen said. "But I don't think any of us will be doing anything until we eat and rest. By All Four, I never encountered such ugly magic before, especially in a child." She shuddered. "And I hope I never do again."

"Then we should go before he returns." Without further words, Kay climbed the ladder. She was so small and thin the ladder didn't quiver under her weight.

Once they were alone, Jenna asked, "Can you climb the ladder, Gwen? You used most of your energy in that battle."

Gwen's dress hung loose on her, a sign she'd had to consume her own reserves to continually heal herself. The boy who'd attempted to take the pottery shard out of her skin hadn't seemed drained after using so much magic. Even once Jenna had dared link with Gwen and feed her strength, the balance of power had been in the boy's favor. How had such a powerful magician come to Challen? Had he really been inside a water clock with Kron and come forward hundreds of years in time? More importantly, where had he gone, and would he return?

Gwen put on a hopeful. "As long as there's food on the other side, I'll walk through a dozen of Kron's portals."

"Walking is easier than climbing. Do you need my help?"

With an odd glance, Gwen replied, "I would appreciate it."

Jenna gripped Gwen's upper arms and assisted her to her feet. The elbow-length sleeves prevented them from making skin-to-skin contact and establishing the link. Gwen arched her eyebrows as if she suspected something. She didn't remember their last life together, did she? She wouldn't lean on Jenna so trustingly if she did.

Jenna had to keep it that way, link or no link.

They shuffled over to the ladder. Jenna held it steady while Gwen ascended. Her skirt smelled like mud from their journey here, along with blood and rotten flesh from the battle with Sal-thaath. It would be good to return someplace where they could all bathe. Gwen definitely needed to eat first, though.

Once Gwen was off the ladder, Jenna climbed up herself. Fresh air greeted her as she poked her head out of the ground. That was the most hospitable part of their surroundings. The only plant life was some yellowish-green moss that did a poor job of keeping the soil in place. No birds called in the air, no insects crawled over the moss or flew in Jenna's ears. Even the bones she'd seen earlier had disappeared. She wasn't sure if they were still in Challen or had actually crossed over into Selath, the Dead Land. Either way, there was more plant life in the middle of Wistica, the capital city of Challen. Anywhere else in Challen would feel more lively than this place. She hoped Kron would get them out of here quickly. But all he did was pace around and stare at the dirt.

"What's he doing?" she asked.

"Looking for materials to make a doorway," Ysabel replied. "He needs something physical to anchor his magic to, he says."

"We might be here a while, then." Maybe Jenna should start carrying seeds with her, so she could force-grow them at need. But even she would be hard pressed to grow anything in this barren land.

Gwen swayed in place. "By All Four, I could sleep for a year."

"You can't do that, Gwen. We need you." Jenna suppressed a yawn. Weariness crept up her body.

Kay circled back to them. "I feel her, don't you?"

"Feel who?" Jenna asked when Gwen didn't respond.

"HER. The one who invades my dreams."

"Salth." The one who had given her name to Selath, the Dead Land. The magician who was an ancient enemy of Kron and the mother of the child who'd attacked them. Maybe she was trying to siphon off their magic even now. Each of Jenna's limbs felt as heavy as a draft horse. Was this fatigue catching up with her, or something worse?

"Gwen?" She nudged her. "Can you stand straight?"

With a groan, Gwen collapsed.

"Gwen? Gwen!" Jenna shook her. When she didn't respond, Jenna muttered, "Freeze it," and placed her hand on Gwen's cheek. If Gwen was unconscious, she wouldn't be able to read Jenna's memories, but hopefully she could still draw strength from her. The link didn't form.

"Kron! Jenna yelled. "Salth is drawing magic from us! Get us out of this frozen place before we lose Gwen!"

"I need something to make a portal—wait. What a fool I am!" He ran back toward the entrance to the hole, muttering in a language Jenna didn't recognize. She hadn't known words could change that much over hundreds of years.

Ysabel came over to them. Her dress was more modest and less fitted than a farm girl's, and a scarf covered her hair. Her dark brown eyes contained flecks of gold and green, as if Fall Herself had scattered leaf bits in them. "Would it help if we shared this?" She held out one of the silver watches Kron had altered so it no longer told time. "Kron told me this was an artifact that could protect me from the time magicians."

"Let's wrap Gwen's hand around it and see if she wakes."

Jenna kept one hand on Gwen's cheek while pressing Gwen's good hand—the one without the embedded shard—around the amulet. "Fight it, Gwen," she said. "We've come too far to let that strange boy win now."

Kron returned with the ladder and touched each short piece, making them fall out. He set them aside while he planted the long ends in the earth. Next, he joined several short ends together by lining them up and pressing them together. Jenna could use her magic on dead wood, but not as effectively as Kron. Hopefully it wouldn't take much longer for him to finish the portal so they could leave.

A shiver passed through Jenna as the wind rose. She clutched her brand-new hat with one hand while maintaining her grip on Gwen. Something tapped her hand. She glanced upward. A handful of seeds with ash-white sails fluttered out of her reach. By the Four, where had they come from? More importantly, what were they? She didn't recognize them. The seeds were smaller than her fingernail, but the white coating struck her as ominous.

"Kay, can you change the wind and bring those seeds back?" She asked. "I'd like a sample."

Kay gulped, turning even paler than normal for her. "Use weather magic this close to Salth! She'll kill me for sure."

"She can't age you while you wear Kron's artifact."

"That's not how I die in my dreams."

The wind taunted Jenna by picking up, blowing the seeds toward Challen. She really ought to chase after them and capture at least one for study....

Gwen groaned. Jenna returned her attention to her, stroking her cheek. "Come on, Gwen, wake up. We'll be out of here in a few heart-beats. Kron's almost done with the portal. We just have to pass through, and then you can eat and rest."

With a gesture, Kron sent a crossbar up against the two ladder posts to form a doorway. He touched it in several places, and the scenery be-yond shifted to Ysabel's mother's dining room. It seemed so long since they had been there Jenna needed a moment to realize they'd been there for lunch earlier that day.

Ysabel's mother and Gwen's aunt sat silently in front of an empty table as they stared at the door. Off to the side, next to the lit fireplace, stood Callie, Robbie's nursemaid, holding Jenna's child. He smiled sleepily, as if he knew his mother was coming for him. Jenna hadn't expected them to meet her at Ysabel's house instead of the hotel, but by the Four, she couldn't wait to take her son herself.

"Mama? Home?" Ysabel whispered. "Are they real, or a cruel joke by that frozen boy?"

"They're real, Dearest." Kron beamed at her. "All you have to do is cross through the portal to go home."

"Portal?"

His smile slipped. "Don't you remember how I used to portal us everywhere we needed to go?"

She shook her head, still staring longingly at the domestic scene. Jenna had to admit the barren scenery surrounding them made the portal seem like an illusion.

"It's real," she told Ysabel. "We used Kron's portal earlier to get to the Chikasi River."

Ysabel tiptoed closer, prodded the portal with a finger, and then hur-ried through, followed by her anilink. The older women waiting on the other side gasped as she appeared. Ysabel's mother recovered first, leaping up to embrace her daughter. Gwen's aunt flushed and fanned herself.

By All Four, I hope it's not her heart. Gwen will never forgive her-self if her Aunt Gabri goes to the God of Winter, even if Gwen's too weak right now to heal a broken toe nail.

A maid entered the dining room through another door, bearing a pot of hot chocolate. The rich scent wafted through the portal. Gwen blinked her eyes. "Chocolate?" she whispered.

"Yes. Lots of food and lovely chocolate, just a few steps away. Can you manage it?"

Gwen struggled to her feet, leaning on Jenna.

Kay came over, hesitated, and asked, "Do you need my help?"

Jenna shook her head. Kay was the shortest of the four and used to the next-to-nothing weight of a needle and thread. Jenna had helped her family stack hay and stocked the shelves of her late husband's store. She could manage Gwen on her own.

As Kay passed through the portal, Kron came forward. "Here, let me help you."

Jenna clutched Gwen tighter. "She's my responsibility as a sister Avatar."

"That doesn't mean you have to do it all by yourself. Come on—"

"Yes, Gwen, come on, take a step."

Even at Jenna's urgings, Gwen refused to move. Kron grasped her by the other arm, and together he and Jenna maneuvered her through the portal by stepping sideways. Jenna had to admit it was easier with his help.

The surroundings changed instantly as Jenna stepped through the portal. A chilly breeze vanished. The moss under her feet gave way to a thick rug. Most importantly, whatever force that had been trying to steal her magic disappeared. It felt as though she and Gwen each lost at least ten pounds.

"By All Four Gods and Goddesses!" Lady lo Havil pressed her hand to her bosom. "What's wrong with my niece?"

"She's exhausted, Lady lo Havil." Jenna steered Gwen to the closest chair. "She used her healing magic in ways I didn't think possible.

Dame s'Ivena Lathatiltin—" that was Ysabel's mother—"Could you please send for more food? We'll all need to eat again."

First, however, Jenna had to provide a meal for her son. Her dress was damp with leaking milk. Robbie whimpered as she pried him away from Callie.

"I can handle him, Ava," the wet nurse protested. "You should rest and eat too. You look like you've been out in Chaos Season too long."

"I'm supposed to be out in a Chaos Season. Who else will heal the plants?" Jenna looked for a dark corner to hide in. It would be scandalous for her to nurse her child in the middle of a crowded room, especially with a male present, but she couldn't wait any longer. Maybe if she ducked behind the damask curtain, no one would notice what she was doing.

Jenna stirred up dust as she slipped between the curtain and the wall. She pulled away from the window so she wouldn't display herself to anyone outside, but she peered around the thick curtain to see if anyone noticed her. Robbie latched on to her as soon as she positioned him properly. At the same time, Ysabel cried out in a frightened voice, "Father's coming home!"

CHAPTER TWO

Deathbushes Sprout

"Your father?" Ysabel's mother asked. "How dare he show his face here after handing you over to Salth's son? Maybe I'm not a Fallswoman anymore, but Fall will hound him to death for that!"

Literally, perhaps. The Goddess of Fall had no love for men and had never incarnated one of Her Avatars as male. In Challen, men who harmed women risked being attacked by the closest animals.

"Hopefully not while he's still on his mare," Ysabel said. "Father might lash her. She's coming up to the stable where he boards her. He'll be here in half an hour."

At least they had some time to prepare. Robbie continued to suckle, pulling harder. Jenna shifted him to the other side while thinking what they should do.

"My father knows I escaped from Salth and her son." Ysabel crossed her arms as if she was holding herself. "He's talking with some of his fellow Salth-lovers right now. I can hear them through his mare." She gasped. "By All Four! If he doesn't give an Avatar to Salth by the end of summer, she'll claim him instead!"

"Nonsense," Kron said. "She doesn't have that much power in Challen. The Four limit what she can do."

"Not according to my father. He says she controls Chaos Season."

Kron frowned. "That's true, but you control that. I mean, you and the other Avatars can take her magic and prevent it from permanently harming Challen."

Gwen lifted her head as a maid handed her a cup of chocolate, so hot and rich Jenna could smell it from where she stood. "Then, Ysabel, you have to come with us," Gwen said. "We can protect you."

"Then who's going to protect my family, if I'm not here?"

"What are you planning to do, summon more cats to guard them? Will they be able to protect you from your father too? Remember, if something happens to you, our quartet is useless."

Jenna shifted so Robbie was hidden behind the curtain, then poked her head out. "There's only one thing you can do. Stop your father from being a threat."

Gwen gave her a curious look, but then nodded. "We have to turn him in to the local Watch."

"Turn him in?" Ysabel glanced back at the house. "But...he's my father. Even if he wants to give me to his false goddess, I can't betray him. And none of the Watch in Tradetown would take the side of an unmarried woman against her father."

Gwen drained her cup. "First we should protect you and the rest of your family. Even the servants, if he's the type to take his anger out on them." She turned to Ysabel's mother. "Is there a secure room where your household can hide from him?"

She scowled. "He has keys for every frozen room. Even if we had a safe place from him, how long would we have to stay in there? That's not enough, young Avas. I've done all that Fall asked me to. I married a man I didn't want, I bore him children, I preached about the Four in secret and spied on my husband when he dealt with Salth-lovers." She sighed, suddenly looking old. "I've had enough, Avas. I want to go home to Wistica and play pianoforte again. I may be out-of-practice for concerts, but I can still teach and write music."

Robbie finished nursing, a sure sign the talk had gone on too long. Jenna fumbled with the impossibly tiny buttons on her dress. "Dame s'Ivena—" she deliberately left off the Selathen surname– "Please decide your future later. We should escape now."

"I could portal us straight to the Temple," Kron offered. "Or the Avatar's house in Wistica. I know both of those locations well enough."

Ysabel's anilink streaked around the corner and leapt straight up into its mistress's arms. She caught him, then looked up, her eyes even bigger than before.

"A squad of Salth worshippers is coming down the street," she said. "My father is leading them."

Ysabel's mother sucked in her breath. "We need time to gather the household and pack some chals and a few essentials. Then you may make any of my doors into a portal to the Temple, Sir Evenhanded. I'll plead our cause to Fall Herself."

"We need a distraction," Gwen said quietly.

Jenna glanced at Kay. "Let us handle that."

Kay's eyes grew larger. "Us?"

"You can do it, Kay," Gwen said. "You have memories using your magic. All you need is practice."

Kay swallowed hard but nodded in agreement. Jenna hoped she could rely on the reluctant Winter Avatar. "Could someone hold Robbie for me?"

"You have a baby? How wonderful!" Ysabel beamed. "I'll hold him. Pouncer, get on my shoulder."

"He's very young." Jenna still hated letting his nursemaid take care of him, let alone someone she'd just met. But Ysabel looked so eager she couldn't refuse. Once Jenna eased her child into her arms, Ysabel cradled him, supporting his head with the confidence of someone who had helped raise her younger siblings like Jenna had. Kron's expression became pained as he watched her murmur to Robbie.

"Ysabel, I need you to help me with our own family," her mother said as she left the room. Ysabel trailed her, followed by Callie.

"Jenna, Kay, do you need me to link with you?" Gwen asked. She'd regained some color in her face, but she still looked drained.

Jenna shook her head. "Just rest." She suppressed the urge to stroke Gwen's soft cheek. She'd lost such privileges after her last life.

Maybe by protecting her, I can make up for my crime. Kay's weather magic was more powerful than Jenna's talent with plants, but as long as there was a single blade of grass or seed available, she'd do what she could to protect her sister Avatar.

Resolved, Jenna led Kay down the stairs and out the front door. A strip of lawn no wider than a carriage separated the house from the street, and a pair of shrubs cut into spiral shapes guarded the entrance. However, Jenna sensed strange seeds in the grass, seeds that had potential to grow into plants very quickly under the right conditions. The soil wasn't as rich here as in the rest of Challen, but Jenna could temporarily feed the seeds with the grass. She could fix the lawn later, once Ysabel and her family were safe.

"Kay, can you bring the rain back?" she asked.

"Are you sure it's safe?"

"You mean, is Salth going to sense your magic? She can't attack us here in Challen, remember? I'll need both rain and sun if I'm going to force-grow some seeds."

Kay frowned, gesturing as if she needed to pull clouds to her. The sky darkened. A downpour drenched Jenna before Kay thinned the rain to a drizzle and allowed sunlight to return.

Jenna strode forward until she stood in the center of the lawn. Back on the farm, she used to pull off her boots so she could feel the earth with her feet. Noblewomen, however, wore boots with lots of little buttons that took forever to undo. Jenna had to squat and press her palms into the lawn to connect with the seeds.

These seeds were unlike any she'd ever worked with. They were light, with a leaf-like wing attached to the seed pod. The shape reminded her of a maple seed, but the color was as white as death. Maybe they were the seeds she'd seen earlier. How did they get here so quickly? Despite the hard seed pods protecting the seeds, the new plants inside seemed to sense her magic. She didn't even have to focus on the seeds before they germinated. Each new plant drew upon its seed pod and wing so fiercely for nourishment they they crumbled to dust. These plants were hungry, hungry as animals, and just as willing to seek out their food.

Jenna didn't like that at all.

There's something not right about these plants. I shouldn't encourage them to grow….

"Hold, two of them!" a man shouted. "Two of the harpies who attacked the most talented, most wondrous Sal-thaath!"

Further shouts answered him. Jenna didn't speak Selathen, but she did know their word for "Avatar," and that was the only word she could pick out. They had to be talking about her and Kay. Even if they were here for Ysabel, they wouldn't mind giving Jenna and Kay to Salthaath, the boy who'd attacked Gwen, as well. Jenna had no other plants she could use as weapons, and she couldn't count on Kay to defend them. It was up to her and the strange plants to stop the Selathens.

Summer, help me, I beg you. Help me make these plants grow faster than weeds.

Each sprout sank a tiny root into the dirt and stretched down deep. At the same time, the seed leaves opened, drinking in faint sunlight shining through the drizzle. The roots spread out and grabbed other plants next to them. The grass turned yellow and brittle, but the new plants shot up tall and thick, sending out heart-shaped leaves—and fine needle-like barbs covering their stalks. Jenna retreated before her own defenses attacked her. But the deathbush—the best name she could give this strange plant—continued to grow supernaturally fast even without her magic. In heartbeats, the stalks towered over her, each shoot half as thick as her waist. The Selathens would think twice about chopping the deathbush down. The spines would prevent them from getting too close. The only problem was the sidewalk to the front wasn't blocked. Ysabel's father charged down the path toward Jenna.

Before she could react, Kay stepped forward, her hand raised and her eyes paler than normal. Jenna shivered as a chill enveloped her for a couple of heartbeats. The sidewalk glimmered with a thin sheen of ice. Ysabel's father slipped, fell, and slid into a deathbush. He yelled in Selathen.

Jenna cautiously stepped forward, grasping leaves of deathbushes to keep her balance. Ice melted in gaps around her. If Ysabel's father regained his feet, he'd be able to catch her. Jenna probed the deathbush, analyzing spikes to see if they contained toxin. They did, but she wasn't sure what effect it would have on a human. From the pained expression on Honored Lathatilltin's face, he'd develop a rash at least. She hoped the toxin would stun him, but she wasn't going to rely on that. Instead, she urged the deathbush to send out side shoots to block the sidewalk. It obeyed eagerly. The plants grew so quickly she could no longer see Ysabel's father. Would he be able to break through them? Jenna backed up, repeating the process with more deathbushes. The ones farther away from the sidewalk continued to grow, smothering the grass. Some of them stretched toward the houses on either side of Ysabel's, blocking the men from bypassing them. Jenna hoped the deathbushes would stop growing before they covered Ysabel's house.

"I can manage from here," she told Kay. "Head back inside and see if the others are gone. Once they are, we can kill these deathbushes."

Kay nodded and slipped into the house. Jenna faced the deathbushes again. She had to maintain the fence until everyone inside had portaled to safety. That would be easy. The hard part would be killing such vigorous plants when they were no longer needed.

Jenna returned to the top step and peered over the plants. More men were coming with axes. Another one brought a torch. By The Four, would he be foolish enough to set the plants on fire? They could spread the flames to the houses too. She rang the door chime several times. "Kay? Better come out here again. We might need some rain."

"Yes, bring the other wench out here too," a man called at her in accented Challen. "We'll sacrifice you both to Salth!"

"You'll have to catch us first." The Four would surely protect Their Avatars, but Jenna preferred defending herself.

She tugged on the nearest deathbush. Avatars performed mock fights with wooden staffs, and if she had a weapon, she could stave off anyone who managed to break through the deathbushes. To her surprise, it refused to give her a stalk. She'd never met a plant able to resist her magic. She decided not to force the issue until the men chopped a path to her—if they managed that.

Two men chopped at the branches blocking the path to the house. Jenna smiled as the men's expressions of triumph turned to dismay, a dismay that deepened as they rubbed their arms. The thorns must have pierced them through their jackets.

A couple more men picked up the abandoned axes, but they couldn't make headway against the deathbushes either. When they gave up, no more volunteers stepped forward. The group dispersed. Jenna scanned them, looking for Ysabel's father, but he wasn't there. Perhaps he had been taken away earlier to have his injuries treated.

Kay opened the front door. "Jenna, Ysabel's family passed through. Kron's going to send us directly to our house in Wistica. He's changing the portal now."

"Thank the Four." Jenna surveyed the jungle that had replaced the lawn. The deathbushes had been exactly what she'd needed to delay the Selathens, but they were already spreading where they didn't belong. She'd have to tame them if possible or destroy them if she couldn't bring them under control.

Kay came out farther to stare at the sky. "A Chaos Season is forming."

"Here? Right now?" At last she'd have a chance to help tame the magical weather storm and restore the plants around her. Gwen could use the magic to speed her recovery.

Kay seemed more dismayed than pleased by the coming Chaos Season. "By All Four Gods and Goddesses, we're not ready for this! I'm not even sure Gwen and Ysabel are still here!"

"Freeze it," Jenna muttered. Without Gwen to share magic, Kay would be the only one who could use the magic of Chaos Season. "Could you check? I'm going to take care of these bushes."

Jenna grasped two deathbushes close to her and told them to drop their leaves. Probing the rest of the plant, she noticed how deep and thick the roots had grown. That meant the plants might grow back if she didn't destroy the roots too. Repressing a groan, she sent her magic into them, shutting them down. They resisted her like Robbie fighting a nap. Some plants had even started to create their own seeds. She had to focus on one plant at a time, wilting its leaves and shriveling its root, before she could move to the next. Thank the Four the deathbushes competed with each other. The central plants had the hardest time reaching the sun, so they were shorter and less robust than the others—and easier to kill.

"Jenna?" Kay called. "Ysabel and Gwen are already in Wistica."

"Can't they just come back?"

"Ysabel went to the Temple with her family. I think she has to help them find lodgings."

We went through so much trouble to rescue Ysabel, and she runs off to her family before we can tame our first Chaos Season. Jenna hoped this was going to be a mild one. Clouds had gathered overhead, but down the street, the sun shone brightly.

"Kay, could you use some of the power of Chaos Season to ice up the rest of these plants?" Jenna gestured at the half-dead deathbushes. "At least that will weaken the storm."

This time Kay didn't object. She raised one hand above her head while pointing at the ground. Ice encased the deathbushes, making them glitter with strange beauty. Jenna flinched as she touched a plant to make sure it would die. Somehow, it still thrived.

"Can you try heat this time?" she asked.

Kay obliged. Ice melted and turned to steam, making each breath feel like a weight in Jenna's lungs. The plants sucked up the water and grew plump again.

"One more time with ice, please."

"I don't think I can do much more on my own," Kay gasped. "I haven't used so much magic since…since…my last life, I suppose."

"Make it as cold as you can," Jenna said, "See if you can freeze these plants on the inside too."

After a few moments, Jenna worried she might freeze on the inside herself. She didn't have a cloak, and her fingers and toes went numb in heartbeats. Still, she managed to send a final burst of her own magic through all the deathbushes, making sure they froze all the way through. This time, she was sure they would die and not shoot up again from their roots.

The cold didn't last long before rain fell again. Jenna abandoned the plants and looked at Kay. She was shaking, something unheard of for a Winter Avatar.

"Come on." She put an arm around the much shorter woman. "Let's portal someplace warmer where we can rest and eat."

Kay guided her back to the dining room. Kron waited by one of the doorways. Through it, Jenna saw the drawing room of the Season Avatars' house in Wistica. Gwen, already comfortable in a chair and holding another cup of chocolate, beckoned to her with a smile. The older Season Avatars—Sophia, Charles, and Dorian—stood next to her, staring at Jenna with mouths agape.

"We're the last," Kron said.

Jenna ran straight through the portal, towing Kay with her.

CHAPTER THREE

The Other Season Avatars

As soon as Jenna crossed the portal, she released Kay and collapsed into the closest vacant seat. Then she scanned the room for Robbie and Callie. They weren't there. Had they gone upstairs to the nursery, or had Ysabel accidentally brought Jenna's son to the Temple instead?

"By All Four Gods and Goddesses, what's going on?" Sophia, the current Ava Fall, said. Her white mourning gown made her complexion pale, especially when compared to her dark brown hair and eyes. Despite her sharp words, there was an edge of fear in her voice.

"How did you even get here?" Charles, Jenna's counterpart, asked. "I thought you were headed to the western border of Challen. Did you get that far, or did you have to come back?" He blinked a few times, as if just waking up, and stared at Kay. "Say, who is this? And how did you enter the house? I didn't hear the butler announce you."

Hadn't Gwen explained everything to them yet? She'd not only come through the portal first, but as Ava Spring, she was the leader of their quartet. She was supposed to handle everything that affected their entire group. Once she had taken care of that, Jenna could find her son and tell Charles about the strange plants she'd let sprout in Tradetown.

Kron stepped through the portal, and it collapsed behind him. The older Avatars stared at him with suspicious gazes. Brighteyes, Sophia's crow, fluttered on his perch near the window, but he didn't attack.

"Fellow Avatars, this is Kron Evenhanded, an artificer who can use magic on manmade objects," Gwen said. "Kron, this is Charles vin

Estcher, the Avi Sum; Sophia vin Estcher, the Ava Fall; and Dorian gran Garnell, the Avi Win." She gestured at each of them before continuing, "Looks like we'll need more chocolate. And maybe some bread and cold cuts too. Jenna and Kay had to use their magic so we could escape, so they must be ravenous. Permit me?" She pulled the bell cord without waiting for an answer. Not surprising that a nobly born Ava Spring would make herself at home so quickly.

Kron studied the older Avatars for a heartbeat before smiling. "You three must have been Carver, Sylva, and Domina in the life when I first met you."

Dorian raised his eyebrows. "Which lifetime was that? I don't recognize any of those names."

"And how would you remember another life?" Sophia asked. "Only Avatars remember their previous lives in such detail."

Jenna bit back a grin. The older Avatars wouldn't believe the truth: Kron had come forward in time eight hundred years, from the time when the Four had first given Their Avatars magic.

"But where's Magstrom?" he asked. "The Spring Avatar for your group."

All three of the other Avatars looked away. They still wore pure white for mourning. Jenna touched her green-and-white striped dress uncomfortably. Technically, she should still be in full mourning for her late husband, even though they'd only been married for a few moons. After wearing half-mourning at the king's ball, Jenna couldn't stand going back to all white again, and Gwen had been too distracted to nag her about following proper etiquette.

Kron asked again, "What happened to Magstrom? What's his—or her—name now?"

No one spoke for several heartbeats. Even when the butler appeared in the doorway, Gwen gestured for food, chocolate, and blankets instead of telling him what she wanted. Sophia finally said, "If you mean Margaret, she's with the God of Winter now."

"What? She's dead?" Kron tugged on his satchel. "How can that be?"

Dorian glared at him. "Wait. You're the one Gwen told us about, the one who found that old pot and all the shards. How did one of those get to the One Oak to kill my wife?" Ice coated his fist.

Gwen forced herself to her feet. "We have a pair of enemies in the Dead Land," she announced. "Ancient ones who have been causing Chaos Season for centuries. One of them, a magical but twisted child named Sal-thaath, caused all the evil with the shards. He came forward in time with Kron. Remember how Kron's water clock disappeared from the University of Wistica, along with the pottery shard that had caused Margaret's death? Sal-thaath wanted to use the shards as a way to hide himself from the Four so he could move at will in our country." She shivered as she displayed her hand where the final shard was still embedded. Her palm looked raw and was crisscrossed with more lines than a letter written by a miser. "If he'd been able to take this shard from me, he would have succeeded."

Everyone frowned as they stared at Gwen's hand. Spring Avatars never bore such ugly wounds. It would take a lot of magic to remove those scars. Jenna longed to press Gwen's palm with healing kisses. Perhaps later she could offer to link with Gwen and let her drain Jenna's reserves to restore herself. Maybe Kay and Ysabel would join them. If they were in the link, Jenna would be less tempted to remember her last life and share her crime with Gwen.

"If all that is true," Sophia said finally, "What should we do?"

"We must face them in the Dead Land, the way you did in your very first life as Avatars," Kron replied. "But the Four insisted all twelve of you are needed to defeat Salth and Sal-thaath. With one of you gone—"

"Don't you mean five?" Charles said.

"Five? Five dead?"

"The twelve of us are never all alive at once. One quartet serves the Four, one quartet replaces them, and one quartet rests with the God of

Winter." Charles spread his hands. "Our predecessors died about thirty years ago."

"Even if they've been reborn, they'd be younger than these girls here," Dorian said.

Kron collapsed onto the closest chair. "Then by All Four Gods and Goddesses, how are we supposed to face Salth and Sal-thaath without all twelve Avatars? How?" He glared up at the ceiling. "Tell us, Spring!"

Jenna held her breath, but Spring didn't appear. Nothing happened that could be a sign from the Four.

"The Four never speak directly to us anymore," Sophia said sadly.

In the corner, Kay bowed her head.

Gwen sat down again. "Are you quite sure the Four said we all have to be incarnated at once?"

"Spring told me to bring all twelve of you to face Salth—and Sal-thaath."

"Then maybe it's not the right season for that to happen." Gwen perked up as the maid brought in hot chocolate and pastries. "Otherwise, I'm sure the Four would have arranged matters differently."

Kron shook his head at the silent offer of chocolate. "Then why did I come to this time and place, if not to help put an end to Salth's destruction?"

"Ask the Four."

Gwen's tone was dismissive, but he seized her suggestion. "I should go to the Temple anyway and check on Ysabel. Maybe she's ready to come back here." He transformed a doorway into a portal and stepped through. The portal faded, leaving an astonished maid on the other side.

Jenna claimed her own cup of chocolate and headed upstairs to check if Robbie was here. After a few false turns, she found him sleeping in a tiny bedroom while Callie watched over him, sewing him a new nightshirt. The one he wore was a bit tight on him. Jenna made a note to send it back home. Her cousin might need it soon for her own child.

Reassured her son was safe, Jenna remembered her other duty. She returned to the parlor for more chocolate and another pastry. Gwen and Kay were gone, so she approached the other Avatar of Summer. A touch of gray appeared at his temples. As a member of the older set of Avatars, he had to be in his fifties, or maybe even sixties. However, he only looked a decade, maybe fifteen years, older than Jenna. Their Spring Avatar had managed to stave off the signs of age while she was still alive, but now they would be sicken and age like anyone else. Charles didn't seem too concerned about it, though, as he stared out the window at the rain.

Jenna bowed her head. "Avi."

"Ava." He studied her for a heartbeat, then glanced away to where Dorian argued with Sophia. Charles lowered his voice. "All ready to take over from our quartet, are you?"

Some Avatars clung to their season of service, unwilling to make way for the next set. Others gladly gave up the role so they could live with their families, in Wistica, or anywhere away from the rest of their quartet. "What will you do when we replace you?" she asked.

"Grow grapes and make wine," he replied. "My family's estate is the perfect place for a vineyard."

"So, you don't mind stepping down?"

"I can't say everyone in our quartet—I mean, trio now—feels the same."

Jenna shrugged. "None of us have a choice about it."

"That makes it even worse." Charles finished his drink. "So, are you looking for advice, perhaps?"

"No, memories. I found a strange plant in Tradetown this morning. It helped us get away, but it makes weeds look like slow growers."

Charles lifted his eyebrow. How seriously was he taking this?

Jenna described everything she remembered about the plant, from the distinctive shape of its seed to the way its leaves felt and smelled. Remembering she had some extra seeds saved, she pulled one out of her reticule and displayed it to him.

Charles took the seed reluctantly and handed it back to her in a few heartbeats. "I've never seen this type of seed before."

"Never? Not even in another life?"

"No. So, this must not be a native plant of Challen."

"Is that bad?"

He gulped his wine. "With something that grows so quickly, yes." He grinned. "Thank the Four I don't have to worry about it anymore."

"What? Won't you and the others stay on to guide us?"

"Are you sure you really want that?"

Jenna hesitated. Even the Spring Avatars couldn't link across generations, so no matter how closely an Avatar worked with her predecessor or successor, she could never know them as intimately as the others in her quartet. Sometimes Avatars serving the same God or Goddess helped each other, but often they became rivals, each wanting to demonstrate the most skill. Jenna was sure she could hold her own with Charles, but Ysabel and Kay hadn't practiced using their magic as much as she had. Maybe they could learn a lot from Sophia and Dorian—or maybe the other Avatars would intimidate them.

"Maybe the four of us should talk about it and then decide," she said.

Sophia wandered over to join them, carrying full glasses of wine for herself and her husband. "At least you returned at a good time," she said. "It will be good to have your quartet at the soltrans."

"The soltrans? When is it?"

Charles stared at her as if she'd mixed up sunflower and mustard seeds. "Tomorrow."

"So soon?" By All Four, how had she lost track of the seasons, especially when her birthday was on the summer solstice? "I suppose that's why you're here instead of back at the One Oak."

Charles nodded.

Jenna leaned forward. "You'll need Gwen to stand in for Spring, of course. But who's going to represent Summer? You or me?"

CHAPTER FOUR

A Temple Visit

"We didn't expect any of you to be here in time for the soltrans," Sophia said. "So I was going to stand in for Margaret while Charles continued in his normal role for Summer."

Gwen hadn't returned yet, but she wouldn't mind if Jenna spoke for her. At least, Jenna hoped not. After hundreds of years together, she ought to know how Gwen would react.

"Gwen would be more suitable, since she's an actual Spring Avatar. And since I'm part of her quartet, I should be the one facing her."

"I don't mind letting you two take our parts." Charles looked at his wife. "Better the new Avatars over the old. The sooner we can establish their season, the sooner we can retire."

Dorian turned his head, glaring at Charles. "Not all of us are in such a rush to give up being Avatars, Charles."

"But Margaret wouldn't want—"

"She's not here, freeze it!"

Jenna's cup of chocolate frosted over. She hastily set it down before her fingers turned numb.

Sophia sighed. "No, she's not here, Dorian. That's why we can't function as Avatars for much longer. We have to step aside for the next set."

"But they're not ready. Their Ava Win's been a seamstress for the past few years. How can she control the weather when she spends less than an hour a day outside, feeling it? Ha!" Dorian spat into the fireplace. "The first strong wind will carry that slip of a girl into the Salt Waters, and then we'll need another set of Avatars anyway."

Gwen and Kay, still in the hall, paused before reentering the parlor. Had Dorian seen them? It didn't matter; Jenna automatically sprang to the defense of her sister Avatar.

"Kay already has hundreds of years of experience handling the weather," she said. "Just give her a moon or two to practice, and her memories will strengthen. The same goes for the rest of us. Once we take over, you'll be free to travel or do anything you want—"

"What I want," Dorian said slowly, enunciating each word carefully, "is to have my wife back and continue using my magic."

Jenna shook her head. She felt sorry for him, but obviously the Four weren't going to give him his wish. He should resign himself to waiting for their next life together. Since they were both Avatars, they would meet again. Of course, maybe the Four would play a cruel trick on Dorian and Margaret and arrange things so they couldn't marry each other, like reincarnating them as the same gender.

"At least you know you'll see her again," she said. She didn't want to reveal too many details about her relationship with Gwen to Avatars she barely knew.

"In our next life. But how many years will I have to wait for Margaret?" Dorian paced, hands clasped behind his back. "Why do I have to live in a world without her? If the Four truly value us and honor our feelings, They should have taken me with her."

"Dorian! By All Four Gods and Goddesses, you shouldn't say such things." Sophia's face turned white as a lily. "What if They take your words seriously and act on them?"

He stared at her. "Would you really object?"

Her nostrils flared, but she didn't speak.

A flash of light made them all turn around. Kron reappeared in the doorway, by himself. His expression was strained.

Gwen, followed by Kay, stepped into the room. They'd managed to sponge some of the dirt off of their clothes. "Where's Ysabel?" Gwen asked.

"She wouldn't come with me. She wants to stay with her family."

"Have they found a place to live yet?"

He shook his head. "They sent a servant out to look for rooms, but no one seemed to know where to find boarding houses in Wistica."

"I have an idea, but I'll have to consult with Aunt Gabri about it," Gwen said. "Is she still there?"

Kron nodded.

Gwen let a sigh escape. "All right, I'll portal over with you."

"Not by yourself, you're not," Jenna said. "I'll come with you in case you need to draw on my magic."

Kay glanced at the other set of Avatars and added. "I'll come too."

Jenna wasn't sure how much help Kay would be with Ysabel and her family, but she appreciated the offer. Gwen nodded in acceptance. She snatched the last pastry from the platter and split it into thirds, offering pieces to Jenna and Kay. "Let's go. Kron, will this portal take us directly to them?"

"If they haven't left the Temple."

"The Temple?" Sophia asked. "The Four allow you to use your magic in Their holy place?"

"It's a good thing They do, since that's the only building in Wistica that hasn't changed in eight hundred years," Kron said drily. "I don't know what would have become of me if it wasn't there."

As Sophia gaped at him, Jenna and Kay followed Gwen through the portal into the Temple. They arrived in a side corridor not far from the central altar area. Voices and running footsteps echoed in the stone hallway.

"Is something wrong?" Kay asked.

"I don't know." Gwen raised her skirt to ankle height and strode forward as if she meant to clear out the Temple single-handedly—not that Jenna would let her do that, of course. She hurried to overtake Gwen.

She came out into the altar room just behind the Ava Spring. In front of them was a sight Jenna was sure had never been in the Temple before. Trunks and carpetbags, some left open, had been piled in the center of the room where worshippers normally stood. A footman attempted to organize the pile, while a maid and a cook chased a handful of young children as they raced from altar to altar. Ysabel's cat patrolled around Fall's altar, hissing at any child who got too near, and Ysabel's mother knelt in front of it, forearms bare. Ysabel herself wiped water up from the God of Summer's altar with a cloth. Cut roses and a shattered vase lay next to the altar. Small wonder she kept glancing around, shoulders hunched as if she expected Summer to appear and scold her for the mess.

Since Summer was Jenna's God, she felt obligated to assist. "What happened?" she asked as she knelt to pick up the roses.

Ysabel blushed. "My family."

Kay frowned. "By All Four Gods and Goddesses, what are you doing? You should be more respectful of Their Temple!" A strong breeze spread rose petals and their perfume around.

Kay complains about the mess even as she makes it worse. Jenna collected a few petals before they blew out of their reach. *She'd better work on her control before we have to tame a Chaos Season.* In previous lives, Kay had been able to guide thread through a needle with a breeze. How long would it take her in this life to regain confidence in her abilities?

"I'm sorry," Ysabel said. "I didn't expect to meet the Four under these circumstances. But Mama's not done praying to Fall yet, and my brothers and sisters are getting restless."

"Then we'd better find somewhere else for them to go." Gwen peered around. "Where's my aunt?"

"If you mean the lady with the outlandish hat, she stepped outside for fresh air."

Gwen nodded and headed off for the main entrance of the Temple, where the mock fights were staged. Jenna finished gathering the flowers and stood up so she could find a new vase for them. Before she could leave, the scents of apple cider and smoke overwhelmed the roses. Jenna glanced around for their source. Blinding light appeared near Ysabel's mother. Jenna turned away, and everyone else stopped what they were doing.

"She has accepted me back!" Ysabel's mother cried. "I'm a Fallswoman again!"

She held out her left arm. Above her marriage tattoo of her and her husband's initials was a new one. It said "Fall" in large scarlet letters so ornate Jenna could hardly read them. The marriage tattoo was now surrounded by a pearl-white border.

Ysabel dropped her cloth. "Mama...is that...is that...Fall did that, just now?" She ran over and touched her mother's tattoo with trembling fingers. Her mother stared at her arm and tilted it from side to side, an elated expression on her face. Jenna and Kay exchanged glances of their own. It wasn't often that one of the Four marked a Fallswoman or Summersman personally. Summer was the most reclusive of the Four, but Jenna couldn't help wishing He would appear, just for a heartbeat.

The servants and children gathered around Dame s'Ivena—no need to add her married name now. "Mama, what does that mean?" a sulky girl of about fourteen years asked.

Ysabel's mother grinned. "It means I'm not married to your father anymore."

The children's eyes grew wide. Then they all spoke at once: "Why not?" "But Mama, when are we going to see Papa again?" "When are we going back home?"

"We'll find another home."

The sulky girl stamped her foot. "I want to go back to Tradetown! All of my friends are there!"

"It's all right, Bethany." Ysabel embraced her sister. "Wistica is a very nice place to live. You'll make new friends—"

"I don't care." Bethany struggled out of Ysabel's grip. "You ruined everything. It's not fair."

Jenna exchanged sympathetic glances with Ysabel. If Jenna had ever acted like that, her mama would have taken a switch to her. She hoped Bethany's governess or mother would put some sense into her.

Gwen returned, supporting her aunt. "I have good news," Gwen said. "Aunt Gabri has kindly agreed to let Ysabel's family stay in our Wistica house until they can find a more permanent place to settle."

Lady lo Havil grimaced as she surveyed the children, but she didn't contradict her niece.

"Thank you, Gabri," Ysabel's mother said. "Don't worry. The children have had a few shocks today, but they'll calm down quickly."

Bethany scowled at her older sister. Ysabel sighed and touched her mourning brooch. She attempted to hug Bethany, but when the child refused to acknowledge her, she left her to stop one of the toddlers from eating a rose Jenna had overlooked.

"I sent an urchin to the lo Havil house for the carriage," Gwen said. "They should be here soon." She looked at Ysabel. "Which things are yours? There must a footman or two back at the Avatar's house brave enough to pass through the portal for your belongings."

"My belongings?"

Gwen put on an earnest expression. "We need you. It's our quartet's season now."

"So soon?" Ysabel glanced back at her family. "I thought I would have more time. You'll need my help sorting things out here, won't you, Mama?"

"Fall needs you more. Go with Her and the rest of the Four, dear." Her mother opened her arms for an embrace. "Don't worry about us. Now that I'm a Fallswoman again, She'll look after me."

"A Fallswoman!" Lady lo Havil fanned herself. "By All Four, Mattie, what happened? You must tell me everything!"

As the two older women started talking, Ysabel hugged each of her family members—besides Bethany—including the servants. Jenna realized she still held the roses from Summer's altar. Kay silently gave her a replacement vase. Jenna arranged the roses, then curtseyed to the altar. *Summer, if Fall gave Ysabel's mother her dearest wish, will You grant mine? Please don't let Gwen remember her last life. Let her accept me in this one. We can't marry this time, but we're still bound to each other.*

Ysabel set a trunk and a carpetbag aside before following Jenna and the others into the hall. "Where are we going now?"

"Back to our own house here in Wistica," Gwen replied. "The summer soltrans is tomorrow."

"Will you and Jenna battle?"

"They always do," Kay said. "Even when it's not the soltrans."

Jenna felt herself flush and caught Gwen doing the same. She was grateful for the chance to distract the others. "Actually, the Avi Summer doesn't mind if we perform this soltrans, but the Avi Winter complained—and he doesn't even have a role in the summer soltrans!" She turned toward Gwen. "I say we ignore Dorian. People will want to see us at the Temple, not the older Avatars."

Kay shrank back. "We shouldn't ignore Dorian. He has strong magic."

"So do we, and we're a complete quartet."

"Maybe it would be wise to give the older Avatars a final soltrans." Gwen spoke in a firm tone that indicated she'd made up her mind. "My father and I perform the soltranses for our neighborhood, but he doesn't feel comfortable fighting me. All we do is tap our staffs together a few times and move on to the reconciliation. I need to practice more before I perform at the Temple." She yawned. "Besides, I need to rest and recover my magic."

Jenna forced her disappointment down. They would have plenty of opportunities to engage in the soltrans in other years. She wasn't ready to risk linking with Gwen by herself yet.

"There's always the fall soltrans," Ysabel said hopefully. "By then we'll be fully established as the new Season Avatars."

Gwen halted in front of the portal and drew them off to the side before someone in the Avatars' house noticed them. In a low voice, she said, "First we have to prove we can tame a Chaos Season. The Four have given each of us a special challenge in this life. I have to keep this froze pottery shard in my hand so Sal-thaath can't take it, and I'm not sure how it will affect us when we face Chaos Season." Gwen turned to Jenna. "You have a child to raise, and…caring for him will drain your energy."

Jenna flipped her braid to her other shoulder. She knew what Gwen was too well-bred to say directly. Although they'd hired a wet-nurse to care for Robbie, Jenna still nursed him as much as she could. Her body needed to produce both milk and magic and would need as much food and rest as she could give it.

"I can handle it," she said.

"You don't have to make it so hard on yourself."

"He's my child." *Especially since his real father hasn't acknowledged him yet.* "I want him to know who his mama is and not run to a servant for comfort."

Gwen narrowed her eyes at Jenna before returning to Ysabel. "I know you're going through some…family difficulties at the moment, but we'll help you as much as we can."

"Thank you." Ysabel touched her brooch. "If only Lathtin was here to see this. Other than my mama, he's the only one who knew I was the next Fall Avatar."

Gwen drooped. "He's…absent? What happened to him?"

"He caught scarlet spots while he was trying to figure out how outbreaks spread. Papa wouldn't even let him come home when he found out Lathtin had been in sick neighborhoods. You would have liked him, Gwen. He wanted to go to the University and study medicine instead of taking over Papa's watch shop."

"Such a shame," Gwen murmured.

Yes, it was a pity the first youth Gwen had shown interest in was no longer alive. Of course, her family would have probably rejected him anyway for not being a nobleman. Maybe Gwen would end up a Fallswoman in this life despite her best intentions. Jenna wondered if that would make things easier between them—or worse.

"May the Four give your brother a good sleep and a gentle rebirth," Gwen said to Ysabel before turning to Kay. "Kay, you're stronger than you give yourself credit for. We know you can tame a Chaos Season. You just have to embrace your magic and tap into your memories."

"But my dreams—"

"Are just dreams." Gwen beckoned them all closer. "I know Kron wants us all to help him attack Salth in the Dead Land, but let's worry about taming the next Chaos Season. That's more important—and we only need four of us to do it."

Jenna hesitated. There was something else their quartet might need to tame. Or she specifically. Maybe the deathbushes were a unique plant and she'd never seen them again. But if their seeds were the ones she'd seen being blown over Challen, then they could be anywhere by now.

She took a deep breath. "Gwen, I haven't told you about the deathbushes yet, have I?"

"Deathbushes?" Gwen raised her perfectly arched eyebrows. "What are those?"

"A plant I've never seen before. Grows very fast, even without my magic, and has possibly poisonous thorns." With a few additions from Kay, Jenna described how the plants had been critical for delaying Ysabel's father so they could all escape. She finished by saying, "I'm sure I killed all of them, but at some point I'll have to go back to check."

Ysabel's face paled. "Papa is very harsh, and he gave me over to Sal-thaath…but he's my father. It doesn't seem right to wish him ill, even if he does deserve it. Besides, this plant might kill animals as well as people."

"The plants are dead, Ysabel. I'd swear it on the Four."

"What about their seeds?"

"Even their seeds." Jenna stared at the tips of her boots peeking out from under her dress. "But there might be more of them blown all over Challen by now."

Gwen shook her head. "Freeze it, why didn't you say something sooner? Maybe Kay could have traced them."

"If you don't watch a wind for as long as it's in motion, you can't tell where it's been," Kay said.

Gwen studied Jenna for a moment. The anger in her blue eyes faded. She must be coming up with a plan to manage the deathbushes. In every life, no matter what the crisis, she took charge. Jenna couldn't imagine being so serious all the time. That was why it was her task to make sure Gwen took time from duty to enjoy herself from time to time. When would she get that chance?

"You said you don't know these plants?" Gwen asked. "You haven't worked with them before?"

Jenna shook her head. "Charles didn't recognize them either."

Gwen took a deep breath. "I…I should link with you then, to make sure there's no lingering toxin."

"I'm immune to all poisonous plants."

"But Robbie isn't. You could pass a poison to him when he—he…" Gwen flushed. "Feeds."

Jenna gasped. She hadn't thought of that.

"I'd better check," Gwen said. "Let me link with you."

Before Jenna could give—or deny—permission, Gwen touched her. As she examined her, Jenna closed her eyes and forced herself to remember handling the deathbushes, making every detail vivid in her mind so as to block out any other memories. Gwen's touch, light as a petal, caressed first one of her hands, then the other. Resolve fled. They'd been husband and wife in so many other lives all Jenna could think of was the ecstasy the link could give them….

Gwen released her, flushing scarlet from throat to forehead. "I…I'd almost forgotten about that," she said quietly. "It would be easier if I'd never remembered it."

"You would have…eventually."

"For all the good it would do us."

As the only child of a noble family, Gwen needed to give them an heir to the estate. She was too concerned about duty to declare herself a Fallswoman, someone forsaking the normal life of a spouse and children. A relationship between her and Jenna was impossible.

"It'll never be like that with William, or anyone else," Gwen said.

"You can teach him to pleasure you."

She shook her head. "Not that one. He won't care."

They stared at each other helplessly for a moment before Gwen gathered her skirts and fled.

Jenna took a few steps to follow her, then halted. The last thing either of them needed to do was link as a pair again. She took a deep breath. They would need both Ysabel and Kay in the link next time to chaperone them. Hopefully that would allow her to tame the attraction she still felt for Gwen.

It's just a memory, an echo of our previous lives.

Jenna hoped that was all there was to it. That was all there could be between them. She didn't deserve more.

CHAPTER FIVE

The Deathbushes' New Trick

The next morning, Jenna patrolled the front steps of the Temple, making sure everything was perfect for the summer soltrans. Today, she was forbidden to wear a single stitch of white for her departed husband; everything she wore was green, from her emerald hairpins to her forest green boots. Thank the Four the color suited her. Lex, who was not only the king's brother and Avatar of the Fip God of War but also Robbie's true father, would attend the soltrans. Jenna hadn't had much chance to talk to him at the king's ball last moon. This time, she hoped to show him his son. Renewing his interest in her would be the best birthday present she could give herself.

The day was warm enough for a short-sleeved dress but not so warm Jenna's sweat would stain the silk. Her gloves were uncomfortable, but she tugged them up to hide her marriage tattoo and its unlucky white border. Then she opened her moss green parasol to block the summer sun. At least its heat would encourage crops to grow—and other plants. Like the seedling growing through a crack in the ancient stone steps. The scent of thyme, just like the smell of the deathbushes in Tradetown, made her look closer at it. She thought she recognized it, but she couldn't believe it had spread to Wistica, on the other side of Challen, in less than two days.

Suspicious, Jenna called, "Kay, come look at this!" She was the only other Season Avatar to have seen the deathbushes.

Kay trailed Dorian as he gestured at the cloudless sky. At Jenna's call, she hurried over. "What is it?"

"Do you recognize this plant?"

"Why are you asking me?" She looked puzzled. "That's your magic, not mine."

"This reminds me of the deathbushes I grew in front of Ysabel's house. They were much taller, though. What do you think?"

"I'd say wait half an hour and see how fast it grows, but it really shouldn't be here," Kay replied. "The other plants shouldn't be here either.

"Other plants?" Jenna rose and glanced around. Sure enough, more shoots had sprung up in every nook and cranny of the Temple, not caring if they stood in sun or shade. Jenna frowned. That seemed unnatural. Most plants had their own set of requirements for soil type, amounts of sun and water, and other things they needed to grow. Weeds, on the other hand, could grow practically anywhere. The deathbushes definitely fit into that category.

A flood of people, each wearing some shade of green, crept up the street toward the Temple. The soltrans would start at noon, less than half an hour from now. She didn't have much time to investigate.

Jenna snapped her parasol shut and climbed up the stairs to the Temple porch, where the duel would take place. A few deathbushes grew here as well. Despite the thorns, she tugged on them. Her calluses didn't protect her as much as she hoped they would. Thorns pricked through her silk gloves and stung her briefly before her magic neutralized any toxins in the deathbushes. The roots snapped before she could pull out the entire plant. Frowning, she tossed the plants into a dark corner and continued into the cool interior.

The door to the small anteroom for colored robes and wooden fighting sticks stood open. Sophia and Charles had already dressed for the ceremony and were in the middle of choosing sticks. Sophia looked odd in yellow for the Goddess of Spring instead of red for Fall.

Charles wore dark green like Jenna. He swished each fighting stick a couple of times before setting it aside.

"Hurry up, Charles," his wife said. "If you don't settle on one soon, the soltrans will be over before we can perform the ceremony."

"It's hard to believe this will be our last ceremony, isn't it?" he said wistfully. "I suppose we should make it a good one."

"Then why are there deathbushes sprouting all over the Temple?" Jenna asked, stepping forward.

He started. "Sprouts? Where did they come from?"

"I don't know. You didn't grow them?"

"Grow plants directly on the Temple?" He shook his head. "By All Four, that wouldn't be proper now, would it?"

"You know how weeds will sprout up from any space between paving stones, or how ivy clings to crannies of an old house? That's what they're doing. I just pulled some." Jenna pointed to the corner. "Didn't you see them when you arrived earlier?"

Sophia and Charles glanced at each other. "No," they both said.

Even if these weren't deathbushes, Jenna's recent experience made her wary of other fast-growing plants. "I better examine them more closely. Will you help me, Charles?"

"Jenna, you know we're not supposed to be seen before the soltrans starts," Sophia said. "It would spoil the drama."

Charles set his fighting stick down. "I'm afraid we have to make an exception this time, Dear." He straightened, shrugging off his lazy posture. "Not when the next Ava Sum keeps finding new plants she's never seen before."

Jenna's skin burned. Did he think he was a better Avatar than her? Both of them had hundreds of years of experience with plants from their past lives. The few decades he had over her in this life didn't matter. "Well, if you know what these plants are, you can perform the Fall soltrans in my place too." *And if I'm right, and these plants are invading Challen, you should let me perform this soltrans.* Mouth clamped shut, she followed him back outside, squinting in the bright light.

"Now, where are these strange plants?" Charles asked. He gaped. "Never mind."

The deathbushes had shot up another couple of thumb-lengths while she was inside, and the scent of thyme was strong enough to make Jenna want to lick the petals. Kay sat next to a deathbush, grinning as if she'd just learned how.

"Kay?" Jenna called. "Where are the others?"

She didn't answer.

Jenna approached her, feeling dizzy for a couple of heartbeats before her head cleared. It couldn't be hunger, as she'd hadn't used magic. Could the deathbushes be affecting her too? She was supposed to be immune to any poison a plant could create, but if the deathbushes were able to affect her, the other Avatars and non-magical people would feel it even more.

"Kay! It's almost time for the soltrans!"

Still no response.

Heart beating faster, Jenna turned back to see how the older Avi Sum was handling this. By the Four, he had actually plucked one of the leaves and was sniffing it! Even she hadn't dared that. Either he was braver than he seemed—or as foolish as he sometimes appeared.

"Charles?" she called. "What can you sense about these plants?" She wanted to confer with him in case he'd learned something she hadn't, but her sister Avatar's welfare was more important. Of course, Gwen should be the one checking on Kay. If she been affected by the plants, Jenna wouldn't be able to cure her. All she could do was destroy the deathbushes and hope that helped.

She didn't wait for Charles to respond. Instead, she went over to the deathbush that had Kay enraptured and grabbed it. She should have been able to yank it out, roots and all, but the slender stalk didn't snap. What was this plant made out of, stone? She tried again, this time sending her magic down through the plant to weaken it. These deathbushes couldn't have grown here for very long, but in that short time, they'd sent their roots down deep into the crevices of the Temple, finding weaknesses Jenna had never suspected were there. Even as she watched, the roots extended in all directions until they encountered more of their kind. Then they twined together like lovers embracing.

She followed a few more roots as a horrible idea entered her mind. Maybe these plants had been sent here to disrupt the ceremony. The roots were thin, but stronger than they should be, supernaturally strong. If she didn't kill the deathbushes down to the roots, they would not only continue affecting people but possibly weaken the Temple foundation.

I can't let a single seed of these plants live, but I'm going to need help. Charles would be of limited use, since his quartet couldn't lend him their strength. Jenna would need to link with Gwen, Ysabel and Kay to destroy all the deathbushes. She hoped all of them would be too busy with the plants to explore Jenna's memories during the link.

She released her physical and magical holds on the deathbush, grabbed Kay by the arm, and hauled her up toward Charles. The Ava Win was so small and thin she was as easy to handle as a bale of hay. After Jenna helped her up a few steps, Kay blinked and pulled out of her grip.

"What happened?" she asked, looking around. "Did I miss the sol-trans?"

"It hasn't started yet. We need to get rid of those deathbushes first."

"But they smell so nice…"

"They're also trying to destroy the Four's Temple," Jenna said. "Where's Gwen and Ysabel? We need to link."

A pained expression appeared on Charles' face.

"Destroy the Temple?" Kay clenched her fists, and her ice-blue eyes darkened to gray. "I don't see how plants could do that, but we can't let that happen."

"It's the roots," Charles said. "They're crumbling the foundation. I'll see what I can do on my own to untangle them. Dorian," he called, "We need more heat to dry out the soil."

Dorian tilted his head. A wind sprung up, tugging at Jenna's hair. Wasn't that the opposite of what Charles wanted? She glanced questioningly at Kay.

"He's using the wind to wick moisture up and drive the clouds away." She frowned as she studied the sky. "It's a very unruly wind, though. Almost feels like a Chaos Season trying to form."

"Freeze it, not at a soltrans!" Jenna glanced around, searching for Ysabel's cat or Sophia's crow. Anilinks were sensitive to Chaos Season and often provided the first warning one was happening somewhere in Challen. Neither animal came out to fetch them, though, and the tension slowly left her shoulders.

"Maybe I was mistaken." Kay hunched into herself.

"That's all right. Do you want to join Dorian or link with me through Gwen?"

Kay swallowed, her eyes bigger, as if she didn't like either option.

Jenna rolled her own eyes. "The link won't hurt you." *You don't have secrets to keep from your sister Avatars.*

"But…if …if Salth can attack the Temple, we're not safe anywhere!"

Kay had a point, but Jenna couldn't let herself get caught up in her sister Avatar's fear. She was willing to use it, though. "We'll be safe with Gwen. Where is she?"

"Somewhere inside the Temple with Ysabel and Kron. He wanted to show them where he arrived in his water clock."

"Then let's find them." Jenna sprinted back up the steps toward the main area of the Temple, the big room where the altars were. Gwen, Ysabel, and Kron weren't there. The Temple wasn't that big, but it was very old, with narrow passages. Jenna hoped they weren't stuck somewhere.

When Kay caught up to her, she asked, "Can you sense any air currents inside the Temple, perhaps made by them moving around?"

She shook her head.

Jenna sighed. "Well, let's split up. Call out when you find them."

She yanked her skirts up to knee length as if she was getting ready to help mow hay. She sprinted past the Four's altars without pausing to worship any of them, not even Summer. The Four would understand. But she knew it was disrespectful to yell for Gwen while she was in the main room. As soon as she reached the exit at the other end of the room, she called, "Gwen! Kron! Come here! We need you!"

Her voice echoed for a few heartbeats before she heard a faint voice. "Jenna? Is that you?" It had to be Ysabel; Jenna would have known Gwen's voice no matter what.

Jenna ran toward the sound. "Come out, all of you! We need to link!"

Ysabel emerged first, dust smeared on her hem and sleeves. Even Pouncer bore a streak of dust on his face. "What's going on?"

"Deathbushes."

"Can they wait until after the soltrans?" Gwen asked.

"They're growing fast enough to bring down the Temple during the soltrans. Come, link with me so I can show you."

"The link," Gwen murmured. "This must be serious."

Ysabel and Gwen exchanged glances. Jenna felt her face growing warm. By the Four, was her reluctance to link that obvious? Did the other two remember what had happened to Gwen in their last life together? What would happen when Gwen recovered that memory? *Don't think of it don't think of it don't think of it...*

Jenna put on a smile to reassure them, then realized they might not take her warning seriously if she seemed calm. With a frustrated grunt, she turned and led the group back through the main room, stopping to collect Kay, who'd remained prostrate before the God of Winter's altar. She rose without protest to accompany them outside.

Jenna blinked as her vision readjusted. The day seemed much brighter this time, and hot air shimmered before her. Dorian stood off to one side, hands held out in a circle above a cluster of deathbushes. Charles knelt next to another patch, his face frozen in a scowl. He must be finding the plants as difficult to work with as Jenna had. The older Avatars had left the biggest outbreak of deathbushes to her and the rest of the quartet. This one was at the bottom of the stairs, spreading over the last step as if forbidding anyone to cross it. More citizens of Wistica lined up next to the plants, staring at them but not touching them.

"Are you the new Avatars?" a dark-skinned girl asked. She looked like a full-blooded Fip, her face all angles, but she stared up at Jenna and the others with awe in her eyes.

Gwen smiled at the girl and sketched the compass rose of the Four. However, she didn't touch her. Gwen probably didn't trust that her healing magic was safe.

Jenna took the lead. "We are, and we have to remove these plants." She raised her voice. "Everyone, please stand back."

She didn't wait to see if people obeyed. She knelt and grasped the closest deathbush, extending her awareness into its root system. For such a small plant, the roots traveled surprisingly deep. They reached partway under the Temple to link with other plants. Jenna could sense a ring of them surrounding the building. She wasn't sure what would happen if their root system grew stronger, but she planned to make sure that wouldn't happen.

Gwen touched her. *What do you see?* Ysabel and Kay joined the link, but they didn't speak.

Jenna showed them the root system. *At the rate these plants are growing, they could crumble the foundation of the Temple during the soltrans.*

And then Avatars and bystanders could get hurt. Gwen paused. *We can't affect the Temple with our magic, but Kron could. Should we ask him to reinforce the building, or would that be blasphemy?*

He's not an Avatar, Ysabel protested.

But the Four speak to him. Summer even gave him the violet brace-let for Gwen. Maybe They favor him over us. Kay's fear, guilt, and heartbreak all mixed together.

Although having Kron repair the Temple was a good idea, the others were missing the point. *These deathbushes were put here to attack the Temple. Plants like this don't normally have such long, fast-growing roots.*

Then we'd better take care of them now, Gwen said. *I'll ask Kron to strengthen the Temple building if he can. I'll have to unlink us so I can talk to him.*

Gwen released Jenna, and the link disappeared, taking Ysabel's and Kay's thoughts too. Jenna used the respite to breathe deeply—the link had gone better than she'd expected—and to check on the root system again. The stringy roots, as thin as thread, spread over the foundation stones of the Temple and wound their way into every crack, leaching minerals from the stones. One of the cracks traveled halfway across a stone as it split wide enough open for Jenna to insert her finger. She gulped. Did she imagine it, or did the stair beneath her tilt? She hoped Kron's magic could repair the Temple. The stones seemed more like part of nature than something manmade.

Gwen and the others returned. *Ready?*

I hope Kron is, Jenna replied. She showed them the damaged foundation stone. *Will he be able to sense what's wrong, Ysabel?*

How would I know?

But we thought you knew him, Gwen said. *You were his wife.*

I don't remember that life at all.

By the Four, that had to be uncomfortable. No wonder Ysabel seemed reluctant to be around Kron. Jenna hoped he would assist them anyway.

He said he'd try it. He's going into the deepest level of the Temple to be closer to the damaged stones. Gwen didn't need to speak, but they all caught images in her mind of pitch-dark halls so narrow a man could get stuck in them. If the Temple collapsed with him down there, they'd never find his body.

He's going to do his part, Gwen said. *It's time we do ours.*

Everyone sent wordless agreement.

Gwen harvested magic from Ysabel and Kay, then sent it to Jenna. Power flowed out of Jenna's fingertips and into the deathbushes. She didn't worry about destroying the leaves or even the seeds right now; she reserved her magic for the roots. If she didn't obliterate every thumb-length of root to the finest hair, the plants could return and do further damage before anyone knew they existed.

She'd suspected the deathbushes had to contain their own magic to grow so quickly. Apparently, this magic made them resistant to hers as well. Direct attempts at killing the roots didn't succeed. Jenna changed tactics. Instead of trying to destroy the whole root system, she focused on the surface layer of the roots, killing off the smallest rootlets and blocking all the tiny channels where they took in water and nutrients. The entire system was extensive, about the size of one of her family's fields. But with the magical support of her sister Avatars, Jenna swept her power across the roots in heartbeats. Then she went back over the roots a second time to make sure she'd destroyed all of them. Maybe she should give them some time to die before attempting to pull them away from the stones. She feared if she removed the roots too soon, she'd damage the foundation before Kron could restore it.

Gwen, can you check to see how Kron's coming along with his magic? Jenna asked.

I'd have to break the link to do it. Are you finished? Maybe if we watch, we'll see something happen—or feel it affect the roots.

Ysabel said, *Maybe we can see more of what's going on if I tap into an animal's senses.*

They all agreed she had the best magic for that task. Ysabel recruited several moles to tunnel near the foundation stones. Jenna maintained her link with the deathbushes' intertwined roots to make sure all of them died. Parts of the net dropped out like a tree shedding leaves. Jenna focused her attention on the remaining sections.

Ysabel helped them interpret the moles' senses. Vision was unimportant to this animal; it relied more on smell and touch. The moles dug easily—maybe a little too easily—through the soil as Dorian dried it out. As they drew closer to the foundation, the soil became moister and packed more readily. As roots rotted, Ysabel sent other creatures to break down them down. The temperature rose, and the moles scurried away out of Ysabel's control. Alarmed, Gwen broke the link before Ysabel could gather more details.

Jenna swayed as she rose. For a heartbeat, she thought it was the Temple shaking, not her body's response to using so much magic. Gwen, Ysabel, and Kay blinked as they readjusted to being four separate people, not one linked entity. Once Jenna steadied, she examined the deathbushes at her feet. They drooped but weren't completely dead. Freeze it, what did it take to destroy them? She lifted her skirt and crushed a plant underfoot, wishing her own boots were sturdier. Charles stretched as he stood up from a sickly yellow deathbush. Behind him, Dorian lowered his lands, and the temperature plummeted from scorching hot to seasonal warmth. Jenna shivered, her silk dress suddenly clammy.

"Everything still looks level," Gwen said. "I think it's safe to assume Kron succeeded. I'd better check on him, though. Ysabel, will you come with me?"

"That isn't part of the normal summer soltrans, is it?" A deep voice asked. "Is something wrong?"

Jenna whirled to face Lex, the Avatar of War and the only other person with the authority to intrude upon the Temple during this ceremony.

CHAPTER SIX

A Weapon Test

"Le—Your Highness," Jenna managed to blurt out. "I wasn't expecting you here."

He raised an eyebrow. By The Four, he looked impeccable in his scarlet jacket with a row of golden eagles flying over his heart. The touches of gray in his beard and hair gave him a regal presence. Even the plain sheath for the dagger on his belt lent him power. He should have been the ruler of Challen, not the Avatar of War. But as an Avatar, he was more accessible than the king would have been.

"Here at the soltrans?" he asked. "Or here on the Temple steps?"

"Here specifically, Your Highness." On a step above Jenna, Gwen sank into a deep curtsey, so graceful she must have spent hours as a girl practicing it. Jenna's childhood skills of shelling peas and bundling hay would never be appreciated in her new setting.

Gwen rose to stare directly at Lex. "Your Highness, you shouldn't be here. The Temple requires foundation repairs, and we're not sure they're complete yet."

"But you were still planning to hold your ceremony anyway?"

Gwen rested her good hand on Jenna's shoulder, touching only fabric. "We just discovered the problem and are taking measures to address it. In fact, I was on my way to check on our…artifact expert right now. Ysabel, will you join me?"

Gwen curtseyed again and departed with Ysabel before Lex could respond. He stared after her until she disappeared inside the Temple.

Jenna bit her lip. Gwen was pretty, clever, nobly born, and wealthy in her own right. No one would be surprised that Lex courted Gwen instead of her.

By the Four, why shouldn't he court me? Even if I was born a farm girl, I'm an Avatar too. I'm just as pretty as Gwen—maybe prettier, since I'm taller and fill out my dress better. She smiled. *Best of all, I have something Gwen doesn't: Robbie.* She beckoned Callie, who calmed the fussy baby as she waited in a corner, out of the sun.

She approached Jenna, curtseyed awkwardly to Lex, and said, "Ava, did you need something?"

"Yes, Callie. Your Highness, I'd like to introduce you to my son, Robbie." She leaned closer to Lex and whispered, "Your son too."

His expression hardened for a moment before freezing. "You assured me last summer there would be no issue."

"I only said I had means to prevent bearing a child." She tilted her head and looked him in the eye. "I chose not to use them."

"If this is true, then you've done something very foolish for a Season Avatar."

Faster than Jenna thought possible, Lex drew his dagger and sliced Robbie's hand. Callie screamed. "Robbie!" Jenna sprang forward, wishing she had a fighting stick, or even a stalk from a deathbush. How was she supposed to protect her son when her magic wasn't useful as a weapon?

"By the Eagle, it's true," Lex said. He held his still-clean dagger up. "See, he's unharmed."

Robbie let out a wail, then stopped as he saw the dagger. With big eyes, he reached for it. All fingers were still attached, and his skin wasn't marked. No sign of blood or a cut. Chuckling, Lex returned the dagger to its sheath.

"This is the Allweapon, War's own weapon, Ava," he said. "Unlike your Four, War selects His Avatars from the Fip royal family. His weapon will not harm a possible future War Avatar."

Jenna grabbed her son from the nursemaid and inspected his hands. His nails were a bit long, but he didn't bear any new scratches. Her heart still raced with fear, and she put some venom in her voice as she said, "I'd have thought a god's weapon would be ...longer."

Lex gave her a cool look. "It changes into whatever type of weapon is needed for battle. For daily use, I most often carry it as a dagger, but I've also used it as a sword or battleaxe. I've shown War pistols and rifles, but He has not seen fit to change His weapon into that form yet." He studied Robbie. "Perhaps someday this child will use it as such."

"Robbie?" How could Lex even think of a helpless little child going to war?

"Isn't that what you had in mind when you seduced me back in your little town—or something even higher? My brother will not appreciate this complication to the succession, even if I'm sixth in the line for the throne and this child was born out of wedlock."

Jenna's cheeks warmed. "Robbie is listed in the Hall of Records as the son of my absent husband, Thomas t'Reve." A pity she couldn't update the record to indicate Robbie's real father. Imagine him someday sitting on the throne! Even if it never happened, he had so much more waiting for him than Thomas's old general store back in Bull Rock.

Lex crossed his arms and stared down at her. "If the succession fails, War could use that false record to create civil war here, something I'm sure you Season Avatars don't want." His mouth hardened. "If you weren't an Avatar, it would be easy to make that child—disappear."

"Disappear!" All the heat of Summer pulsed through her veins. "You so much as trim this child's hair with your dagger, and I'll plant a score of acorns in you and feed them on your flesh!"

"Easy, Ava. I do not threaten, but warn. Swear by your God that you'll never tell anyone else who his real father is, and I will protect the both of you." He sighed. "Does the Spring Avatar know?"

Jenna nodded. "She realized it after dancing with you."

"Eagle's Talons. That may affect the alliance War and your Four need." He glared at Jenna. "Ava, you should not have borne this child. Frankly, I'm astonished your Gods haven't punished you yet for your audacity."

Jenna clutched her child to her chest. "First of all, Your Royal Avatarness, Gwen wouldn't marry you even if all of the Four asked her to. She still remembers the Fip Annexation from a previous life, and it wasn't as glorious as the ballads say."

"Has your country been at war since?" he snapped.

"It might as well be, when you take our farmers and harvests from us!" she countered. "And second, what's this about an alliance between our gods and yours? They haven't told us anything about that." *If Spring wants to treat with War, why wouldn't She marry Him Herself? Or is this why Gwen's engagement is in trouble?*

By All Four, would They expect Gwen to marry Lex? How could either of them stand that? How could Jenna stand by and watch two lovers, one from this life, the other from a previous one, make each other miserable?

I would pledge myself a Fallswoman if I thought Gwen would do the same for me, so we could be together in this life, just like all the others we've shared. But she's determined to marry, even if she hasn't decided who the lucky groom will be. I'm a better match for Lex than she is. All I have to do is make him realize that.

The crowd suddenly quieted. Jenna glanced up to the open space at the top of the Temple stairs. Gwen, Ysabel, Kron, and Kay crept down toward Jenna. Four low notes rang out from the bell tower. As the last one faded away, Sophia entered from the left, while her husband entered from the right.

Jenna grabbed Lex's arm and whispered, "The soltrans is starting. We should clear the stairs."

He nodded. "Are you going up to the boxes?" The building straight across from the Temple boasted large windows at the same level as the Temple stage. The Fip royals had a private room reserved for their use, and nobles squabbled for seats near the windows so they could watch the soltrans in comfort.

Jenna gestured toward a shaded section in front of the Temple marked off by green ribbons. Dorian already stood there, arms crossed as he scowled at Sophia.

"We prefer to stay outside," Jenna told Lex. "We feel closer to the Four that way."

"As you will, Ava." He bowed, though not as deeply as her rank required. "You have given me much to think about. Enjoy the solstice."

He could have at least wished me a happy birthday too. Even if he follows the Fip God of War, he should know all Avatars celebrate their birthdays on the first day of their seasons.

Sophia waited until Jenna's quartet joined Dorian before beginning her praise chant to the Goddess of Spring:

Thank You, yellow-haired Mother of Us all,
Thank You for the blessings You have let fall;
We praise You for the sunshine and the warmth,
We thank You for the new life from the Earth....

"We should update the words so they rhyme again, the way they did a long time ago," Ysabel whispered.

"We'd best establish ourselves as Season Avatars before we challenge tradition," Gwen whispered back. "Our quartet already breaks several traditions as it is."

Ysabel blushed. Half Selathen, with a twin brother born the day before the fall equinox, she was the last person anyone would think of as a Season Avatar. Gwen turned her head to study Jenna, who met Gwen's gaze without flinching. Maybe as a widowed mother, she was unusual for an Avatar too. Gwen would probably be just as happy to see Jenna remarried to someone else. *To Lex, or to anyone?* Jenna hoped Gwen wouldn't change her mind and want Lex after all. They had enough issues from their last life without introducing jealousy in this one.

Then again, if the Four did want Their Avatars to ally themselves with Lex, or if Robbie was destined to become a War Avatar, what did that mean for Challen?

The sun continued to shine as Charles challenged Sophia and they tapped their staves together in ritual combat. Even so, Jenna felt cold inside.

CHAPTER SEVEN

The Question of Kron

To Jenna's disappointment, Lex didn't attend the special dinner later that evening at the Season Avatars' house in Wistica. There wasn't enough room to hold a dance, but Ysabel's mother, after several protests that she was hopelessly out of practice, consented to perform a private concert for the Avatars and select guests after the dinner. Several unattached nobles and wealthy businessmen stopped in to introduce themselves to Jenna and the rest of her quartet. Jenna smiled and flirted with all of them, but none of them appealed to her more than Lex did. She hoped Gwen, Ysabel, and Kay would have better luck. After the concert, the four of them gathered in Gwen and Jenna's room with leftover cake and wine to compare notes. Gwen also linked with Ysabel and Kay so they would be less drawn to deathbushes in the future.

"Found a more suitable fiancé yet, Gwen?" Jenna asked as she poured four glasses of a fine red, taking care not to spill on the bed quilt.

Gwen shrugged and unpinned her chignon, spilling blonde hair down her back. Gold hairpins clinked as she dropped them in a glass jar on the nightstand. "I've met some of the guests already on previous trips to Wistica. Most of them too old or too conceited or too foolish for my tastes, if I were to choose for myself."

"You should choose for yourself!" Jenna insisted.

"You don't have to worry about your family's estate," Gwen retorted. "Someone needs to manage it for me. I'll be spending most of my time at the One Oak or here in Wistica or on a Grand Tour with you three, so I need someone I can trust."

"But then your husband will have to live apart from you." Ysabel tucked her feet under her skirt.

"True. I think most of these men have enough to do managing their own interests, though some of the newly rich seek the prestige of an alliance with the lo Havils—or the One Oak. Gold diggers, Aunt Gabri would call them." Gwen sipped her wine thoughtfully.

Jenna shook her head. That wasn't what she wanted for Gwen—or for any of her sister Avatars. Surely there had to be enough handsome young noblemen for all of them. At thirty-eight, Lex wasn't young, but his royal rank and Avatar status—not to mention his broad shoulders and arms—more than made up for that.

"I never told Jon I was an Avatar." Kay stared out the window, as if he might be waiting beneath it. "I wonder how he reacted to the letter I left him. I haven't heard back from him yet."

"How long have you known him?" Ysabel asked.

"Nearly four years. I met him while I was trying to leave Wistica, right after I gained control of my magic and the nightmares started." Kay clutched a pillow to herself. "I tried hiding aboard a locomotive to escape, but he found me. Instead of throwing me off the train, he let me stay and even shared his meals with me." Her eyes shone bright. "I'm not looking for a nobleman. Jon is prince enough for me."

Jenna admitted it was a romantic story, though Kay could do better than a train engineer if she chose. "At least Ysabel's unattached. All the young men will court her."

"Mama only married because Fall came to her in a dream and asked her to." Ysabel deftly moved her cake plate before Pouncer could steal a bite. "She told me I shouldn't marry unless it was my choice. But I never wanted to be a Fallswoman like her. I want lots of children."

Even after your own sister wanted nothing to do with you? Jenna had an older sister and two younger brothers, but she didn't want many children, only one or two more.

Gwen drained her glass. "Kron has a unique aura—whitish-yellow. I've never seen anything like it before. Given that he came forward hundreds of years through time, I should probably make sure he's still...vigorous before the two of you get marriage tattoos."

Ysabel sat upright. "I never said I was going to marry him! By All Four Gods and Goddesses, I don't remember marrying him at all."

"I wonder if I married Jon before," Kay said wistfully. "Sometimes when you meet someone, it feels like you knew them in a previous life. But we Avatars are the only ones who can be certain about it."

"That's the oddest part of it all." Despite the warm summer night, Ysabel shivered. "I've never met anyone other than an Avatar who remembers so much about our previous lives. He claims he was there when the Four gifted us with our magic. Not even we remember that far back." She glanced at each of them, her flecked eyes holding a mute appeal. "He frightens me a little with his persistence."

Kay put her hand over Ysabel's. "Have faith in the Four. Fall won't let anyone hurt you."

"And neither will we," Jenna said.

Surprisingly, Gwen didn't add her support. She played with the bracelet of live violets she still wore as protection from the frozen shard in her wrist. "Ysabel, I didn't know what to think of Kron either when we first met. That's why Summer gave him this to give to me, as a sign we could trust him."

Ysabel let out a shaky laugh. "Then where's my bouquet from Kron and the Four?"

"Be grateful you don't need one."

"If the Four trust him, that alone should be enough reason for us to accept him," Kay said. "Besides, wasn't he our first teacher? It seems a shame to turn him away, especially if he wasn't born into this time or place. Where else would he go?"

"Back to the University where we found him, I suppose." Jenna poured the last of the wine for herself. "We don't need a teacher anymore. We have more experience with our magic from our previous lives. All we need to do is practice, and our skills will bloom like flowers."

"He has a type of magic we'll never have." Gwen finished her cake and set the plate aside. "Maybe it would be helpful for us to have him at the One Oak."

Ysabel's eyes widened.

"We won't try to link with him," Gwen said, "but he could be helpful in other ways. I'm not saying you have to let him court you, Ysabel, but we shouldn't be too quick to send him away."

We might not be able to send him away. Jenna remembered how he'd made it to Tradetown before they could. He might choose to move to Midpoint and call on the One Oak daily until Ysabel either accepted him or told every animal in the area to harass him in turn.

"If everyone thinks that's the best thing to do…"

"By the Four, it's not what we want, Bel, it should be what you want," Jenna said. "Do you really want a skinny man old enough to be your father for a suitor when there are plenty of nobles to choose from?"

Ysabel blushed, but she said, "What about the War Avatar, Jenna? Isn't he too old for you too?"

"He's got rank and muscles. That makes up for it." She sighed as she remembered a hot summer day beneath the biggest rose bush in Challen.

"Is it true his weapon is magic?" Kay asked, pale blue eyes gleaming.

"Which one?"

Ysabel and Kay laughed. Even proper Gwen smiled knowingly. Pouncer took advantage of the moment to steal the last of the cake. By the time Ysabel took it away from him, everyone else had settled down.

Ysabel took a deep breath. "I've decided. Kron can stay at the One Oak, but not in the Fall Wing. And…and he has to stop talking about a life I don't remember."

"That's reasonable," Gwen said.

"It does seem a shame not to let him tell us about the Four, though." Kay turned to Ysabel. "I think in his way, Kron is devoted to you."

"He doesn't love me! He loves Bella. I haven't been Bella in eight hundred years." Ysabel chewed on her lip. "Maybe he won't love me now that I'm Ysabel."

"If he wants to court you, he should start over," Jenna said. "He's acting as if you've been waltzing with your bodies pressed close together for an entire evening when you've barely been introduced to him. Someone should tell him that."

Three pairs of eyes stared at her.

"An excellent idea, Jenna." Gwen beamed at her, making her heart sing. "You should do it."

"Me?"

"It was your idea."

"Could you, Jenna?" Ysabel looked at her with eyes as irresistible as a kitten's. "It would make things so much easier for me."

How could she refuse? She had the most experience with men, so it shouldn't be too hard persuading Kron to be more subtle with his pursuit of Ysabel.

"I will," Jenna promised. "I should talk to him anyway about the strange plants I found here and in Tradetown. Maybe he knows something about them."

"Thank you, Jenna." Gwen raised her glass. "A toast to Jenna, our sister Summer Avatar, on her birthday! May the Four favor her in every season and grant her many more."

"Hail!" Ysabel and Kay toasted her as well. Kay covered up a yawn with her glass.

"We should all get some rest," Gwen said. "Tomorrow's going to be a long day of travel."

The last time Jenna had traveled from Wistica to the One Oak, she had sailed northwest up the Chikasi River on a steamboat. This time, the Avatars' schedule coincided with one of the locomotives traveling from the capital city to Midpoint. They would have to get up at dawn, but they would arrive at Midpoint in time for a late supper. They might even be able to reach the One Oak tomorrow night if the weather and horses cooperated. With two Fall and two Winter Avatars along, they shouldn't have any problems—unless Dorian and Kay quarreled. Jenna hoped they would be able to avoid each other on the crowded locomotive.

Ysabel and Kay said goodnight and left for the room they were sharing. Gwen and Jenna were sharing not just the room, but the bed. If they bumped into each other in the middle of the night, would they link and share dreams? Would Gwen learn the truth about their last marriage?

"I don't need a blanket in this warm weather. Here, you can have it." Jenna pushed the comforter into the middle of the bed.

Gwen disappeared behind a screen and returned a few moments later in a silk nightgown—pale yellow, of course. "I certainly don't need it either. Ready for bed?"

Jenna quickly changed before Gwen turned down the lights in the sconce. "Now I am. Good night, Gwen."

"Pleasant dreams, Jenna."

Jenna's dreams of their previous marriage were anything but pleasant.

* * *

Later that morning, still exhausted and suffering from a wine-induced headache, Jenna sat at the far end of the locomotive station, as far away from the line of people buying tickets as she could be. Using a light shawl to cover herself, she discreetly nursed Robbie. Callie, Gwen, Ysabel, and Kay surrounded her, sheltering her from the stares of the few other people boarding the train with them.

Kay kept watch out the window. "Jon might be on this train," she said, "but normally he doesn't come this far east."

Ysabel smiled. "I'm sure you're looking forward to seeing him again."

The whistle of an oncoming train gave Kay a chance to slip away without answering. Jenna handed Robbie over to Callie, then followed her outside. Puffs of steam and roiling black smoke obscured their sight of the train. Jenna wasn't surprised when the wind changed and blew the smoke away. Kay watched the train approach, but before it pulled into the station, she retreated to the back of the group.

"What are you doing?" Gwen asked. "Don't you want to see him?"

"Of course I do. I'm not ready for him to see me."

"But you look beautiful," Ysabel said.

Now that Kay could count on regular, bountiful meals to give her energy for magic, she'd gained some slight curves. Her short, black hair shone, and her hat ribbon and dress matched her light blue eyes. With her hands worked into white kidskin gloves, she appeared almost as confident in her outfit as noble-born Gwen. Jenna had left her family farm for a townswoman's life before Gwen had found her, and she still expected to find manure and dust on her gowns. Kay, as a former seamstress, was more comfortable with silk and lace than she was.

She stared down at her clothes and let out a sharp laugh. "I don't look anything like the seamstress he courted."

"You think he won't accept that you're an Avatar?" Gwen asked. "He and my former betrothed would get along famously, then, despite the difference in their stations."

"Do you want me to talk to Jon?" Jenna offered. "I can let him know you still care for him."

"Oh, could you?" The tension left Kay's face. "You know much more about how to handle men than any of us do."

If I know so much about men, why doesn't Lex want anything to do with me? Jenna put on a smile. "Why, thank you, Kay."

As the train eased to a halt, Jenna stood on tiptoe and peered at the engine. The cab window was so small she wondered how the driver could see where they were going. Three men poured out of the engines, all of them in soot-stained clothes. Jenna would have been hard-pressed to tell them apart. Kay, however, gasped and fell back.

"Which one is he?" Jenna asked.

"The one on the right."

Kay's Jon was the dirtiest of the lot; he must have been the one shoveling coal. His jacket was off, and his shirt stuck to his chest and arms, exposing pure muscle. Jenna had to stop herself from licking her lips. No wonder Kay was reluctant to let him go.

"He's not going to be on our trip," Kay continued, disappointment and relief warring in her tone. "He'll get a layover if he's been working all night."

"Then I'd better talk to him before he disappears." Jenna darted forward so quickly all Gwen could call after her was "Be quick!"

Jenna reached for her skirts, intending to run after the men, before remembering she should show more dignity as an Avatar. That didn't stop her from calling, "Jon!" She didn't know his last name, so she hoped he wouldn't be offended by the familiarity. "Stop! I want to talk to you!"

The passengers on the platform stared at her, mouths open in shock. Jon continued into the station as if he hadn't heard. When Jenna followed him inside, the door to the ticket window closed.

She dashed over and called, "Jon! Jon!"

The elderly ticket seller woke from his doze. "Huh? Ava, the train is boarding. You should be outside—"

"They wouldn't dare leave without me." She hoped. She flashed a man a brilliant smile. "I need to speak to one of the crew members who just came in, the one named Jon. Do you know where he went?"

"The fireman? One moment, Ava." He called, "Jon, clean up! You have a very important visitor!"

A few heartbeats later, Jon appeared. Soot still ringed his eyes, and his wet hair stuck up. He'd thrown a jacket over his shirt. He stared at her warily, with no signs of recognition from their first locomotive trip to Rainbow River, where they'd found Kay. Wasn't Jenna beautiful enough to be memorable?

"Lady? No, Avatar," he said. "You're one of the new Avatars."

Gwen would say it would be proper etiquette for someone else to introduce them. Seeing as their mutual acquaintance was unavailable, Jenna didn't mind doing it herself. "Jenna t'Reve, the next Summer Avatar." She gave him a pointed look. "Sister Avatar to Kay Seltich, the next Winter Avatar."

"Kay." He swallowed. "It's true, then? She's the next Winter Avatar?"

"As sure as I'll be wearing green for the rest of my life. And she wants to know if she can be sure of you."

He laughed harshly. "Me? Married to an Avatar? She might as well be a Crown Princess of Fip. She's moved into a better world now, as far above me as a star."

She leaned closer. "She still loves you."

His eyebrows flew up in surprise, but all he said was, "That may change once she meets more wealthy nobles. I know we discussed marriage, but she shouldn't consider herself bound by that."

"Why not tell her directly and let her decide?" Jenna asked. "She's free to make up her own mind. Her family doesn't expect her to make a brilliant match for them." Jenna wondered if Gwen would really choose her own spouse or end up with someone her family picked out for her. Her own parents had just been relieved when someone offered to marry her before her belly swelled.

Before Jon could speak, the train outside sounded two toots. He shook his head. "No time for that now. If you plan to take that train, Ava, you'd better board before they leave without you."

"They wouldn't dare!" she said indignantly.

He left the ticket window without responding.

Jenna hurried outside to find the passengers had all disappeared. One of the conductors beckoned her over to the first-class carriage. She ignored the folding footstool and climbed into the train on her own without getting her dress tangled on the steep steps. The train jerked forward as she made her way to the Avatar party. Two older nobles shared their carriage, but although they eyed the women, especially Gwen and Jenna, with interest, they stayed in the corner and read their newspapers.

Jenna slid into an empty seat next to Kay, who stared at her with hopeful eyes.

"He said…he said…you're like a star."

Kay beamed. She and the other Avatars leaned closer.

"And?" Gwen asked.

Jenna shrugged. "And…I let him know you could choose whom you want to marry."

"So, when is he coming to the One Oak?" Kay asked. "When can I see him?"

Jenna stared at her. "You wanted me to ask him that?"

"Well, didn't you?"

"I didn't know that was what you wanted."

Kay sighed so heavily Jenna glanced up to see if a raincloud was going to appear in their carriage.

Freeze it, maybe she wasn't as good at arranging other peoples' romances as she thought she was. Hopefully her upcoming talk with Kron about Ysabel would proceed more smoothly. He sat on the other side of the train in his own seat, behind Dorian, as he stared out the window. Jenna watched him as Gwen and Kay discussed how to arrange to have Jon transferred to a position based in Midpoint and if it could be done without his realizing who was behind it. Dorian looked haggard, with dark circles making his complexion appear sallow. He leaned back against the seat with his eyes closed, but he tossed and turned restlessly.

The train followed the Chikasi River for several hours. The train's path was straighter than the river's, veering around obstacles but never straying too far from Challen's main travel route. They passed fields and orchards. Jenna eyed them critically, but the locomotive traveled faster than a galloping horse, so she couldn't examine the plants closely enough to determine how healthy they were. She didn't see any deathbushes, though she would have liked to walk through the farmlands and touch the plants to learn more about their health.

If the plants were plentiful, the people weren't. Occasionally Jenna spotted someone working in a field. Twice they stopped at hamlets where the biggest building was the granary. They had a few moments to walk on the platform while goods were loaded or unloaded and the train took on water and coal. At the second stop, Jenna asked a farmer how his crops were this year. He complained about the weather and pests and the state of his soil, but he didn't mention any strange plants until the end.

"Oh, and the weeds this year are growing so fast, you'd think the Summer Avatar was growing them on purpose."

Charles suffered an acute coughing fit.

"What do they look like?" Jenna asked.

Before he could answer, the train let out a warning whistle.

"Send a sample to the One Oak!" she called before boarding the train.

As they pulled away, the farmer waved his hat at her, a puzzled look on his face.

They stopped for luncheon at a larger town called Apple Valley. The inn overlooked the Chikasi and featured a large balcony with tables. Jenna leaned on the railing and admired the view. The sun's warmth faded as someone joined her. She turned her head and saw Kron.

"I almost think I recognize this turn of the river," he said. "There were more trees here in my time, but they were oak and birch, not apple. I think the bend was sharper then too."

She nodded, unsure of how to respond.

He gave her a wry grin. "So, I hear you're the one to talk to about romance."

Her face heated up from inside. "I'm not the Avatar of Love."

He laughed, not unkindly. "No, Summer is too shy to woo anyone. He must have chosen you for your boldness."

"Me?" she said, flattered.

"Well, you are still very much like Janno, though I doubt you chase women the way he did."

"Of course I can't do that anymore!" The idea sparked images in her mind of her wooing Gwen the way Lex had wooed her. She couldn't take it as far as Lex had, however.

"And I bet Gwen would disapprove as much as she did when she was your mother."

"My mother? By All Four, I don't need more details from that life." She tilted her head back to the table, where Ysabel sat watching them. "What about Bel? Has she changed since she was your Bella?"

"More than I imagined." He pressed a protruding nail into the railing with a finger. "She…she doesn't want to listen to me the way Bella did. She seems more confident now, even after all of the trouble with her family." He sighed. "One thing that hasn't changed is her desire for a family."

"Most people are reborn with no memories of their previous lives," Jenna said. "We keep some, particularly those dealing with magic. But we remember personal details too. Most of us have been both men and women, but Ysabel has always been a woman in every life."

Kron nodded. "Not surprising. Fall has been hostile to me every time I've seen Her. I wouldn't want to meet Her alone, without Spring to temper Her." He hesitated. "She must have a reason to hate men so much."

"Only the Four know what that is." Jenna made the sign of the Four over her heart. "Anyway, Kron, we don't remember as much about our early lives as we do more recent ones. I hate to say it, but…Ysabel doesn't remember the life you had together however long ago it was."

"I suspected as much." His voice developed a dangerous edge. "And I wonder why."

By All Four, did he think Fall Herself was blocking Ysabel's memories of him? Jenna shivered. He could be right, but she wouldn't want to oppose any of the Four. Time to move away from potentially blasphemous territory and onto the advice she wanted to give him.

"You have to start over with her," she said. "Pretend you're two strangers who have just met."

"I don't know if I can do that, Jenna."

"You have to." She met his gaze head on. "You're a stranger to her, and to us. If you want the chance to win her heart again, then restrain yourself."

He stood straight. "By All Four, do you think I would force myself on her? I don't need you or a child goddess to teach me how to behave decently. I knew that hundreds of years ago. If your Challen men must be punished before they learn good manners, then I pity the rest of you when you wed." He turned to go back inside the restaurant, then faced Jenna again. "Or perhaps I should pity the man foolish enough to marry you."

Jenna glared at him, half-tempted to pull off the top railing and batter him with it. She flinched when the door rattled behind Kron as if he meant to send it flying toward her. She retreated to a corner of the balcony next to a rosebush, hoping its scent would calm her. All she could do was stare at the stems and wonder why she'd shown her own thorns to Kron.

Gwen came up to her and offered her a glass of dry red wine. "By All Four, Jenna, we just wanted him to court Ysabel more slowly, not run away from us. We might need him again."

A faint smile brightened her face, so she couldn't be too upset. Jenna couldn't help feeling she'd failed her sister Avatars, especially Gwen. She was the one who'd wanted her to help Ysabel and Kay, but Jenna was only making their lives harder.

"I'm sorry." She stared into her wine. "I shouldn't have been that harsh with him. He's done everything he can to help us."

"I was suspicious of him at first too, remember?" Gwen asked. "Without him, we wouldn't have rescued Ysabel in time."

Of course, that didn't mean he had a right to claim Ysabel as his bride. That had been in another life. They'd only been married once, not like Gwen and Jenna. But Jenna couldn't marry Gwen this time. Maybe she shouldn't be jealous that Kron had a second chance with his love. She didn't deserve one with Gwen.

"I…I'll go beg his pardon." Jenna set the glass aside without having touched a drop. She would have given it back to Gwen, but she didn't want to risk linking with her and letting her feel Jenna's guilt.

CHAPTER EIGHT

The One Oak's Welcome

Kron accepted Jenna's apology, but he chose to sit with Dorian for the afternoon train ride. Nothing good could come from associating with that discontented Avatar, especially since Dorian seemed very interested in what Kron had to tell him and asked several questions about Salth, the Dead Land, and the Avatars' first life. Jenna joined a card game of Seasons with her sister Avatars and misplayed most of her hands trying to listen to Kron and Dorian. By the time the entire party disembarked at Midpoint, she was grateful for the chance to move around. Gwen's Aunt Gabri had chosen to stay behind in Wistica to help Ysabel's family settle in, so Gwen posted instructions to her servants at her country house. Then everyone boarded carriages for the last leg of the journey. Soon Jenna's opportunities for more journeys would be limited.

She stared through the twilight at the oaks lining the path to the old house, which had been built shortly after Challen had been annexed into the Fip Empire. The first Summer Avatar who had lived here had started a tradition of force-growing an oak tree from an acorn as a counterpart to the Fall Avatar's anilink. The tree helped the Summer Avatar extend his or her reach across Challen. Each new Summer Avatar grew a new tree. Over the centuries, the trees had created their own little forest. Tomorrow, or as soon as Jenna had settled in, she would have to select an acorn from storage and find the perfect spot to plant it. She hoped she could find a clearing, but since the trees were considered too sacred to cut down, they crowded together, choking off new life.

Jenna hoped the house and the old Season Avatars wouldn't do that to her.

Before they'd boarded their hired carriages in Midpoint, Sophia had summoned an owl and persuaded him, despite derisive cawing from her crow anilink, to carry a message to the One Oak ahead of them. Jenna wasn't surprised to see the grooms waiting to assist them, but she didn't expect the other servants—from the butler down to the lowest scullery maid—to be lined up in front of the entrance and dressed in clean uniforms. Lanterns posted along the drive cast a crescent of light above them.

The butler stepped forward and bowed to each of the older Avatars before turning to Gwen and bowing again. "Ava, welcome home, and congratulations on finding the rest of your set. All Avas this time, I see."

"Yes, Frederick." She beckoned Jenna, Ysabel, and Kay forward. "Jenna t'Reve, Ysabel s'Ivena Lathatilltin, and Kay Seltich, I would like you to meet our new butler, Frederick Pippen. If there's anything you need when we're here, it's his job to arrange it."

Gwen led them to the chief housekeeper, Dame Elga H'even, a woman with iron-gray hair and a back as straight as a hoe. The housekeeper then took over the job of introducing every single servant to them. Jenna lost track of the names after the third maid, but Gwen spoke to and blessed each of them, taking care to use her unscarred hand. Jenna nodded at the servants, but she wasn't sure if she should bless them. Since her magic dealt with plants, it wouldn't be as effective here. Ysabel and Kay followed along, with Kay too shy to speak.

By the time the introductions were done, Jenna was exhausted and ravenous. The servants had set up a cold buffet in the dining room, but first she had to help Callie settle her overtired child. Robbie fussed so much it was difficult to get him to nurse. Once he calmed down, Jenna strolled with him through the public rooms of the One Oak, reacquainting herself with the layout and furnishings.

The original house had been built around a central courtyard, with each Avatar assigned to a separate side of the house. The front of the house was Spring's side, with Summer on one side and Winter on the other. Jenna turned toward the Summer side, distinguished by floral wallpaper and potted plants throughout. She passed a small parlor to head into the study. Books and journals lined the room from floor to ceiling, occasionally interrupted by pressed and framed leaves and flowers. Jenna grimaced at the thought of having to read everything to find clues about the new plants—if there were any clues to be found. Hopefully Charles would help her.

She noticed a door leading into the central courtyard. Did it lead where she thought it did? Shifting Robbie to her other arm, Jenna opened the door and peeked inside. Warm, humid air greeted her, along with scents of moss, soil, and various herbs. The atrium. It was dark inside, with not enough starlight to show her the rows of plants and the seed bank in the corner of the atrium. Tomorrow she would come here to choose an acorn, but if she couldn't find any information about the deathbushes, she would have to try growing them here under controlled conditions and learn the best way to destroy them.

"Jenna, aren't you going to eat?" Gwen glided up behind her. "You'd better come to the dining room before all the food disappears. I don't think the staff realizes yet how much food seven Avatars can eat every day."

"I'll be right there. Where's Callie? Robbie's ready for bed."

"Speaking of that…" Gwen lowered her voice. "Apparently Charles and Sophia share the Summer Avatar's suite. You'll have to take another bedroom."

Jenna sighed wistfully. From what she remembered, the Avatar suites were bigger than her family's farmhouse, big enough to boast two fireplaces, a sitting area, and a dressing room. She wouldn't be surprised if Charles had had one of the new water closets installed.

She itched to have a place of her own she could fill with pretty dresses. Hopefully now that they were settled, they could send for seamstresses to make new wardrobes for everyone.

"I suppose you don't have to worry about that since Margaret is with the God of Winter," Jenna said.

Gwen shook her head. "No, Dorian shared the Spring Suite with her. He says he wants to stay there with all of her things so he doesn't forget her."

"How sad."

Gwen sighed. "From the way he glares at me, I think he'd like to eject me out of the Spring Wing altogether. I have a feeling my bedroom will be freezing tonight."

"Maybe you should stay in the Summer Wing with me," Jenna suggested. "We can keep each other company, the way we did while we were traveling so much." It would be dangerous continuing to share a room with Gwen, as they might accidentally link. But having Gwen close by would make this huge house more homelike.

"No, I'm not going to let him drive me out of my own wing." Gwen's voice developed an edge. "I'm not going to toss him out of the Spring Suite, but I'm the current Spring Avatar now. Once the four of us prove we can tame a Chaos Season, then the older three Avatars need to step down so we can be officially recognized. We've been doing it this way for hundreds of years. Dorian knows what to expect. He should give way to Kay as gracefully as the real seasons do."

"And has he ever done that?"

Gwen sighed. "Not in any life we know was his."

"What are you going to do about him?"

"Normally, I'd let the Avatars from his own set handle Dorian. But with Margaret gone, Charles and Sophia can't manage him." She lowered her voice. "You'll see what I mean in the dining room."

Callie waited in the hallway, and Jenna gratefully passed her sleeping son to him. Robbie seemed to have gained twenty pounds on the walk back. Ysabel and Kay, on the other hand, were absent when

Jenna entered the dining room with Gwen. As Gwen had predicted, most of the food was already gone. However, the wine still flowed at the end of the table occupied by the three older Avatars. Charles leaned back in his chair, snoring. He must have had a magic talent to sleep while Sophia and Dorian, backs toward the door, argued with each other.

"By All Four, they're not ready!" Dorian said. "I don't think they'll ever be ready. There's something wrong with their set."

Gwen raised a finger to her lips, but Jenna didn't need the caution. She flattened herself against the wall, wishing her dress didn't stand out so much against the pale yellow wallpaper. Maybe the best thing to do would be to sneak out of the room silently before the other Avatars noticed them. Jenna's stomach rumbled again. She needed to eat now, and her curiosity was almost as strong as her hunger.

Gwen tapped Jenna's arm—the sleeve prevented her from linking—and sank to the floor. Jenna copied her. They faced each other. Gwen scowled, but Jenna didn't think the anger was directed at her—for once.

"What do you mean, something's wrong with their set?" Sophia slurred her words. "Have you noticed we're the ones without a Spring Avatar?"

"You frozen fool! How can I forget for a heartbeat that Margaret's gone? She calls out to me in my dreams, pleading for help."

"Help? Dorian, she's with the Four now." Sophia patted Dorian's hand. "They will take care of her until the two of you can be reborn together."

"That's the problem. They don't have her!"

Sophia snorted in a most unladylike manner. "How much wine have you had?"

"Less than you. We'll talk more about Margaret in the morning, when your winehead has cleared." His tone hardened. "Even with wineheads, we're still better suited to handle Chaos Season than the girls are."

"Nonsense. Youth doesn't matter when they have their memories."

"Are you sure of that? Because the way the Fall and Winter Avatars were wandering around, they didn't seem to remember the One Oak at all."

"It was their first time here in this life, Dorian. Every set changes the house a little. In another day or so, it will be home to them."

"And it's still our home." Dorian punctuated "our" by slamming the glass down on the table. A piece of the base broke off and bounced against the wall.

"And I still think we should leave after they've proved they can handle a Chaos Season," Sophia said. "So should you. Go visit that adorable grandson Margaret helped deliver."

"Margaret needs me to stay here."

Sophia shook her head. "Let her rest with the God of Winter, Dorian. She deserves it. You'll see her soon enough."

"So will a lot of other people."

"By All Four, what do you mean?"

Jenna crept closer to the buffet table, followed by Gwen.

"The Spring Ava didn't heal anyone at the soltrans, did she? Maybe that frozen shard stole her magic, just like it stole Margaret's life."

Gwen winced.

"But she said they linked, all four of them."

"Ha! I'll believe that when I see it. Wasn't there some blasphemy involved with the Fall Avatar?"

"She might be the first Avatar who's part Selathen," Sophia said slowly, "but that doesn't matter."

"You mean, you hadn't heard she had a twin brother?"

"A twin…brother?" Sophia laughed. "By All Four, Dorian, you've had too much wine. Avatars can't have twins; that would interfere with their magic. My Goddess would never allow a twin brother anywhere near one of Her Avatars. We're lucky She allows us to marry."

Gwen and Jenna exchanged glances. Dorian had learned a great deal about their quartet. It didn't matter, though. They'd worked with Ysabel and knew her magic was effective. If it wasn't, they would have lost her—and Gwen too—when Sal-thaath captured them.

"It gets worse," Dorian said. "Their Winter Avatar doesn't want to use her magic at all."

"That is bad," Sophia agreed. "Without Kay, they have no chance of taming a Chaos Season. But we can't do it without Margaret either."

"I can pull the magic from the weather—"

"And then what would you do with it? How would I heal animals and Charles restore the harvest? No, our group is done, Dorian." Sophia rose, grasping the edge of the table as she swayed. "Thank the Four. Even Margaret would say you mourn her too much."

"You never knew her the way I did!" The air grew colder, as if Dorian intended to make it snow inside the house. "You and Charles may have linked with us, but she never let you two see her most private thoughts!"

"That didn't matter. She made no secret of being ready to step down. Healing people is never-ending, weary work, Dorian, even harder than tending plants or animals. She wanted a rest. Let her have it."

Sophia staggered out. Dorian poured himself another glass of wine as he mumbled to himself. Jenna couldn't make out everything he said, but she heard the word "sunshine" several times. Gwen crept forward. As he stared into his glass, frosting it over, Gwen rose behind him and touched his ear. He fell forward and would have landed on his wineglass if Gwen hadn't moved it at the last heartbeat.

Jenna crept out from under the table and straightened herself. "Thank the Four I can finally eat. I'm starving."

"I could use some more bread and cheese myself." Gwen wiped her hands on her dress as she stepped away from the snoring Dorian.

"I don't think my curse affected him. If there was anyone I might wish it on, it would be him, no matter how much he's grieving."

Jenna grabbed a loaf of bread and sliced off a piece as thick as her thumb. "What, not your tender fiancé William?"

"At least he doesn't have a grudge against my sister Avatars."

"Dorian's in mourning, Gwen." His snow-white suit made Jenna feel guilty over wearing pure green. She should switch to half-mourning for Thomas, her absent husband. "He hurts so much he thinks his wife shares his suffering. Don't you feel any pity for him?"

"I would, if I didn't think he loves his magic as much, if not more than, his wife."

Jenna chewed on that as she ate. She washed down the last of her sandwich with some wine. Finally she said, "Well, it doesn't matter what he thinks or says about us. He can't tame Chaos Season without the rest of his set. All he can do is teach Kay—oh." Jenna widened her eyes. "He's the last Avatar who should work with her. One day with him, and she'll hide in some windowless room and never come out again."

"If we're lucky, he won't have anything to do with us." Gwen stared at him. "The four of us can practice with Kay. I see no reason why Sophia can't assist Ysabel or Charles help you. But we should discourage Kay from having Dorian teach her."

"I don't think that will be a problem," Jenna said. "They've barely spoken to each other."

"Good. Let's keep it that way." Gwen touched Dorian's neck. "I have a feeling he'll sleep in late tomorrow with a fierce headache. We can get up early and practice our linking."

"Why Gwen, are you using your magic to hurt him? I thought Springs consider that an abuse of their magic."

Gwen flashed a wicked smile. "No, I wouldn't do that to an Avatar. I'm just letting him harvest what he planted—or drank."

Jenna couldn't help grinning herself at Gwen's less-than-proper behavior. She hoped the four of them could prove their skill quickly.

The sooner they tamed a Chaos Season, the sooner they would be recognized as official Avatars. Then it would be easier to deal with Dorian.

CHAPTER NINE

The Atrium

Jenna didn't rise at dawn—faint wailing from the nursery roused her in the middle of the night, and even though Callie arrived first to pick up Robbie, he didn't calm down until Jenna rocked him in her arms for an hour. She dragged herself out of bed when a maid came in with fresh water.

"Good morning, Ava." She curtseyed. "I'm to be your personal maid, if you're willing."

A personal maid. Jenna hadn't had one before, at least, not in this life. She struggled to remember what Gwen would do. "Ah, good morning."

"Clover. I'm called Clover." The maid was in her mid-twenties. She had a broad smile, despite the gap between her front teeth. "I thought you might not remember me from last night."

Jenna nodded ruefully. "By the Four, I barely remember the One Oak. At least, not this room."

Since Charles and Sophia still occupied the main summer suite, Jenna had been given a slightly smaller room. With its own fireplace, dressing area, and sitting area, it was as big as her family's cottage, which had held seven before her eldest brother had married. Her family would swell with pride if they had the time to visit. She would have to send them a letter and some chals once she'd settled in.

"Ava, will you eat here or in the breakfast nook?" Clover asked.

"Here." She didn't want to face one of the older Avatars with their words from last night fresh in her head. "Tell me, are my sister Avas awake?"

"All of them dined an hour ago, Ava."

Freeze it, Gwen would not be happy with her. Jenna found a simple dress suitable for working in the garden, braided her hair, and downed her breakfast quickly. She had to check on Robbie before starting her own work.

Robbie had just woken up a short while ago himself. Callie was attempting to feed him gruel, but he spat it back out, getting gruel not just on himself, but the table and his nursemaid. Jenna would have liked to stay and feed him herself, but all she could do was blow a kiss at him and leave before he started fussing for her.

As Jenna flew down the stairs, she debated if she should start force-growing her oak first or join Gwen and the others for linking practice. They had probably already begun and would lose focus if they had to stop and regroup to include her. Force-growing her tree would be easier on her if she could spread it out over several sessions. The sooner she started it, the sooner she would be ready to link with all the plants in Challen. The Avatars would have to gather at her oak during a Chaos Season, so she should pick a good location. Once the tree was established, they could include it in their practice link sessions. It made sense to Jenna to take care of her tree first before finding the others. Hopefully Gwen would agree with her.

Jenna let herself in to the main atrium occupying the center courtyard. She hadn't been able to view it properly last night, so she took a few heartbeats to admire it. Ages ago, the Avatars had put in a glass roof. Although direct sunlight exposure was limited to when the sun was overhead, the Winters ensured the room stayed warm and humid constantly. Sconces along the walls provided additional light. Plants that required more sun were grown in a separate greenhouse away from the main building, but Jenna preferred to work in this atrium as much as possible.

Four rows of tables lined the atrium. These tables were filled with different types of soil taken from various parts of Challen. Wooden sticks divided the tables into sections with different seedlings or plants in each one. Jenna walked up and down, reading the labels Charles had printed in a neat hand. Most of them were for peas and beans. Given his family background in producing wine, she would have expected more grapes. Maybe they were in the greenhouse. All of the plants in here were well-known to her. It didn't seem as if Charles was studying any of the strange plants. The Avatars had only returned yesterday, and she had the samples. It irked her that Charles wasn't interested in learning more about the deathbushes. Being near the end of his own term as reigning Avatar was no excuse, as he could bring the knowledge into his next life.

Jenna had brought a few deathbush seeds down with her, and she broke off their wings as she debated what to do with them. Most of the time, Summer Avatars wanted to make crops thrive and weeds wither. She needed to figure out what conditions would stop these seeds from sprouting. It would give her some ideas about how to handle them the next time she found them.

She found a couple of small cups and filled them from a barrel of water in the corner. Setting the cups down on a bench, she opened a cabinet that had stood there for three hundred years and had the scratches and dents to prove it. She grabbed a container of salt from one shelf and a stoppered pitcher of vinegar from another. One cup received a generous handful of salt; the other, enough vinegar to make her nose crinkle. Although she'd be able to tell the samples apart by the smell, Jenna followed Charles' example and wrote out labels for each cup. She put a deathbush seed in each cup and set them in the darkest corner of the atrium. Neither plant would likely sprout under the harsh conditions, but she didn't want to disturb what he was working on. That might give the older Avatars a reason to think her group couldn't handle Chaos Season.

Jenna labeled more paper, wrapped the remaining deathbush seeds in it, and placed them in a cubby of a shelf, high up where no one would take them accidentally. Then, with a sigh, she trudged to a corner where the door to the underground seed vault was. The small room was kept cool—but not too cold—by a block of ice. More baskets and boxes filled the vault. The light coming in from the open door was too dim for Jenna to read the labels, but she let her nose guide her to a tightly woven basket of sawdust. The sawdust protected the acorns. Time to bind herself to the One Oak—again.

Jenna wondered what would happen if she used two oaks at once, one here and one in another part of the country. Would that make her more sensitive to what was happening with Chaos Season, or would that be too confusing? Would she be able to force-grow the second tree if she wasn't able to visit it frequently?

Kron's portals would come in handy for something like that. I could have trees growing in every corner of Challen and visit them all in a single day. Maybe they could even travel around the country to take care of small Chaos Seasons. It would be less effort for Kay to unravel them on the spot instead of reaching through weather systems to sense a Chaos Season. She would have to propose the idea later, after making sure Gwen wasn't mad at her for avoiding link practice.

For now, Jenna had to focus on finding the acorn that best fit with her. She could plant other trees later if Kron was willing to make portals to their locations, but for now she needed at least one tree to help her tap into the plants of Challen. Her magic could make acorns sprout no matter what the season.

She reached into the basket, sneezing as she stirred up sawdust. The acorns had been gathered in the fall. They were past their prime but still capable of sprouting. Charles had done well in selecting and storing them. She touched a couple that seemed promising, but they tumbled away when she chased after them. Then one gave itself into her hand, the embryo inside reaching for her as if it thought she was the sun. Jenna pulled the acorn out of the basket and held it up in front of her face.

"Did you come from my last tree?" she asked it. "I'm sure you did. Well, little one, let's create some plant magic together."

The acorn seemed to swell in her hand, as if ready to burst open. She didn't need to place it in water to tell it was sound.

She tucked it next to her bosom and cleaned up, ready to find a suitable spot to plant her acorn. Before leaving, she glanced at her test cups and raised her eyebrows.

"By All Four, how do they do that?"

The deathbush seeds had already sprouted, with roots stretching over the sides, questing to do more damage.

CHAPTER TEN

A Sprout Duel

Jenna grabbed the sprouts out of both cups, heedless of the liquid spilling out, and squeezed them in her hands. *Die!* She urged them. *You were never meant to sprout.*

Several roots peeked out of each hand and curled over her fingers as if they planned to draw nourishment from her directly.

"Freeze it!" Freezing wouldn't work; she needed fire. Surely even these unnatural plants would burn. It was too warm for the fireplaces to be lit. She'd have to take these sprouts to the kitchen and hope they didn't harm the cooks.

She ran to the door and struggled with the latch. Roots wrapped around her fingers as if they knew how to hinder her. Once she managed to throw the door open, she bolted down the hall. Where was the kitchen, and how could she get to it? Her memories didn't extend to the servants' areas.

She spotted a housemaid polishing a sconce and ran up to her. "Show me to the kitchen right now!"

The maid dropped her rag. "Ava, you startled me! The kitchen? You don't belong there. I can send for food—"

"I don't need food, I need a fire!"

The maid opened the door to the Summer Study. "I'll lay one right away."

Jenna paced, pulling at the sprouts while the maid laid kindling and struck a match. As Jenna broke the plants apart, she tossed them into the fireplace. The still-damp roots wouldn't catch fire. Every flame that licked a root died.

As she reached for more tinder, the maid asked, "Should I call someone to help you, Ava?"

"Get the fire going first." Jenna took a deep breath. "Then find the current Avi Summer and the rest of my quartet." She didn't want them to find her in such an embarrassing state, but these plants were more dangerous than she'd thought. She needed to kill them before they developed thorns.

By the time the maid finally got the fire going, Jenna had managed to rip half the plant away from one hand. Her other hand was little more than a claw. The roots wrapped around her fingers were surprisingly tough. As she attacked them, they curled toward her free fingers.

"Better get Charles—the Avi Summer first," she said. "I've never dealt with such stubborn plants before."

The maid glanced again at Jenna's hand before running off.

Jenna scraped the roots against the rough bricks of the fireplace. She shredded a few roots along with her skin. The root tips turned toward the scrapes, questing like worms to bury inside. She renewed her efforts to remove them.

As if the link had drawn her, Gwen came in, followed by Kay and Ysabel. "Jenna!" She rushed forward. "By All Four, what are you doing?"

"Get this frozen plant off of me! Be careful." She grimaced. "It thinks my skin is soil."

"And you can't get it off on your own?" Gwen's tone was incredulous, but she came over. Scars on her palm were visible as she raised her hand with the cursed shard still embedded in it.

"I don't think your magic will work on plants, Gwen," Jenna said. "Even with the cursed shard."

Gwen met her eyes. "What if I send you the curse through the link, and you curse the plants? Are you willing to try that?"

"Is that possible? No, is it a good idea?" Jenna wasn't sure what would happen if she used the curse. What if it permanently twisted her magic? Even after getting the bracelet, Gwen didn't heal others as often as an Ava Spring normally would. Worse was the scar that hadn't disappeared. Springs could heal themselves of anything short of a mortal injury. They weren't supposed to have scars left over from some magical duel.

"We've already linked with Gwen before," Ysabel said. "Why not try it now?"

"We didn't touch her …injured hand before," Jenna replied. "That bracelet is supposed to protect us from her curse. I mean, the curse she carries."

Gwen's eyes darkened. At the rate Jenna kept accidentally offending her, they wouldn't be able to link for the next several lifetimes.

The roots squeezed Jenna's fingers. If she didn't get them off soon, she might lose her whole hand. That, along with the fear of alienating Gwen, made her decide on the brave course—or the rash one. "But maybe we should try it," she said. "I can't think of a better idea."

Kay glanced worriedly at Gwen's hand, but she didn't speak.

Please let this work, O Four, Jenna prayed. *And please don't let the curse infect our magic too. Ysabel and Kay shouldn't suffer for my foolishness.*

Gwen pushed her violet bracelet halfway up her arm, then offered Jenna her scarred hand. As Jenna reached for it, her wrapped hand brushed against the flowers. The roots shied away for an instant, long enough to let Jenna wiggle her numb fingers.

"Did you see that?" Jenna asked. Hope flared. "Maybe we don't have to link."

Gwen's expression flickered. Was she disappointed? She put on a stoic face while Jenna brought her hand up against the bracelet, almost but not quite touching it. The roots slithered up Jenna's arm, but they refused to release her.

"Let me try something," Kay said. "Gwen, will you link with me?"

"Of course," she replied.

Jenna felt as wanted as a weed.

Gwen laid a hand—her good one, Jenna noted—on top of Kay's. Moving together, they brought their hands closer to the roots, close enough Jenna worried she'd be drawn into their link. Then she felt the cold streaming from Kay's fingers. Kay seemed to be targeting the plants, but Jenna shivered as goosebumps appeared on her arm. Gwen brought her scarred hand in from the other side, forcing the roots back down toward Jenna's hand. They clung to Jenna for a few heartbeats before dropping onto the tiled floor.

"Toss them into the fire!" Jenna said as she rubbed life back into her tingling fingers.

Ysabel stabbed the center of the root mass with the fireplace poker and threw the plants into the fireplace, closing the screen before they could escape.

"By All Four Gods and Goddesses." Jenna sank onto a chair before her knees gave out. "I've never had problems controlling plants before, not in this life or any I remember."

"What happened?" Gwen moved closer to her, reaching for her hand. "Let me see that."

"It'll be fine." Jenna forced a smile and hoped it didn't look shaky. "I'm getting feeling back in my fingers already."

Gwen let out a huff of air, shaking her bangs off of her forehead. "I'll use my good hand, Jenna. You don't have to worry about the curse."

That wasn't her chief worry. But protesting too much would make the others suspicious, so Jenna let Gwen touch her hand. While Gwen examined it, Jenna told everyone about her disaster of an experiment. Talking not only kept her mind away from incriminating memories but kept the link between her and Gwen light, so Gwen couldn't see any memories from Jenna's previous lives.

Gwen gave her a curious look as she released her hand, now with full feeling restored, but all she said was, "So, you put the deathbush seeds into something you thought would kill them, and they sprouted instead?"

She nodded. "I have to learn the best way to stop them in case they return."

"Do you have any more of those seeds?" Ysabel asked.

"I put them on a shelf in the atrium, away from water." Sudden fear jolted her out of her chair. "By All Four, what if they've—"

She ran for the atrium, convinced the seeds had already sprouted and were ready to swallow the house. To her relief, they were still dormant, though she could have sworn she put the paper full of seeds farther back on the shelf. She eyed them for a moment, then took the packet and placed it in the seed vault, an iron safe. A few other twists of paper were already in there, but she took them out and placed them in the cabinet. It wouldn't do for the deathbushes to destroy the best strains of wheat, grapes, and other foodstuffs in Challen.

"I hope that's safe enough for now," she said as she relocked the door. "But I'm going to have to let them sprout sometime."

"Only in a fireplace, I hope." Gwen crossed her arms. "That seems to be the best way to keep them under control."

"Because my magic didn't."

Gwen silently rubbed her hand as Jenna and the other Avatars watched her. Maybe she had passed her curse on to Jenna during that brief link after all. Were Ysabel and Kay affected too? Neither of them had said anything about it.

By the Four, it had better be the curse. Whoever heard of a Summer Avatar who couldn't control plants? And Gwen feared she was going to be useless in this life.

Gwen gave Jenna a level look. "Maybe you should have come to us first and practiced the link. You probably could have handled it if we'd strengthened your magic."

"I shouldn't need the link to take care of a handful of sprouts!"

"No, you shouldn't," Gwen said. "But has anything gone the way it should in this life?"

"There's no reason to be ashamed of the link." Kay laid a hand on Jenna's sleeve. The link couldn't form between the two of them, so maybe she meant to be kind. "What would I do with all the magic of Chaos Season if I couldn't channel it into the three of you?"

"Chaos Season." Ysabel lifted her head. "If Chaos Season is weather gone wrong, then these plants are the Chaos Season of all flora."

Jenna smiled at the analogy. "By All Four, I'd hate to see what Chaos Season would look like as an animal! Probably something so mixed up it has both feathers and fur."

"But hopefully not vicious like your plants."

"Speaking of plants…" Jenna put her hand over her bosom, feeling for her acorn. It was still there, but the embryo within was uneasy at the presence of strange magic. "I think I should plant my oak tree as soon as possible, in a protected place."

"We could link with you and help you force-grow it," Gwen suggested.

"Usually only the Summer Avatar puts magic into her tree. It strengthens the bond between them if no one else is involved."

"We could link with you beforehand," Gwen said. "Or afterward, if you need more magic."

Jenna repressed a sigh. Gwen was only trying to be helpful. That meant she didn't know about her last death. How long could Jenna keep it that way?

"Maybe after I'm done," she said to appease Gwen. "First, I have to find the perfect spot."

CHAPTER ELEVEN

An Oak Sprouts

Jenna swept out of the room without checking to see if the others were following her. They all did. They were probably curious to see where they would gather in the future to tame Chaos Seasons. She wished they would leave her alone for this. Her confidence in her own magic had been shaken more than she wanted to admit. If it turned out she needed their help for this simple task, would she really be fit to be the next Summer Avatar?

Once she was outside, she sat on a bench and pulled her boots and stockings off. Direct contact with grasses and other plants eased her worries, not to mention it helped her determine the health of the land. It seems good to her, but she decided to ask another expert.

"Ysabel, how does the soil feel to you?" Jenna asked. "Is it alive enough?"

Ysabel squatted and stuck her fingers in the soil. "The little lives are there."

"Good. But we're still too close to the house. This tree wants space."

That was one problem about living in the middle of an oak forest with Summer Avatars—they took such good care of the trees that the oaks lived for hundreds of years. Summer Avatars had to discourage many acorns from sprouting in order to keep the trees from overrunning the estate. This was the wrong season for harvesting trees, so Jenna left the buildings behind and headed toward the Chikasi River. She preferred giving her tree a view of the river and tried to do so in every life.

She paused at the top of a small hill. A few oak seedlings poked out of the wild grasses and wildflowers living here. Below, a curve in the river sheltered a small dock used both for receiving supplies for the estate and launching rowboats.

"Remember that boat Kron made when we went to rescue Ysabel?" she asked. "I wonder what he did with it."

"For all I know, it's still where he left it," Gwen replied. "So, here? No other sites closer to the house?"

"Trees need space, Gwen," Jenna replied as she paced out an area to clear.

"Well, we need to be able to respond to Chaos Season promptly. If it takes us ten minutes to find your tree every time Kay senses Chaos Season, we give the storm more time to do damage—irreversible damage."

When Jenna had been ten summers old, a whirlwind had descended on a neighbor's farm, flattening both the barn and the house. The neighbors had lost all of their livestock, two children, and one of their parents. Half a moon later, the Ava Spring had ridden out to offer the survivors a purse of chals and her deepest regrets. Chals could help the family rebuild their barn and buy more goats, but even Spring Avatars couldn't bring the dead back to life.

"Freeze it, I wish we didn't have to worry about Chaos Season," Jenna said. "It's hard enough making sure harvests are good and everything is in balance without Chaos Season upsetting everything all the time."

"Kron says the Four said we can defeat Salth if all twelve of us Avatars face her. If she and her son were gone, Chaos Season would be done too," Ysabel said. Her flecked eyes grew dull. "Only how can that happen when we're never all incarnated at once anymore?"

"We shouldn't give up hope." Gwen rested her gloved hand on Ysabel's shoulder. The Ava Fall showed no discomfort. By All Four, why did Jenna have to be the only Avatar who didn't want to link with Gwen?

The Ava Spring continued, "If Fall can let Ysabel be born with a male twin, maybe the Four will let the absent Avatars be reborn sooner than we would expect them. The next time we go to Wistica, I'll return to the Hall of Records and search myself for more births on solstices or equinoxes."

Jenna didn't bother to point out that Margaret couldn't be reborn until the rest of her quartet visited the God of Winter, or that the third set of Avatars would be too young to use their powers if they'd been born after this group. She turned her frustration on the plants instead, clearing all of them in a five-foot circle around her.

"Freeze it, I forgot a shovel." She'd have to return to the house, find one, and come back out here. Suddenly Gwen's complaint about the distance seemed more reasonable, even if this was the best spot for Jenna's tree. "Bel, where's your anilink? Is there any way he can bring a stable hand out here to dig the hole?" It was nice to remember that as an Avatar, she could command others to perform physical labor for her now.

Ysabel smiled. "There's no need for that. I can summon little diggers to help." She strode into the cleared area. "But you'd better move away, Jen. You scared the animals away with that blast."

Grimacing at the nickname, Jenna positioned herself between Gwen and Kay.

Ysabel knelt and laid her hands on the dirt. After a few heartbeats, several squirrels scampered over and dug where she showed them.

"That's good enough," Jenna said when the hole was about as deep as the length of her hand. "I can manage the rest."

She waited until all of the squirrels had returned to the forest so they wouldn't be tempted by her acorn. Then she took Ysabel's place, gently twisted off the acorn's cap, and placed it, point down, in the hole. *Grow, my chosen one. Grow tall and strong enough to protect all of Challen.*

She smoothed the dirt over the acorn herself, then glanced hesitantly at Kay. "I could use some gentle rain, if you don't mind."

Kay glanced around as if she thought the woman from her night-mares would kill her on the spot. Finally, she edged forward and spread out her hands. Jenna watched the space below them, expecting a cloud to form there. Instead, something struck her nose.

"Sorry." Kay blushed. "I need to work on control."

By All Four, you do. As more cold drops fell on her, Jenna forced herself not to yell at Kay. Gwen and Ysabel retreated a few steps to stay dry. Jenna didn't have that option. The embryo inside her chosen acorn cried out for joy as it sucked in its first drops of water. Having already missed the best sprouting time, it was eager to grow. Jenna needed to force-grow it past the most vulnerable stages.

She put her hands on the mud, reaching for the sprout and encour-aging it upward, toward the sun, and downward to create a strong root network. A green tip burst through the soil. Jenna directed nourishment at it. She grinned as it became a twig, then shot out its first true leaves.

"Back off on the rain a bit, Kay," she said. "My tree needs sun too."

The leaves worked frantically to make nutrients. Although the tree grew much faster than it normally would, Jenna longed to see it reach its full potential. She rested a finger on the still-delicate sapling, watch-ing it lay down rings of growth around its trunk. Soon it was as high as her waist and as thick as her thumb. But that wasn't enough. The tree grew taller and wider. When it was as tall as her, branches split apart from the top. Now she could press both hands on it, urging it to keep going. It obliged. She stared at its most intimate parts, mesmerized by the dance of life going on at levels no one else could see…

"Jenna t'Reve! That's enough for one day." A hand grabbed her arm and pulled her out of the link with her tree. "It doesn't have to be full-grown today, or even this moon. Conserve your strength."

She blinked and shook her head, reorienting herself to the larger world. Her dress was muddy and soaked through, and her hair had come undone. Even her feet were cold.

Jenna glared at Gwen, who watched her with a slight smirk. "You could have handled that more gently."

"How can I when you won't let me link with you?"

Jenna scowled half-heartedly at her. Her blood still sang with the tree's happiness. She stepped back and admired it for a few heartbeats. Its bark was unmarred, and its leaves bright green and glossy. It was still small for an oak, but it had managed about twenty or thirty years' worth of growth in less than an hour. At this rate, it would be full grown before the end of Cornmoon. She patted its trunk affectionately. After having put so much effort into this one tree, it felt a little like a child to her.

Thank the Four Gwen can't make Robbie grow up so quickly. I'd hate to miss a heartbeat of his childhood.

Jenna stepped away from her tree. Exhaustion and hunger struck her at the same time. She reeled and would have fallen if Gwen hadn't caught her by the arm, again managing it so they didn't link.

"We missed lunch," she said. "I hope the other Avatars left some food for us."

"I wish they'd bring me some," Jenna said. At this heartbeat, she did agree that her tree was too far from the house. She used visions of roast duck, fresh bread, and berry pies to keep her feet moving one in front of the other.

A side door let them enter directly into the atrium. Jenna found the energy to make sure no more plants had overgrown their containers before heading into the house. Should she change first or eat? Eat, she decided.

Old memories guided her to the dining room, but the butler stopped her before she could summon a servant for more food. "Avas," he said, looking back and forth between Gwen and Jenna, "here you are. You have a very important visitor waiting in the Spring Parlor."

"Very important?" Gwen raised her eyebrows. "Who is it? Where's their calling card?"

"This gentleman doesn't need a calling card, Ava." For a heartbeat, the butler twitched as if about to break into a full-fledged squirm. "It's the king's brother, the...other Avatar. He claims our nation is at war."

CHAPTER TWELVE

An Alliance of Avatars

"Le—The Avatar of War? He's here?" Jenna's heart hammered. Why had he come? "How did he get here so quickly? He must have left soon after us!" Maybe he'd missed her, or maybe he wanted to see his son. No, hadn't he said something about war? When had that happened?

Gwen scowled and planted her hands on her hips. "The treaty states we are not required to assist the military. Our duties are to Challen and its people."

"I don't think that's what he has in mind, Ava," the butler said. "But he wants to discuss it with all of the Avatars at once."

She sighed. "And I suppose everyone else is already gathered. How long has he been waiting?"

Jenna looked down at her bare feet and muddy dress. They reminded her too much of the first time she and Lex met. "Well, he's going to have to wait a few minutes. I'm not respectable enough to meet him."

She didn't wait to hear where he was. Instead, she bolted for her suite. Thoughts of not being thought respectable enough for Lex—or anyone noble—taunted her. As an Avatar, she should be above such concerns. She should be respectable enough for anyone.

There's nothing wrong with enjoying the pleasures of the body. Summer Himself would approve, even if He doesn't practice such things. Pleasure is part of His season. She sensed the truth of it even though it had been lifetimes since she'd had direct contact with the God she served. The problem was convincing the rest of Challen pleasure wasn't only for breeding.

I wonder if Lex will stay long enough to see his son. If I find Callie, I'll tell her to dress Robbie in his best outfit and make sure he's been changed recently.

When Jenna entered her room, Clover jumped up from her seat, letting an old dress of Jenna's fall from her lap. "By All Four, Ava, I wasn't expecting you so soon!"

"No one told me the Avatar of War would call. I need to wash and change quickly so I don't look so much like a farm girl."

"There's no shame in being a farm girl, Ava." The maid poured fresh water into a bowl, then fetched a towel. "Especially when everyone knows Summer prefers Avatars with dirt under their fingers."

That was true, but her words made Jenna scrub her hands a little longer than she would have otherwise.

Clover laced her into a pale green dress with matching slippers. "Should I redo your hair, Ava?"

"Just pin it back in place. I better not keep him waiting." Beauty could do only so much if she angered him.

She nearly ran out the door without saying anything else, but remembering what Gwen would do, she said, "Thanks, Clover. Could you please find Callie and ask her to dress Robbie in his best outfit and bring him to me in an hour?"

Clover smiled. "Of course, Ava."

Jenna wished she had time to nurse him now, even though she wasn't aching or leaky yet. If her milk dried up, she'd have to either let Callie nurse Robbie all of the time or ask Gwen to restore her milk. Neither option sounded appealing.

She descended to the main level. The butler was waiting by the stairs and ushered her, not to the Spring Parlor as she would have expected, but the Map Room in the Winter Wing. Here the Winter Avatars kept records of the weather patterns they felt across Challen and plotted places where they expected Chaos Season to strike. Shelves with journals lined the room, and all of the chairs had been pushed to the walls to show off the mosaic of Challen in the floor. Lex paced over it as if he meant to reconquer their country. Gwen sat with a polite smile on her face and tension in her eyes as she watched him. All of the other Avatars—and even Kron—watched him silently as well.

Jenna walked around the edge of the mosaic to ask Gwen in a whisper, "What's going on?"

Lex halted and stared at her. "Summer Ava." His tone was harsh. "You are the last one to report for duty, even though I have word you are the one most involved in this battle."

The accusation stung, even if she wasn't sure what he accused her of. It was almost enough to distract her from his broad shoulders and rugged face. "Your Highness." She curtseyed just low enough to avoid an insult. "I wasn't aware there was a war going on among the plants. And even if there was, you could give us enough notice to receive you properly."

He narrowed his eyes. "How could you not be aware, when your own Spring Ava reports the plants you grow yourself are fighting you?"

Gwen had already told him about what had happened this morning? She should know better than that. A Summer Avatar who couldn't control her plants was as worthless as a cursed Spring Avatar. Jenna would have to have words with her later. For now, she tried to cover up how unsettled the incident had made her. "These plants are new to Challen, but once I've had time to study them, I'll be able to bring them under control."

"They are invaders in a war of magic—and gods."

"Gods?" all of the Avatars echoed. Kron nodded as if he'd known this all along.

"Yes. Hold while I prepare myself."

Lex commandeered an empty chair and sat in the center of the Challen mosaic as if to remind them who really controlled their country. Jenna half-wished him to fall onto the blue tiles representing the Chikasi

River. He tilted his head back and spread out his hands, palms up. A shudder passed through him. Slowly he turned to stare at Gwen. His eyes were covered with a steel sheen that hid his dark brown pupils. By All Four, where had that come from?

"The Goddess and Child of Time are not satisfied with Their rule over the Dead Land." Lex's voice had deepened so much he sounded like an organ, yet Jenna was still able to understand him.

Gwen traced the compass rose of the Four over her heart. Jenna copied her, but it took her a few heartbeats before she realized what was happening. *The God of War is speaking through Lex.* She shivered, thankful the God of Summer had never asked such a thing of her.

"They seek to unseat the Four Gods and Goddesses of Challen," Lex continued. "If the Four permit Time to break through Their border, then Time will invade the rest of the world, conquering not just the human lands but the divine realm."

Goddess and Child of Time? He must be referring to Salth and Salthaath, the ancient enemies of Kron.

"Salth is not a full goddess," Kron said, "She has not Ascended."

"Neither have you, God of Artifacts."

At that, everyone sucked in their breath and turned to look at Kron. Kron, a god? Gwen said he had a yellow-white aura, too light for a typical spring-born, but otherwise he seemed ordinary.

"I'm not a god," he said. "I'm a magician from a time when humans were born with magic and didn't depend on deities for it."

"You still have star magic, God of Artifacts. If you chose, you could Ascend."

Ascend? What does He mean by that? Kron could become a god? Jenna wished she had her own chair. She felt weaker now than she had after giving birth.

"I don't have enough star magic. The Four told me so. Besides," he glanced at Ysabel, "I've no wish to Ascend."

Ysabel flushed and stared at the floor.

"You choose to remain weak when you're at war?" The God of War sounded scornful. "Even if Time is not a full goddess, She is still very powerful. No wonder you failed in your first attempt to subdue Her. I hope the Season Avatars are more reasonable, or else it's not worth My sending My Avatar to ally with you against Time."

Kay's hand shook as she made the sign of the Four over and over.

Face pale, Gwen rose and curtsied as if before the king. "War, You wish to…work with us? Not conquer us this time?"

Lex's eyes turned storm gray. "Have a care, little Avatar. Spring may favor you, My own Avatar may desire you, but you are still mortal and subject to the fortunes of war."

"How would Your Avatar help us?" Kron asked. "And at what price?"

Lex slumped, and the gray faded from his eyes.

Gwen brushed her hand against Jenna's long enough to send her through the link, *Notice how the God left without answering us. I don't trust Him. It's like the gods are at war with each other, and we're caught in it.*

Gwen, what can we do against gods? What if there's a threat to Our Four? No one—except maybe Kron—knew for sure what the Four looked like, but Summer was always pictured as a thin, green-skinned youth. Many pictures showed Him as half-hidden by a tree. Jenna imagined Him as a shy youth who had to be coaxed into enjoying life. He didn't deserve to be bullied by foreign gods.

This is the Four's country. They're strongest here.

Gwen withdrew the link before Jenna could ask what she meant by that.

Lex stirred, staring at each of them. His eyes were back to normal. "What did He say?"

"You don't remember?" Jenna asked.

"When the God fills you, there's no room for anything else—even you."

She shivered, grateful the Four never asked such things from Their Avatars.

"Apparently your God thinks we should work together to defeat Salth and Sal-thaath, Your Highness," Gwen said. "But the Four have not given us a similar sign."

Kron shook his head. "The Four told me long ago twelve Avatars are needed to bring Salth down. They never said anything about a God of War or His Avatar."

"Perhaps I'm supposed to replace a Season Avatar, then."

Sophia stirred. "If the third set of Avatars has been reborn—"

"They'd still be too young," Dorian snapped. "And he's no replacement for my wife."

Lex's eyes narrowed, but before he could speak, Kron said, "Just what kind of magic do you have, War Avatar?"

Lex raised his eyebrows. "You don't know?"

"I've been inside of a water clock for eight hundred years. I wasn't expecting the Fip city-state to take over the world while I was occupied with Sal-thaath."

"You're eight hundred years old?" Lex leaned forward. "There's more to your magic than I thought, Delnsman."

"It has nothing to do with my magic." Kron looked sheepish. "I'm an artificer. I specialize in enchanted objects, either creating or destroying them."

"Such as weapons?"

"No. No weapons."

"A pity. We could use improved weapons in our campaign in the Spice Islands. Even traps to counteract theirs aren't helping us."

"And that won't help us with Salth either," Kron said.

Lex steepled his fingers. "How about battle strategy, uncanny skill with weapons, and the ability to inspire superhuman effort from ordinary people?"

"What good will any of that do against someone who can control time?" Gwen asked. "Kron and I defeated Sal-thaath's human allies, but he reversed time and captured us. And he's capable of much worse." She displayed her scarred palm to Lex.

"Eagle Talons!" Disgust crossed his face as he backed away. "I was told your magic could heal almost anything."

How dare he insult her? He has no idea what she endured! "Sal-thaath tried to rot Gwen's hand away," Jenna said. "If her magic wasn't as strong as it is, she would have lost her hand altogether, or maybe even her life."

"I could barely heal myself fast enough to keep up with his destructive magic." Gwen grimaced. "I needed to link with my sister Avatars to beat him, at least temporarily." She glanced at Kron. "If he and Sal-thaath can turn time backward, can they also look forward? If they can find out what we plan in advance, they'll be able to defeat us no matter what we do!"

"There are still strategies we can use, Ava." Lex rose and paced over the mosaic to the western end of Challen. "We can provide the enemy with false information. Better yet would be to find out their weakness. The easiest way to defeat an enemy is to trick them into fighting themselves." He crossed over to stand in front of Gwen. Jenna was close enough to smell his musky aftershave. "I am willing to ally myself with you against this Salth, but I think we should look for other ways to make the alliance permanent."

Gwen's face was expressionless as she said, "I will pray to the Four and seek Their guidance. Excuse me, Your Highness." She left at somewhere between a walk and a run.

By All Four, he still wants to marry her? I thought her scarred hand would put him off. He doesn't deserve her, and he won't make her happy. Why isn't she refusing him outright, like we agreed?

Jenna wasn't sure she would accept him anymore herself. What if the God of War took Lex over while they were intimate? The thought pained her more than she wanted to admit.

Callie appeared in the doorway with a bundle of silk in her arms. Jenna hoped her son could breathe under all that cloth. She pushed it away from his face before taking him from the nursemaid.

Conscious of the other Avatars still in the room, Jenna said, "Your Highness, would you like to see my son, Robbie?"

Lex's ears turned pink. He peered at Robbie, keeping his hands behind his back. "He has a good nose and chin."

He got them from you. "Thank you, Your Highness." Freeze it, she'd hoped he'd show more interest in his child than that. Maybe he would if they were alone.

Sophia rose, curtseyed, and said, "Will you be spending the night, Your Highness?"

He nodded.

"Splendid." Something about her tone struck Jenna as false. "I'll have our staff prepare a guest suite in the Winter Wing for you."

"I trust it will not be snowy," he said.

Jenna laughed, even though the other Avatars looked uncomfortable. At least Lex could make a joke.

He gave her a stiff nod. "Perhaps the presumptive Ava Summer could privilege me with a tour of the grounds before dinner?"

Her stomach growled. Heartbeats later, so did his.

"Then again, some refreshment would be appreciated," he said.

Jenna saw her opportunity. "We could have something brought out to the gazebo in the rose garden." They could speak privately there—though she supposed they wouldn't be permitted complete privacy. Privacy was probably the only advantage her parents' farm had over the One Oak. If she had to have a chaperone here, then she'd pick one before Sophia volunteered for the job. "Callie, please bring Robbie to the gazebo with us. The air would be good for him."

Lex surprised her by offering her his arm. She squeezed it, approving of his firm muscles. She led him through a side door and onto a brick-laid path heading upriver from her newly planted tree. The path wound between patches of clover, ornamental grasses, and wildflowers.

Jenna's face tingled from the warmth of the sun, but she tilted her head and drank in the blue sky, the slight breeze from the river, and the sense that this was the perfect summer day, a tribute to her chosen God.

"You may not channel your God the way I do mine, but you embody Him well," Lex said. "I could think of no one more suitable to be Summer's Avatar."

"Thank you." She turned, checking to see where Callie and Robbie were. Callie had found an ancient pram, but she struggled to push it over the bricks. Since Callie was too far back to overhear Jenna, so she dared being informal. "Lex." She hesitated. "Does your God…visit you often?"

"During peacetime, no. Even during a battle, He can be fickle. He expects me to use His gifts without calling on Him too often. I try not to summon Him unless the need is great."

"To save your soldiers?"

"To save the battle, and then only when failure would cost us the entire war." He stared straight ahead, as if he didn't want to be distracted by flowers. "All of us are in the end expendable to the Gods and Goddesses."

"That's not true. I've served Summer for several lifetimes. He needs me and my sister Avatars to tame Chaos Season for Him. Without us, Challen would starve."

"And so would the Fip soldiers. But I suspect all of the Gods use us for Their own ends. They expect you to obey Them as if you were soldiers, dying for Them without question."

They passed under an arch of elm trees, and Jenna shivered in their shade. "I'd rather not talk of gods right now, Lex. You still haven't told me what you think of Robbie."

He shifted away from her. "He seems like a quiet child. I hope he's strong?"

"By All Four, you've never heard him when he's hungry. I swear you can hear his cries on the other side of Challen. And it's too soon to tell how strong he'll be." She glanced at him. "But if he takes after his father, I suspect he'll be as strong as an ox." She hesitated, remembering what he had told her at the soltrans. "What does the War God look for in His Avatars? Is it just strength, or something else?"

"Many things. Strength and skill with weapons, of course, but also cunning and a warlike temperament."

It was so hard to imagine her sweet child someday channeling a god through him. Perhaps it would be safer to have Robbie study something different when he grew up. Would he be happy with life as a farmer, or would he crave more excitement, like she did?

"How are new War Avatars chosen?" she asked. "Does War do it directly?"

They arrived at the gazebo, a wicker structure painted white, with openings to view the Chikasi River and the garden. Lex strode inside and placed his dagger on the table. "He decides through His dagger. All eligible Avatar candidates take turns handling the weapon. When it changes form, the one holding it becomes the next Avatar." He looked at her, gray eyes cool. "Is that what you seek for our son, Jenna? If you cannot pass your magic to him, you would give him mine? Remember the risk he would run by exposing his true heritage."

She shook her head. "No, that wasn't what I had in mind at all."

Lex spat out something harsh in Fip. Had she offended him? Jenna quickly added, "There was no great plan behind my decision to bear a child. I just…I'd heard some bad news and needed some comfort."

Given that Lex himself had been the bearer of the news—he was the one who'd told her the Spring Avatar was a woman and therefore someone she couldn't marry—that might not have been the best thing to say either. Especially if he ever guessed she had been in love with Gwen for far longer than she'd known Lex.

Lex raised an eyebrow. "You found comfort in my arms, or in the child?"

"Both." If she couldn't count on Gwen's love in this life, then she'd seek it from her children.

"Hmm." He scooped up his dagger again as if it would pain him to be parted from it for more than a heartbeat. Then he left the gazebo and stood at the top of the garden, arms crossed, watching the river below.

Now there's a seed that doesn't want to crack its shell. What was he thinking? Did he care enough to tell her? They might have had a child together, but she still knew very little about him as a man.

Glancing back to make sure Callie still had Robbie, Jenna approached the War Avatar. "Lex?" she asked, letting her voice take on a quaver. "Did *you* want to be the War Avatar?"

His hand went to his dagger hilt, then relaxed. He turned his head to regard her for a few heartbeats. Despite the breeze, his closely-cut hair didn't stir.

Lex finally shrugged. "It doesn't matter. I was born to it as surely as you are to your magic."

"I had a choice, however many lifetimes ago that was. If you weren't the War Avatar, what would you choose to do?"

He stood straighter. "I am of the Fip family. If I hadn't been chosen, I would have either helped my brother administer Challen or joined the military anyway."

Both options sounded more exciting than spending the rest of her life in Bull Rock, which would have happened to her if she wasn't an Avatar. Yet they still didn't tell her anything about Lex. "What would you have chosen for yourself if you weren't a Fip?"

"Why do you ask, Jenna? Is this for the child's sake?"

Jenna stepped closer to him. Lex's aftershave couldn't quite cover the masculine smell of his sweat. "No, not for Robbie. For me." *For us.*

He studied her for a few heartbeats, as if he was checking to see if she still had stalks of hay in her hair. He raised his eyebrows. "For you? You wish to cement the alliance between our gods? A tempting idea, but I fear my brother would not approve my marrying a commoner. Besides, War prefers Lady lo Havil's healing magic over yours."

Jenna wished there were some weeds around here that she could rip apart. Bad enough she couldn't have Gwen, but Lex refused her too?

"You know she won't have you!" *Thank the Four for that.* "You found me fair enough before!"

"That was different." For a moment, his eyes darkened with passion. "A man and a woman can come together and enjoy each other, but for something more permanent, families must be considered."

"You don't like my farming family? How about my three sister Avatars? Our magic should be dowry enough."

"And here you just told me the Ava Spring would never marry me. Why would a marriage between the two of us persuade her to use her gift on my behalf?" He headed past the gazebo, back to the One Oak. "Jenna, I...I do thank you for the gift of a son, even if I can't acknowledge him." He gave her a brilliant smile, which only frustrated her. "I will protect you and Robbie as much as I can. Do not ask me for more."

She stalked after him. "More! I should have given you less."

He didn't acknowledge her. Off to the side, Callie blushed and covered Robbie's ears as if he was old enough to understand her.

Jenna returned to the gazebo, now mocking her with its emptiness. She left it to stalk through the garden, inspecting it for weeds. Whenever she found one, she shriveled it from tip to root. If only she could do the same to Lex and his weapon. Turn her down, ha!

After perhaps a quarter-hour, hunger reminded her she'd already used a great deal of magic earlier that day. She should rest and eat. Unwilling to face Lex or her sister Avatars just yet, she returned to the gazebo. Callie sat in the shade with Robbie. He made sucking motions with his lips, so she picked him up. "I'll take this feeding, Callie. You can have the rest of the afternoon off."

"Thank you, Ava, but are you sure?"

"I'm quite sure," she said. "I'd like to be alone for a while. But where's the food we were promised? Could you have a meal sent out here for me?"

Callie curtseyed. "Of course, Ava. I'll see to it directly."

Nursing Robbie did nothing to soothe Jenna's hunger pangs, but it did give her time to think. Maybe marriages between nobles, including royals, and commoners weren't as easy to arrange as all the songs and stories said they were. Still, as an Avatar, her original birth rank didn't matter. She would be considered equal to nobility once her quartet was officially recognized. Was rank difference really Lex's main reason for not marrying her, or was there another obstacle between them?

Maybe if she reminded Lex what he was giving up by rejecting her, he would change his mind. War's Avatar had as much passion as she did. She remembered it from their time together last summer, and she'd seen it storming in his eyes. Would seducing him again remind him of what he was missing, or would he think she was too loose? Was there something else she should try?

Maybe she wasn't the expert on love the others thought she was. Should she ask the rest of her quartet for advice? Could she trust Gwen to help her make the right decision? The wrong choice wouldn't just affect Jenna and Robbie. If Jenna offended Lex deeply enough, he might withdraw his offer to fight with them against Salth.

CHAPTER THIRTEEN

A Selathen Surprise

Lex met with the Avatars again the next day, but there seemed to be nothing they could do about Salth until all twelve Season Avatars managed to reunite. Frustrated, Lex left. Jenna avoided another private moment with him, and as he was extremely polite to her in public, she treated him the same way in return. When he rode away, everyone else breathed a sigh of relief. Her sigh contained regret instead.

Training continued for another quarter-moon. Every day, Jenna would tend to her oak, force-growing it toward maturity. Sometimes Charles would stroll by to offer her unwanted advice. During that time, her sister Avatars would practice their magic individually. Sophia and Ysabel sometimes rode out to nearby farms to tend to the horses and cows, while other days they would monitor the wildlife near the One Oak. Gwen visited Midpoint to treat the sick and injured there. Dorian continued to grow more haggard every day, despite all the sleeping tonics Charles prepared for him. Gwen volunteered to treat him once, but he rejected her so harshly she didn't repeat her offer. He occupied the Spring Wing, scarcely bothering to leave. In contrast, Kay spent most of her time outdoors, drinking in fresh air and sunshine. Although her complexion remained pale, her manner gradually became more relaxed and confident as she worked through practice weather exercises on her own.

In the mid-afternoon or early evening, when Gwen, Jenna, Ysabel, and Kay had finished their individual tasks, they would gather to practice linking. This did not proceed smoothly. Try as she might, Jenna couldn't commit herself fully to the link. Gwen and Ysabel had no problem sharing themselves, and once they reassured Kay they still accepted her despite the years she'd neglected her magic, she opened up like a blooming flower. Jenna resolved every evening to copy Kay's example, but one glance at Gwen's solemn face would remind her of their last life together, the life she had to keep secret. At that, her soul closed off part of itself, something everyone could sense. They went through the motions of surveying sites remotely and searching for any sign of Chaos Season, but their range was limited. Thank the Four there was no evidence of a Chaos Season anywhere during this time.

The worst part was the way Gwen allowed Jenna to fumble in silence, watching her with those intent blue eyes but never accusing her, never even asking why Jenna had so much trouble with the link. Did she know what had happened to her? There must be plenty of journals and histories describing the tragedy of their last life in lavish detail. Jenna wished she dared root all of them out of the One Oak, but she didn't have access to the Spring Study.

One evening, as the four of them ended yet another unsuccessful session, Gwen stretched and said, "I think tomorrow we should try something else. But in the meantime…Ysabel, are the glowflies awake yet?"

She nodded. "I can feel many of them in the meadow by the stable."

"Freeze it, that's a bad place to walk at night. Our boots and hems will become filthy." Gwen paced to the window. "Perhaps we could take a stroll around the garden before bed. Don't we have some night-blooming flowers, Jenna? I don't think I've seen them yet."

Jenna glanced at Ysabel and Kay, but neither of them met her gaze.

"I should write to my family," Ysabel said.

"And I to Jon," Kay added.

Jenna bit her lip. Looked like this would be the confrontation she'd been dreading all along.

"There's a section of primrose and jasmine near the edge of the garden," she said.

"That sounds perfect." Gwen's bright smile didn't reach her eyes. "Do we need a lantern, or is your night vision strong enough to go without?"

"Maybe we should bring a lantern just in case." She would have preferred the dark to shelter her from the forthcoming probe.

Although the butler frowned disapprovingly when Gwen informed him they would be outside—what did he think would happen to two Avatars on their own property?—he sent for a lantern and maids to fetch their shawls. Jenna abandoned hers before they left the house. The cool air outside was refreshing, not chilly. She took a deep breath, inhaling the scents of the night: soil, manure, the green smell of cut plants, and even a dead fish from the river mingling with the perfumes of nearby flowers. She didn't need odors to guide her to the nocturnal flowers, though; she'd worked in the garden enough over the last several days to know the different sections by heart. Raising the lantern so they could see the path, Jenna led the way, walking quickly to put distance between herself and Gwen.

Despite the difference in their heights, Gwen kept up easily. She remained silent for many long heartbeats, long enough to make Jenna testy. She slapped a whining biter harder than necessary and winced. That would leave a bruise on her arm. "We should have brought Ysabel with us to keep these frozen pests away."

"The bites don't bother me."

Jenna turned toward the wood. An owl hooted in the distance.

Gwen continued softly, "Nothing bothers me as much as your refusal to link with us."

She halted next to a series of lilac bushes. "By All Four Gods and Goddesses, you know I've been trying!"

"Trying, not doing." She remorselessly advanced forward, as if she could pin Jenna on thorns. "You don't commit, Jenna. You never did." She turned away and whispered, "Not to me."

"Gwen…" Spring should never know sadness, never look so forlorn. How could Gwen stand in the center of all the lush green life and yet look like everything lovely in the world had been shut away from her? Jenna longed to embrace her, fold her in her arms until neither knew where one ended and the other began. She held out her arms—and then remembered what would happen if she gave Gwen the communion they both craved. It would barely last a heartbeat before Gwen realized why it could never be.

The full import of Gwen's words sunk in. "Not commit to you?" *O Four, she must remember. Why doesn't she come straight out and accuse me?* Maybe she could bluster past this moment. Jenna turned to the closest bush and force-grew an out-of-season cluster of purple lilacs. Moths who had never encountered such flowers before fluttered around curiously. Once the cluster separated from the branch, she offered it to Gwen. "How many lives have we spent hand in hand already? We've been together longer than any married couple. How else do I have to prove I'm devoted to you?"

She pushed the flowers away. With her hands in gloves, the link didn't form. "Things and fancy words are all you ever give me." Her eyes seemed bigger and darker in the lamplight. "You know what I need from you, Jenna Dorshay t'Reve. Your heart, your soul."

At her words, hope bloomed inside Jenna's heart.

"Not just for me. For all of us."

Hope drooped, just a little.

Gwen pulled off a lace glove and offered Jenna her bare hand. "Jenna, I know when we first met in this life, you must have thought I was nothing more than some arrogant noblewoman who knows better than you."

You are. I still love you, faults and all.

"But however poorly you think of me, I hope to change that. Won't you link to me, fully, so we can truly be the sister Avatars we were born to be?"

Her jaw dropped. Gwen blamed herself, not Jenna, for their problems with the link? Either that was very noble of her or very arrogant—perhaps a little of both. It would be so easy to let Gwen blame herself, but Jenna knew that wouldn't help for long.

I should just tell her what happened. She's bound to find out one season or another. If I apologize first, maybe she won't be quite so angry at me. She'll only give me a rash instead of constant pain....

"Jenna?" Gwen's voice quavered in the silence.

The silence. When had she last heard an owl or cricket?

The two of them exchanged looks. Jenna reached out and touched Gwen's still-extended hand with one of her fingers. *Something's wrong.* The brief link wouldn't allow either of them to delve into the real issue they faced, but Jenna meant it as a symbol for later. She hoped Gwen took it as such.

Gwen tilted her head, probably enhancing her hearing to the extent her magic allowed. "Riders, maybe? Coming to the One Oak?" She straightened. "Someone must need healing." Fixing Jenna with a we're-not-done-yet stare, she raised her skirts and ran back blindly the way they had come.

"Wait for me!" Jenna called after her as she followed.

The gardens were on the opposite side of the estate from the entrance, so Jenna had to run past the entire house. She gasped for breath when she reached the top of the driveway. Gwen already stood there, scarcely a hair out of place. Spring Avatars could be so annoying when their magic made them appear inhuman.

Several horses were coming up the drive. They sounded as if they were being ridden instead of pulling a carriage. Although no lights shone along the approach to the One Oak, the riders didn't carry lanterns with them. Moonlight allowed Jenna to see their shapes. There were five of them, spread apart, not speaking.

Gwen stepped forward. "Welcome to the One Oak!" she called. "Who needs healing? Is the patient here or elsewhere?"

The party halted some distance away, too far for Jenna to make out any detail.

"Who's there?" a man with a Selathen accent said.

"Lady Gwendolyn lo Havil, Ava Spring. Do you need my services?"

Jenna tugged at her sleeve. "Gwen, they're Selathens!" she whispered.

"That doesn't matter. The Four would want me to heal them too."

"Why would Selathens seek us out for healing—or any magic at all?"

"Hmm." Gwen frowned, but she didn't move.

"We seek the Ava Fall," the man replied. "Where is she?"

Jenna initiated the link by grasping Gwen's still-bare hand. *By the Four, what if Ysabel's father is one of them? Didn't he promise her to Salth and Sal-thaath? We better do something!*

Do you believe her father would dare leave Tradetown and travel all the way here, to the center of Challen, where the Four would protect us even if our magic is unequal to the task?

He'll die if he doesn't give an Avatar to Salth, Gwen.

Gwen sighed. *That's what comes of worshipping other gods beside the Four.* Out loud, she said, "You'll have to introduce yourselves first and tell us the nature of your business with the Fall Avatar."

The spokesman pulled a gleaming pistol out and aimed it at them. "This is all the introduction we need, Ava."

CHAPTER FOURTEEN

Magic Against Pistols

"By All Four Gods and Goddesses, how dare you threaten us?" Gwen's voice remained cool as winter, but her hand trembled. "Put that frozen weapon away this instant."

The pistol wavered, as if the man wasn't sure which one of them to target. However, two of his companions pulled out their own pistols and aimed at them. Jenna's heart sank. Avatars weren't bulletproof. Gwen could incapacitate the men if she could touch them, but they would never allow that to happen. Kay and Ysabel weren't here to attack with weather or magically-enraged animals. What could Jenna do with her own magic?

The horses are nervous in the dark, Gwen told her through the link. *I can tell by the way they shift about.*

Gwen knew horses better than Jenna did, but that seemed like no help—at first. What could Jenna do with plant magic to frighten horses? She glanced up. *Of course. The branches.*

Gwen tilted her chin upwards, looking every inch the imposing noble. "Threatening the Season Avatars is a crime against Challen. You could get hanged for this. Be sensible and put your pistols away…"

While Gwen continued her attempts to make the Selathens stand down, Jenna cast her awareness into the trees, seeking dead or dying branches that could be spared—an impossible task in the height of Summer and at the One Oak. A big branch hung over two of the riders. If she brought that down, it could injure both men and horses, perhaps severely. Gwen and Ysabel would object, but their safety had to come first. Perhaps Jenna should use smaller branches first before resorting to the big one.

Sending a silent apology to the tree and a promise to tend to it later, Jenna broke several smaller branches off the big one. They hit one man on his shoulders and the other man's horse on the muzzle. With a panicked whinny, the horse bolted toward the One Oak's stable. A couple of other horses followed it. Selathen curses filled the air.

"Get down!" Jenna pulled Gwen to the ground before she could move on her own. A shot rang out, followed by the sound of shattering glass and a feminine shriek. Jenna wondered if anyone had been hurt. Gwen needed to get to safety before something happened to her. The house would be more defensible than their current location.

"This way!" she whispered, crawling toward the front door.

"No, we'll be exposed, and the butler won't let us in quick enough. Go around the back."

Praying that the bushes wouldn't rustle and betray them, Jenna followed Gwen. When they reached the corner, the front door burst open. "Who's there?" Dorian demanded.

Kron pushed him aside. "Your weapons will no longer work here. Surrender before the Avatars turn their magic against you." He smiled grimly. "Or before I do."

A couple of riders who'd managed to retain control of their mounts started back down the driveway, but as soon as they'd gone a couple of yards, their beasts suddenly halted, planting themselves firmly in place as if Kron had turned them to stone. Either Sophia or Ysabel must have spoken to them remotely. The spokesman pointed his weapon at Kron, swearing even louder.

Gwen rose to her feet, wiping the dirt off of her hands and dress as if this was an ordinary stroll in the garden. Jenna reached for her to pull her back to safety, but she strode toward the leader, every inch of her screaming fierce determination. *You frozen imbecile, you're going to get yourself killed!* Jenna scrambled after her, desperate to protect her.

"Are you the Honored Lathatilltin, the Ava Fall's father?" Gwen asked the Selathen.

Even in the dim light, Jenna could tell he wasn't. He was younger, perhaps in his early or mid-twenties. He shook his head, refusing to meet Gwen's eyes.

Sophia and Charles came out of the house, along with Dorian and Kron. "By All Four, what's going on here?" Charles asked.

"They want to kidnap Ysabel!" Jenna said before Gwen could.

"We don't know that for certain—"

"They came at night and shot at the house, Gwen! That's not how you invite someone to a harvest dance!"

Sophia sighed. "Gwendolyn, send them to sleep until we can sort this out."

"I was about to," Gwen muttered. The Selathen man, eyes wide with fear, shied away from her, but Jenna helped her hold the man's arm long enough for Gwen to push his jacket and shirt up to touch bare skin. He slumped over his mount. The second rider dismounted and fled.

Jenna connected with oaks farther down the drive, searching for some way to impede the fugitive. The gate at the end of the road was iron, so she couldn't affect it directly. She was unwilling to sacrifice a tree to block him, even if she could topple it in time. The gate clanged shut. Kron must have done it from a distance. If Dorian had used wind, the plants would have sensed it too.

"I'll find the runaway." Dorian stalked past Gwen and Jenna.

"Charles, find the butler and some servants to take care of this one and the others by the stable," Sophia said. "The horses won't cooperate much longer."

Gwen remained outside until the servants brought the rest of the Selathens over to her so she could put them to sleep too. Jenna stayed with her for moral support and as a source of energy should she need it. All of the Selathens except for the leader were placed in the kitchen's root cellar. At the butler's advice, the leader was taken to the Spring parlor. Kay and Ysabel joined them there, with Ysabel peering past Kay at the stranger.

"I've seen him come to our house in Tradetown to meet with my father," she said. "Does he have a silver watch with him? That's the sign of a Salth-worshipper."

"We can't search him," Sophia said severely. "That would be most improper."

Kron took up a position near Ysabel. "It won't be necessary. I can feel it from here."

"Is it an artifact?" Gwen asked.

"Not like the ones I make. Salth has never been interested in that aspect of magic. The watch allows her to maintain contact with the bearers." He frowned. "I'd better destroy it, just in case it has some nasty surprise bundled with it."

Kron pulled out a silk handkerchief and draped it over his fingers. Going straight to the man's breast pocket in his coat, he extracted the watch without touching it directly. He studied it for several heartbeats before saying, "I'd better take this to my workshop."

"Can't you just smash it?" Charles asked.

"When it comes to Salth and magic, I'd rather not take chances." He glanced at Ysabel but said nothing else before leaving.

After a few moments, Jenna said, "Perhaps we should secure him before Gwen allows him to wake up." She didn't want to take any chances with her sister Avatars' lives either. "Do we have rope? Or a length of cloth?"

Sophia scowled, as if she was about to state Avatars shouldn't need such tools. To Jenna's relief, Gwen said, "That's a good idea. It will make it easier to touch him if I have to send him to sleep again."

The butler and another servant tied up the man. Once they had left, Gwen darted forward to wake him. While he stared blearily at them, Sophia moved into place next to her, as if she wanted to lead the questioning of the prisoner. The two exchanged pointed glances. Jenna stepped forward to support Gwen if necessary, but Sophia gestured for Gwen to go ahead.

"What's your name, Honored?" she asked.

Instead of answering, he struggled against the ropes. When that didn't work, he spat out something in Selathen.

"His name is Loth Tholltin," Ysabel translated. "The rest of what he said…you don't want to hear."

Honored Tholltin turned to her and yelled more Selathen. She answered in kind. As he spoke again, her cat crept in front of her, fur raised along his spine and fangs displayed.

Ysabel swayed in place. "He says my father has offered a considerable reward for the person who brings me back to Tradetown before the end of the moon. There's also a smaller reward for any of the Avatars in my quartet."

Jenna bristled, one hand automatically going to Gwen's shoulder while checking to make sure Ysabel and Kay were safe. Gwen tensed as well.

"All of these frozen men need to be delivered to the Watch in Wistica at once," Sophia said.

Gwen looked at Ysabel. "Would Kron be willing to portal them there?"

She nodded. "He'd take them straight to the deepest, darkest, dungeon."

"Or the gallows," Jenna said.

Another burst of Selathen from their prisoner. Ysabel listened to it without responding or translating. Her complexion paled, and she swayed again.

Gwen darted back to her. "Someone bring her a chair." She gently brushed the hair off of Ysabel's forehead. "Are you all—oh, By All Four!"

"What's wrong?" Jenna asked.

Gwen looked up, her blue eyes sober. "The Honored Tholltin wants to bargain for his life—by leading us straight to Honored Lathatilltin himself."

CHAPTER FIFTEEN

Lex's Study

Sophia whirled on Ysabel and demanded, "Is this true?"

Charles inspected his nails. "It would be so much more convenient if it was."

Convenient! Jenna wanted to spit the word back at him. They were thoughtlessly discussing the death of Ysabel's father right in front of her. It might be hard for her to love someone who'd handed her over as a sacrifice, but she was obviously upset about the whole affair. She shouldn't be involved in this at all.

As Jenna brought a chair over, she and Gwen exchanged glances. On this, they had to work together for the good of their sister Avatar. Before either of them could protest, however, a quiet voice spoke.

"He must be given a chance to repent." Somehow Kay had glided into the center of the room without them noticing. She spread her hands, appealing to all of them. "Whatever happens, Ysabel's father must be given a chance to save his soul before Winter freezes it forever."

"He won't," Ysabel's voice was equally quiet, swallowed up by the season paintings on the walls. "He's been Salth's man as far back as I can remember."

"By All Four Gods and Goddesses, does he expect Salth and Sal-thaath to save him?" Gwen asked.

Dorian crossed his arms. "According to Kron, they don't save anyone. Just the opposite."

"Why would anyone worship such dreadful...whatever they are?" Charles asked.

"I never understood it myself." Ysabel groped around as if searching for her reticule. Pouncer jumped into her lap and gently batted her cheeks.

Gwen patted her shoulder. "Did you want to see him again, talk to him? You don't have to if you don't want to."

She clutched her cat and buried her face in his fur. Finally she lifted her. "I don't want to, but I have to. My little brothers and sisters would never forgive me otherwise."

"You won't go alone," Gwen said. "We'll all come with you."

Jenna and Kay nodded agreement.

The older Season Avatars exchanged glances among the three of them. Surprisingly, Dorian spoke first. "I'll accompany you as well."

Kay winced. What if she chose to stay behind to avoid him? That wasn't fair. Jenna wasn't the leader of the group, but she knew they should stay together as much as possible, both to strengthen their ties to each other and in case a Chaos Season occurred.

Gwen bobbed her head at him. "I appreciate your offer, Dorian, but I'm sure we'll manage just fine on our own."

"But I insist."

"We do need another witness," Charles said. "Someone impartial."

"Another Avatar wouldn't be impartial."

Gwen's words gave Jenna inspiration. "Maybe not another Season Avatar, but what about the War Avatar?"

"The War Avatar?" Sophia raised her eyebrows. "You would invite him back here?"

"We would have to send word to Wistica and wait for him to return," Dorian said. "That would take another quarter-moon."

"What would?" Kron asked as he returned.

Gwen explained the situation to him, and his expression darkened. He studied Ysabel, still curled up with her anilink, and edged a little closer to her.

"I could be the witness you need," Kron said when she was done.

"The War Avatar would be an even better witness," Jenna pointed out, "second only to the king himself. And if the Selathens try to attack us again, who better to be on our side?"

Sophia shrugged. "All of you can go, if you wish. I'll stay here. I've no desire to visit such a Four-forsaken city." She pulled the bell-rope in the corner of the room. A manservant appeared moments later. "Take the prisoner away and secure him with the others."

"I have a better idea," Kron said. "I can create a portal to the Temple or to the Avatars' house in Wistica tonight to speak to the War Avatar. Perhaps I can bring him the other Selathens as proof of what happened."

"An excellent idea," Sophia said. "We should turn them over to the Watch. The sooner these men are out of here, the safer we'll be."

As Charles, Dorian, and Kron discussed the best ways to secure all of the attackers, Gwen beckoned Jenna and Kay closer. She still had one hand on Ysabel's shoulder, and she offered her other hand—the scarred one, Jenna couldn't help noting—out to them for a link. Jenna took a few cleansing breaths before accepting it.

This attack affects our quartet directly, Gwen told them all. *Someone should go with Kron and the others to make sure the War Avatar listens to us. I don't like splitting the group, but this errand should only take a couple of hours, not days.*

I'll do it, Jenna offered. Thoughts of Lex's muscular, unclothed body popped into her mind, for all to see.

By All Four Gods and Goddesses, he's your child's real father? Kay asked.

A spark of interest from Ysabel shone through her gloom. *How did that happen?*

Jenna clamped down on her memories of a giant rosebush sheltering her and Lex. *I'll tell you some other season.*

Do you think he'll listen to you? Gwen asked.

He will if I have to unclog his ears with a thornbush.

Gwen permitted herself a brief snort of amusement. *Then do so. We'll stay here with Ysabel. If we need you, she'll send Pouncer or another animal through the portal. May the Four keep you safe.*

They released the link and separated, the three of them to huddle together and comfort Ysabel, and Jenna to check on her son. He slept soundly in his cradle. She pulled the light blanket away from his mouth, then returned to her quarters to wash her face, apply fresh powder, and restyle her hair. By the time she returned downstairs, Kron had secured each prisoner's hands behind his back with leather straps.

"Do we need to bring fighting sticks with us?" she asked.

"They won't escape from those bonds," he replied.

Even if they did, with Dorian twitching his fingers as if he was preparing to summon lightning, they wouldn't get very far.

Kron created a portal in a door way, showing the dark courtyard of the Avatars' house. He led the way, with Charles reluctantly following, the prisoners next, and Dorian and Jenna at the end. As Charles roused the household and Kron checked on the prisoners, Jenna edged closer to Dorian.

"What do you want?" he asked.

"I could ask the same of you. Why did you offer to come?"

"Margaret would have wanted me to," he replied.

That had to be an excuse. What was he really planning? Jenna resolved to keep a close eye on him during this errand.

It took a while for the staff to send a messenger to the Watch and prepare a carriage to take them to the Palace. By the time all the arrangements had been made and they were on their way, Jenna was nodding off in the carriage. She jolted awake when they arrived. A pair of guards escorted the Season Avatars—the prisoners were taken in a different direction—to the same conference room where Gwen and Jenna had first met the king. This time, Lex sat in his brother's place. While his uniform was as immaculate as ever, his eyelids drooped. The stuffy, warm air in the room tempted her to yawn. Servants brought them hot chocolate. Jenna stirred spoonfuls of cream into hers to cool it. The drink was still unappetizing, but she forced herself to sip it anyway.

Lex steepled his fingers, not touching his chocolate. "Ava, Avis, I wasn't expecting to see you so soon under such circumstances. Tell me what happened."

Since she had been there for the entire attack, Jenna told the tale, skipping over the reason she and Gwen had been outside in the first place. She watched Lex closely, gauging his reaction. His posture relaxed slightly after she described how they'd defended themselves. Kron added a few terse words about Selathens being foolish for worshipping Salth and how Ysabel's father didn't deserve her. When they were done, Lex stared into his mug as if expecting his god to advise him through it.

"The Selathen threat must be addressed," he said. "This may be the first battle in our war against Time. Even after we capture the Honored Lathatilltin, Salth may send other enemies against us. I will therefore take command and move my center of operation to the One Oak." He glanced at Charles. "With your permission, of course."

"Granted, Your Highness," Charles replied, turning pale.

Jenna came to full alert. Having Lex live at the One Oak would allow them to interact daily. Perhaps she could make him change his mind—or better yet, reach his heart. That frozen man seemed to think love was war and shielded his emotions even from her. Hopefully her sister Avatars would help her woo him without Lex realizing what was going on.

"Do you think Salth can be destroyed outright?" Dorian asked.

"No enemy is invincible, Avi." Lex smiled as if relishing the challenge. "Even Time must have a weakness. It is simply a matter of finding it and applying our strengths against it."

Dorian cocked his head. "What would happen if Salth is defeated, then? What happens to Time?"

Everyone turned to stare at Kron, who shifted uncomfortably in his seat. "Time existed before Salth did." He seemed to draw confidence in his own words. "Defeating her shouldn't cause Time to stop. The only thing that will stop when she can no longer use magic is the death and destruction she's brought to the Dead Land."

Jenna wondered if the Selathens would leave Challen if Salth was defeated. Maybe then they would stop hating magic—and Avatars.

"Wouldn't it be better to seize her magic instead? If we had time magic, imagine what we could do with it." Dorian touched the pocket where he kept his watch, which in turn held a locket of his wife's hair. "Why, we'd be able to tame Chaos Season in a heartbeat!"

Kron winced. "Dorian, Salth is the one draining the Dead Land and sending Chaos Seasons to Challen. Magic is as much a part of her as it is of us; we can't take it from her. And if we remove her, Chaos Season will stop."

"What would happen to us then?"

"I don't know. The Four chose you and the rest of the twelve before Chaos Season started, so They must have other tasks for you."

"This is all very fascinating," Lex said dryly, "but I have much to prepare before I can join you at the One Oak." He turned to Kron. "I trust you will create a portal for me from here to the One Oak?"

"A temporary one."

"I may need to return here in an instant, so I prefer if you keep it open." Jenna knew this was a demand, not a preference. "If you can make another portal from One Oak to Tradetown, we will confront the Honored Lathatilltin tonight. Eagle Talon, it's after midnight! We should rest." Lex rose, forcing them all to stand. "Will you spend the night in Wistica or back at the One Oak?"

"At the One Oak." Kron studied the room. "Your Highness, if you do want to have a portal created between the Palace and the One Oak, it needs to be in a secure area. Will this room do, or do you have another place in mind? Ideally, I need a doorway that can remain dedicated to the portal, so one that's rarely used."

"Then my study would be the best place," Lex said. "Come with me."

He led them into one of the palace towers and up a long staircase. Even Jenna was winded by the time they stopped at a landing with a locked door. Lex opened it with a plain iron key and gestured them inside.

The circular room was covered with maps in every scale, from ones showing the entire world—how strange to think Challen was just a small part of it!—to one detailing every building in the University in Wistica. Jenna studied it, fancying she could see individual students and professors going about their daily business. Bookshelves squared off the other end of the room. A large table dominated the center, with a map of the Dead Land held down by a spotted shell, a toy soldier, an old medal, and, most curiously, a book in the Fip language. Jenna could only speak a few phrases and certainly couldn't read it, but she flipped it open anyway, hoping there would be pictures to give her some sense of what Lex was interested in. A faint whiff of jasmine rose from the pages. Short lines of what appeared to be verse clustered together as if hiding from the world outside the wide margins.

While Kron, Charles, and Dorian moved the bookshelves, Lex came over to Jenna and gently pulled the book out of her hand. "Eagle's Talons, I'd forgotten this was still here."

"What is it? What does it say?"

The tips of his ears turned pink. "Nothing important."

"Is it poetry?" Perhaps an old lover had doused it with her perfume before giving it to him.

"Are you sure you can't read Fip?"

She smiled and looked up at him. "Even if I could, I'd much rather you read it to me."

He shook his head slightly, as if he meant to refuse. Then he glanced back at Kron, who was explaining to Charles and Dorian how portals worked. Something about reaching through a magical space that held all space—it didn't make sense to Jenna. She leaned closer to Lex, inhaling the masculine scents of his soap and aftershave. He bent down so his head nearly touched hers.

"I can't translate it very well," he said, lowering his voice. "It sounds better in Fip. The best I can do is this:

My heart is hidden
Behind the strongest shield
But one glance from your eyes
Makes me surrender.

Come visit me now
In our secret garden
Where we will shed these robes…."

He broke off. "That last line isn't suitable for a public audience."

Freeze it, that was probably the best part. Jenna wanted to urge him to continue, but Kron called out, "The portal's done."

She reluctantly turned to face it. Kron's doorway was smaller than normal. The lintel was level with the tops of the bookshelves, so they would all have to duck to pass through. The green furnishings on the other side indicated the portal led to a small parlor in the Summer Wing. Perhaps that would make it easier for Jenna to encounter Lex.

Charles and Dorian passed through quickly, with only a minimal amount of complaining. Kron held off, as if he expected Jenna to precede him. She had to keep up a pretense of formality in front of him, so she curtseyed to Lex. "Thank you for reading the poem to me, Your Highness."

"A pleasure, Ava." He took her hand and raised it to his lips, sending a tingle down his arm. "Rest well. We have much to do tomorrow."

As she left, she gave him a coy glance over her shoulder. Did he really like poetry? A shame she didn't know much about it. Perhaps she should find a few Challen love poems to share with him.

CHAPTER SIXTEEN

Two Books

Jenna slept in late and woke up to a hot morning, made worse by Kron's insistence all windows remain closed and they stay inside. "I'm going to put defenses at every opening, no matter how small." His face looked haggard, and despite the heat, he drained his chocolate in heartbeats. "I know the Four will protect you, especially this far inside Challen, but I can't rest until I add my own artifacts." For his efforts, Ysabel rewarded him with a shy smile before he left the breakfast parlor.

Gwen half-heartedly proposed another practice linking session, but Ysabel and Kay weren't any more eager for it than Jenna was. The four of them separated after breakfast. Jenna spent an hour with her cranky child before retreating to the Summer Avatars' study. At least the books and journals crammed into the room were silent. If any previous Summer Avatar had encountered something like the deathbush before, it would be recorded here. All she had to do was find it.

Determination helped her skim through two volumes, but there were still another dozen books on the first shelf, and a score of other shelves to go through. Jenna needed another pair of expert eyes, so she summoned a maid.

"I'd like a pitcher of tea, brewed as strong as you can make it and cooled with some of Winter's ice," she said. "Oh, and please tell the Avi Sum I'd like him to come help me in the Summer Study."

The maid curtseyed, keeping her gaze on the floor. "I'll ask one of the cooks to make your tea, Ava. But begging your pardon, the Avi Sum left word not to be disturbed."

"By All Four, why not?"

The maid shrugged. "It's not for me to know the Avi's business, Ava."

The clock in the hallway chimed twice. Early afternoon. Freeze it, it had taken her longer to read the two books than she'd expected. At this rate, she'd need a moon to finish going through the entire study. How much would the deathbushes grow in the meantime?

She sighed. "Just the tea, then."

When she was alone, Jenna pulled the pins out of her hair and let her braid fall to her waist. She caught the end of it and chewed it for a few heartbeats while she studied the shelves. If she couldn't read all of the books this season, she had to pick a few that were most likely to help her. Which ones would those be? Personal journals? Histories from the earliest Summer Avatars?

A title caught her eye: *Invasive Plants: A Record of Plants Originally Foreign to Challen But Now Established In Our Fair Country.* She hoped she hadn't written it in a previous life, as the author obviously liked to use more words than necessary. Still, this book could hold the answers she was searching for—and it was big enough that it would take her the rest of the day to find them. Sighing, she settled into a chair in the corner and began to flip through the book. It was over two hundred years old, according to the date on the front page, but the paper, though soft and yellow, still felt strong. She sent magic into the book, strengthening the paper so she didn't tear it.

Noises came from the room next door, shuffling feet and men's voices. Servants cleaning up? No, she picked out Lex's voice. Why had he arrived so early? Jenna leaned closer to the wall to eavesdrop.

"If this wine is as special as you claim, why keep it here instead of in the cellar?" Lex asked.

"Charles has a feel for grapes, even after they've been picked," Dorian said. "He claims wine ages better if he handles the bottles from time to time. I always thought the bottle would block his magic, but I can't argue with the result. See for yourself, Your Royal Highness."

The men were silent, allowing Jenna to hear glasses clink.

"Fit for my brother," Lex remarked. "I'll suggest to your Summer Avatar that when he steps down, he and his wife should come to Wistica. Their talents would be useful."

Something slammed against a table. "Their magic, not mine," Dorian said. "I'm supposed to forget magic and pretend my sunshine isn't with the God of Winter. What's the use of living if I lose both of them?"

"Come now, it can't be that bad—"

"Bad enough I'd join your army if you want my weather magic."

A pause. "Can you even use it outside this country?"

"According to Kron, we can. Or we did, hundreds of years ago in a lifetime none of us remember clearly anymore." Dorian's voice twisted so much it was easy to picture him snarling as he spoke. "Very convenient, that. No wonder the foolish girls are taken in by him."

Foolish girls? Jenna would have loved to burst into the room next door and show Dorian how foolish she thought he was. But Lex said calmly, "What do you mean? He has a type of magic I've never seen before, and I've traveled from one end of the Fip Empire to the other—and outside of it, too."

Lucky him. Jenna wished she could travel so widely. She'd be happy just to hear Lex's tales of other lands.

"The magic may be real, but everything else he's been telling us about another Goddess causing Chaos Season has to be wrong," Dorian said.

"Not according to my God." Lex's voice dropped, becoming much deeper and colder. "Otherwise, I wouldn't be here."

"The young women will need our support, especially Kay," Dorian said. "She's so scrawny a raindrop could knock her over."

"Your Four Gods and Goddesses make some…unusual choices for Their Avatars. Or perhaps being bound to deities for so many lifetimes makes you…unusual."

Now it was Dorian's voice that sounded dangerous. "And what does that mean, Avatar of War?"

"It means our gods have set us on very different paths. And with that, Winter Avatar, I bid you farewell. I must prepare for tonight's campaign."

The door to the hallway opened, then closed. Jenna pressed herself against her chair, worried Lex might see her and realize she'd overheard them. He passed the study without glancing in her direction.

More liquid splashed into a glass next door. "Unusual Avatars indeed," Dorian grumbled. "We're normal; he's the strange one serving only one life as Avatar. Such odd magic he has; if only he could run it backward….Oh, Sunshine, if you were still here, we wouldn't have to deal with all of these other Avatars trying to take over. Why, Winter, why?"

Glass shattered.

Jenna held still, not daring to turn a page of her book. Winter magic could be very dangerous, especially in the hands of someone as ill-tempered as Dorian.

After the room next door fell silent, she stared at her book for a long time, but the letters on the pages turned into meaningless shapes, offering her no help with either the deathbushes or the other Avatars.

* * *

Jenna took a short break to nurse Robbie, then returned to the study. She eventually managed to skim the book on invasive plants, but she found nothing resembling a deathbush. She searched for methods to kill unwanted weeds, but all she could find were techniques she'd already tried or knew wouldn't work. If only she could find some animal that could safely eat the deathbush—or another plant that could outcompete it. She'd done something like that in a previous life, hadn't she?

She studied the shelves devoted to personal journals. Her first name had always started with a "J," so it was easy to pick out her previous lives: Jilly wo'Leaf, Josh Sunflower, Janet r'Ivis, and of course Jacob Raddesdeath. He'd known the most about killing weeds. With a sigh, she selected one of his journals—not the last one—and flipped through it. A sentence leapt out at her: "Some seeds prevent their rivals from sprouting. I discovered this by accident, as I was trying to find strains of tropical plants that could be adapted to grow in Challen..."

"There you are, Ava!" Clover swept into the study and straightened a pile of books. "It's nearly dinner time. Which dress shall I lay out for you? Something formal, in honor of the War Avatar's visit?"

As much as Jenna would have liked to wear her newest favorite—a hunter green dress with cream trim and a daringly low-cut bosom—Gwen had suggested they all choose practical outfits so they could leave immediately after dinner. "The forest green and light blue poplin will do. I'll also need sturdy boots and a wool-lined cloak." It might be cooler in Tradetown, but Jenna had to be prepared in case Chaos Season occurred.

Before leaving the study, Jenna needed to mark her current page in this journal, so she could reference it later. What could she use? She didn't see any loose sheets or bookmarks handy, but a better solution came to her. She found Jacob's final journal, the one with Glory's death spelled out in shameful detail, and slipped it into the volume she was currently reading. Avatars weren't supposed to damage their documents, but in this case she had to make an exception.

Perhaps after this adventure is over, I can destroy that journal, or at least rip out the appropriate pages.

Twenty minutes later, when she entered the dining room, Jenna was relieved to see her sister Avatars in outfits similar to her own. Charles and Dorian had brought their weatherproof cloaks with them as well. Kron wore a satchel with many stuffed pockets, and Lex had changed into a field uniform in drab earth colors and no medals. Sophia, who planned to stay behind, was the only one in a formal gown and jewels. The head housekeeper frowned slightly as she surveyed them, and even the servers with the first course—a chilled cucumber soup—seemed surprised.

Gwen ate with perfect manners, nobility drilled too deeply into her to need fancy clothes. "Are we all ready and willing to do what must be done?"

Ysabel swallowed hard and managed a tiny nod.

"By The Four, must all of you go?" Sophia asked. "I can't believe one Selathen man requires this much magic to be subdued."

"He may have allies with him, Dear."

"Even so, Charles, the others can manage it just fine without you. Why risk yourself?"

"To see the deathbushes," Jenna said.

He raised an eyebrow. "I thought you said they were all destroyed."

"I hope they are, but if we find one, I'd like your thoughts on how to destroy it."

Sophia glared at her during the rest of the meal. Thankfully, no one else wanted to make conversation, polite or otherwise. They all devoured their way through the meal at twice the normal speed of a formal dinner.

"I apologize for the poor meal, Your Royal Highness," the housekeeper said to Lex as the servers brought out peach and berry pastries. "We've hosted royalty before and can serve you as your rank requires, given the opportunity to do so."

He selected one of each pastry. "No need to apologize, Dame. I've eaten field rations alongside my men. If your chefs could feed an army like this every day, we could conquer the world."

"Perhaps when this business is done, we could have a formal dinner and dance," Jenna suggested. Lex would be honor-bound to take a turn with all of the unmarried women, but she'd wager he'd give her the most dances.

Kron broke in before she could flirt further. "I need another doorway for the portal to Tradetown. Where should I put it? A doorway that isn't used very often would be best."

"How about the Summer Study?" Dorian said with a disdainful glance at Jenna.

"By All Four, I do read!" Why didn't Charles support her? The insult was directed at him too. "As a matter of fact, I've been researching the deathbushes." Did Dorian suspect she'd overheard his conversation with Kron earlier? Maybe she could throw that back at him. "Use the sample room next door to the Summer Study instead."

Kron nodded. "That will do. The rest of you can wait in the study while I prepare the portal."

The study was crowded with seven other people in it. Gwen took the opportunity to scan the titles, as if she planned to read while she waited. What if she noticed Jacob's last journal was missing? Jenna snatched up both of his journals, keeping the fatal one inside the other, and read out loud, "All the weeds grew when sown by themselves or with grains, but when I placed this seed among them, they did not sprout. Only whole seeds worked; those that had been hulled could not defend their spaces from the encroaching weeds."

"Is that about natural weed control?" Charles asked. "What seed was Jacob referring to?"

Ysabel peered around the corner. "The portal's ready."

"I can look it up later," Jenna replied to Charles. She slid the journal with its secret back into place.

Ysabel's cat suddenly growled, and his fur stood on end.

"Freeze it," Gwen said. "Does everyone have their winter clothes?"

From halfway across the room, Jenna could feel the blast of cold air coming through the portal. The ground beyond was covered in white.

CHAPTER SEVENTEEN

Deathbushes and Chaos

Jenna groaned. Chaos Season in the middle of summer always seemed like a special insult. Some people found cold and snow in summer a break from the heat, but she hated how it interfered with the crops. Over the centuries, the plants in Challen had developed some resistance to changes in temperature, but Chaos Season still interfered with the growing season. Once a Chaos Season had been tamed, she always had to restore the crops to their normal state.

"Is it widespread?" she asked.

"I'll know once we're on the other side," Kay said.

Jenna drew her cloak tightly around herself and stepped through, pleased that Dorian and Lex hesitated before following them.

The portal brought them to the back of Ysabel's house. Snow came up to Jenna's knees in an unbroken sheet. The windows looked dingy, and the house had a deserted feeling to it. Ysabel picked up her anilink and studied the house. "The songbirds haven't seen anyone going in or out of the house since we left. I'll wager my father is living in his watch shop downtown."

Dorian announced, "Chaos Season is active in this part of Tradetown and extends toward the Selathen border."

"I hope it doesn't reach the border," Kron said. "Salth could make it even stronger."

"Let's dispel it before that happens." Gwen extended her hands toward Jenna and Kay.

As Jenna trudged through the snow toward Gwen, Dorian said, "This Chaos Season is small enough for me to manage on my own."

Gwen raised her eyebrow. "But you can't restore anything besides the weather."

"I can still do a better job of that than you four will."

Gwen narrowed her eyes. Kay lowered her gaze, and Ysabel touched her between her shoulder blades. Jenna wished she dared tell him to be silent. Every time he spoke, he made it harder for Kay to regain faith in herself and her magic. If he didn't stop, his words might come true.

Jenna glared at him. "Just let us work. We'll show you which quartet the Four favor."

Gwen took her hand. *Less talking, more magic. We need to work quickly before he interferes.*

He does have a lot of experience, Kay said doubtfully.

So do you. And you have something more—us, Gwen said. *We'll make you stronger than him, Kay. Don't worry about Dorian or anyone else, just send the winter back where it belongs!*

Kay sent agreement, though the nightmares of her death still lingered in the back of her thoughts. But when she focused her attention on the snow and cold, her fears dwindled. Jenna and Ysabel anchored her, letting Gwen share their magic with Kay to make her stronger.

Kay studied the gray clouds above them before pushing them away as gently as a mother soothing a sick child. Warm winds swept in from the south. The snow around them melted, running into their boots. Kay turned her focus to the part of the storm brushing the border between Challen and Selath. A cold wind returned and drove off the warmth. The slush they were standing in froze, trapping them in ice.

Kay dropped the link, her complexion red. She squeezed her eyes shut as if they'd been frozen that way.

Jenna couldn't help sighing and saying, "By All Four…"

Don't say it, Gwen sent. Out loud, she said, "It's all right, Kay. Just warm up the air again."

The clouds returned, blocking the sunlight.

"The wind, I need the wind," Kay muttered. "Freeze it, why won't it listen to me?"

Dorian walked on top of the snow over to them. "Having trouble, young Avas?" Amusement glittered in his ice-hard eyes.

Kay stared at the ice binding her feet, silent.

Gwen met his stare dead-on. "Do you happen to know anything about…Kay's current difficulties, Avi?"

I'll bet he does! Jenna sent through the link. *Remember, he wants to keep using his power even though his quartet is broken. Give me a fighting stick and let me at him!* She wriggled her feet, trying to break free. The ice immobilized her boots. If she and the others didn't obtain freedom soon, they'd freeze despite Gwen's and Kay's magic.

Dorian shrugged. "She's out of practice. The weather won't answer her."

True words, but Jenna suspected there was more to the story. Gwen must have thought the same thing. She dropped the link and pushed her violet bracelet farther up her arm, then she extended her cursed hand toward Dorian.

"I'll wager you can make sure the weather answers her, Avi," she said.

"Perhaps." He danced in place, sure-footed despite the slick ice, advancing until he was just out of Gwen's reach. "And I bet you still require touch for your magic, young Ava."

"What's going on?" Kron took a few steps toward them through the snow, frowned, then lifted each boot in turn and touched it. He too climbed onto the top of the snow and walked over it as securely as though he was on land. "Ysabel? Are you all right?"

Dorian scowled and stepped back. A warm—no, hot—blast of air roared at them. Jenna's face burned. At the same time, the ice holding her prisoner melted. Water flooded her boots, numbing her toes. She stamped her feet extra hard as she clambered over the rotting snow.

"Well done, Kay," Gwen said.

Kay shook her head. "It wasn't me."

They all turned to stare at Dorian. The only sound breaking the silence was water dripping from icicles. Finally, Gwen stepped forward, toward the Avi Win. "Leave, Dorian. Go home. We don't want you interfering with our magic."

"I was an Avatar first, before any of you were born." He crossed his arms. "You can't take this from me."

"I wish the Four would," Gwen said. "Maybe then you'd let Kay work in peace."

"Be careful what you wish for, young Ava. Someday you'll find yourself facing your replacement. You won't want to give up your position either.

"Jenna! I say, come round here!"

Everyone fell silent as Charles approached them from the side of the house. He must have gone to the front while they were busy with Chaos Season.

"I think I found the deathbushes you told me about," he said. "By All Four, they do look nasty."

She felt ready to wilt. "Deathbushes? They grew back?"

"Come take a look at them and tell me."

They tramped through more snow to the front of the house. Sure enough, the scent of thyme greeted her. Four deathbushes, spaced as far apart as possible, guarded the front of the house. Withered branches between them showed where other deathbushes had grown. These plants weren't as tall as the ones Jenna had first grown, but they bore more thorns. Their branches trembled as the group of Avatars approached them.

"These are the plants you're so worried about, Jenna?" Gwen tilted her head as she studied them. "Are they poisonous too?"

"The thorns carry some sort of toxin. I'm not sure how strong it is or what it does."

"Well, don't try to test it without me." Gwen's warning made Jenna feel warm inside. Even if she just wanted to be close by if Jenna required healing, Gwen still cared for her.

Gwen continued, "We need to finish taming Chaos Season first before dealing with the plants. Other people might be facing hunger or cold if we don't restore the weather. We can funnel the magic from Chaos Season into Jenna so she can kill off the deathbushes."

Taming the weather was their most important job—if they could do it without interference. Jenna and her three sister Avatars turned in unison to Dorian, glaring at him with enough force to send him back to the One Oak. He simply stood there, arms crossed, radiating coldness.

After a few heartbeats, Gwen sighed. "Charles, please?"

The Avi Summer stopped studying the deathbushes—not touching them, Jenna noted—and took Dorian's arm. "By the Four, Dorian, there's nothing for us to do here. Let them work in peace. We have to stand together against the Selathens."

"The Selathens. Yes. Maybe we should go find them right now."

Ysabel glanced around nervously. "Shouldn't we stay together?"

"It's still daylight here," Gwen said. "If we're recognized in the streets, more Selathens might attack us. I'm not sure I can handle a mob, especially if they have pistols."

Before Dorian could taunt them again, Lex said, "Perhaps Kron, Dorian, and Charles could find Ysabel's father and create a portal back here. I can stay here and guard the young women while they work."

Gwen nodded. "That seems to be the best solution. The less time we have to spend here, the better."

After Ysabel gave the men the directions to her father's store, Jenna and the rest of her quartet retreated to the back of the house so they would be less visible. Lex remained out front, prodding a deathbush with a polearm. Jenna supposed it was actually his dagger in a different form.

"Once we clear this Chaos Season, we can officially be recognized as Season Avatars," Gwen told them as they gathered around her. "So, let's do our best."

At least then Dorian would have to leave them alone. Jenna wished she'd been able to bring part of her tree with her to enhance her magic. She could use another weapon in her fight against the death-bushes.

They joined hands, and Gwen took control, funneling all of their magic to Kay. Slowly, then with greater assurance, she warmed the air and melted the rest of the snow. Jenna sighed with bliss as summer heat returned.

The herb garden's overgrown, Ysabel said. *And the sunflowers for my songbirds aren't blooming.*

I can fix that. Kay shunted magic from Chaos Season to Jenna and Ysabel. While Ysabel gently healed half-frozen baby birds and encouraged the insects to crawl out of their shelters, Jenna revived the plants. Scents of rosemary and mint reminded her of the thyme-smelling deathbushes. She still had to destroy them, but she focused first on restoring the Lathatilltins' garden and all other affected areas before returning to the deathbushes. Cursed plants.

Cursed plants...Gwen, is there any way we can use your cursed shard against the deathbushes?

You'd risk that? Are you sure? Gwen's mental voice turned bitter. *What if it makes them worse?*

Freeze it, she'd been using that same argument to keep Gwen from learning...

Learning what? Gwen, Ysabel, and Kay all asked at once.

Panicking, Jenna tore out of the link. Her body still thrummed with extra magic from Chaos Season, so she raced to the closest deathbush.

"Jenna, wait!" Kay called after her.

She wasn't ready to link with the others just yet. She had to do this on her own. Jenna grabbed a couple of leaves and pushed the magic from Chaos Season into the deathbush, willing it to die.

Two things happened so quickly she wasn't sure which one came first: thorns bit into her hands, and hail pelted her head.

"By All Four!" Jenna released the plant and stepped back, inspecting her palms. Blood streamed from the holes where she'd been pricked, and her hand throbbed with poison.

Frowning, Gwen hurried over to examine Jenna.

"I'll be fine," Jenna said. Already the throbbing was fading as her plant magic helped her neutralize the poison.

"Let me decide that. Besides, you'd like to use that hand again, wouldn't you?"

Gwen clasped Jenna's injured hand between her own. The throbbing vanished. Jenna's skin tingled as Gwen healed the wounds.

"All better." Gwen rubbed her hands as if trying to remove the blood. "That poison would be dangerous to a normal person, though."

"Did any of you notice Chaos Season returned?" Kay asked. "It was a small one, and it's already faded, but it happened when Jenna used Chaos Season magic on the deathbush."

Jenna flexed her healed hand. "Maybe it was a fluke."

"You'll have to try it again to be sure," Gwen said.

They linked again, with Jenna too worried about this new problem to accidentally divulge her secret. Once again, Gwen passed her magic from Kay. The heartbeat she attempted to use it against the deathbushes, the temperature around them dropped to freezing.

"I think these plants are resistant to our magic, Jenna," Ysabel said. "Too bad they're not useful."

"Does that mean we've failed to tame Chaos Season?" Kay hung her head.

"It's not your fault, Kay." Gwen released Jenna and Ysabel to pull Kay into a sisterly embrace.

Jenna watched the two of them. *It's not her fault. It's mine. I should be able to handle these frozen plants. And I will, no matter what.*

She let her cloak slip to the ground. With a growl of frustration, Jenna strode forward, grabbed the closest branch—this time trying to avoid the thorns—and pulled with all her strength until part of the branch broke off. She shifted her grip on the branch until she held it like a fighting stick used at a soltrans. "In the name of the God of Summer, ruler of all the plants in Challen, I command you to die. Die, you frozen weeds, die and never sprout again!"

Jenna lashed out at the deathbush, whipping it until leaves and twigs flew like snow. Its branches reached for her, but she hardened the staff in her hands and bashed them. Her human reflexes were faster than theirs, and although they outnumbered her, she was able to block several at once.

One by one, she broke branches off of the plant, stomping on each of them as hard as she could. Before she could close in on the main stem, something poked her in the back. "Look out!" Gwen shouted.

Jenna turned awkwardly as cloth ripped. Another deathbush had stretched out toward her and snagged her dress. She doubted the plant wanted to dance with her. How could she destroy both plants at once?

The first deathbush leaned over toward her. That gave her an idea. She grabbed the tip and touched it to a branch of the second death-bush, trying to make each plant think the other one was its best target.

The trick worked better than she had expected. The deathbushes entwined around each other. The one closer to her leaned forward, its roots coming free from the soil. High-pitched squeaks prompted her to look down. Mice, moles, and other small burrowing creatures dug through the ground quickly enough to evade the deathbush roots while loosening the soil.

"Well done, Ysabel!" Jenna said. They might be able to conquer these plants yet.

"More are sprouting behind you!" Gwen called.

"What?" Jenna checked for herself. A half dozen sprouts poked out of the ground and shot first knee-high, then past her head.

"There are some on the other side too!" Kay pointed behind Jenna.

Gwen stalked up to the line of deathbushes. "What do you want us to do?"

"Have Kay pull as much water out of the soil as possible. Even magic plants need water to grow."

Jenna dropped to her knees and put both hands on the ground. All the grass in the lawn was dead, more victims of the deathbushes. What could stop them? If she attempted to make the soil itself unfit for plants—something that went against her very nature—would that be enough to kill them?

She scraped away the top layer. It crumbled easily, especially as Kay wicked moisture out of it. The deathbush roots plunged deep within the soil, longer than Jenna herself. She didn't have the strength to drain it that far down.

"Jenna, come out of there!" Gwen released Kay to beckon her. "You'll get trapped!"

Of course I won't get trapped. She glanced at the deathbushes anyway. Wherever she looked, the branches wove together to create a deadly fence. "Oh, By All Four Gods and Goddesses, just die already!" She grabbed her branch and attempted to create an opening she could squeeze through. To her surprise, thorns sank into her branch and pulled it away from her.

"Jenna! Stand back!" Lex shifted his grip on his polearm, and it turned into an axe. He chopped up the deathbushes blocking her escape. They fell apart like matchsticks. *How humiliating to have someone else save me from plants. I suppose War can destroy anything, even deathbushes.*

It didn't take long for him to create an opening wide enough for her to pass through without touching a deathbush. He adjusted his grip on his axe and extended his hand to her. She accepted it and let him guide her through the gap to freedom.

She gasped for breath for a few heartbeats before saying, "Lex, you saved me. How—" she was going to say "romantic," but she didn't think he would appreciate that—"How kind of you."

He met her gaze. "Are you unhurt?"

She nodded. Scratches burned her arms and legs, but they were minor. "What about you?"

He grinned wryly. "Unfortunately, I don't have magic armor, but I do heal rapidly from injuries." He rubbed his arm where his jacket had been torn. "Eagle's Talons, the thorns prick like the War Eagle Himself."

"Allow me to tend that, Avi." Gwen avoided looking at his face as she healed him.

He nodded at her. "My thanks, Ava."

"Thank you for saving our sister Avatar." Gwen watched Jenna as she spoke.

"Should I destroy the rest of the plants?" Lex asked.

Jenna sighed. "Can you dig out their roots too? Otherwise, they'll return."

"The War Dagger would flay my own flesh if I tried to turn it into a shovel. I'll just chop the deathbushes as close to the ground as I can. Perhaps that will give us more time to figure out a more permanent solution."

He attacked the deathbushes again while Gwen turned her attention to Jenna, checking her for more injuries and thorn pricks. While she worked, Jenna admired how easily Lex handled his weapon. Maybe he cared for her more than he was willing to admit.

By All Four, if he does, you're welcome to him.

You still don't like him?

I'm glad he's on our side, but I can't bring myself to marry War. I just can't.

He's too serious for you, Jenna agreed. *You need someone who can make you smile.*

Gwen raised an eyebrow. *Did you have someone in mind?*

Before Jenna could answer, Kay joined the link. *I feel more magic in the air. Chaos Season is about to start—*

A few drops of rain slid down Jenna's face before clouds released a gale's worth of water on them.

CHAPTER EIGHTEEN

Allies Divided

"When will Kron and the other Avatars come back with my father?" Ysabel asked. "It seems they've been gone a long time."

After taming Chaos Season—again—Jenna and the rest of the Avatars were hungry. Ysabel didn't have a key to her house, so Jenna loosened the kitchen door, and Lex burst it open. Most of the food was spoiled, but there was flour, baking powder, and oil. Jenna and Kay prepared fried flatcakes while Gwen sliced cheese and Ysabel mixed chocolate from a tin of powder. Even Lex helped get the stove restarted—though Jenna ultimately had to show him how—and searched for supplies.

Gwen pulled out a watch on a necklace. "We've been here less than two hours. Do you think they walked all the way to the center of town, or found a carriage?"

"I thought Kron would portal everyone back here," Lex said.

"First they have to travel to Father's shop the normal way. That part could take some time." Ysabel set plates for everyone at the kitchen table. No one protested at eating where servants normally did.

Gwen frowned. "Even so, they should have been back by now."

Jenna scraped a burned flatcake out of the frying pan. "Should we try to find them?"

"Send a scout first," Lex said.

Everyone glanced at Ysabel. She set the chocolate aside, sat at the table, and closed her eyes. At some unseen signal, her anilink jumped into her lap. "I don't see them in the streets," she said. "Or the birds don't, at least. Let me contact the rats and mice in my father's shop."

Pouncer rumbled, as if he wanted to hunt mice instead of talking to them.

Ysabel continued, "The mice don't want to leave their holes. There are four pairs of boots and several places in the room that feel wrong to them. Two pairs of boots wandered into the bad areas and haven't moved since. The other two pairs are still moving, with one vanishing and reappearing constantly."

"What does that mean?" Gwen asked. "Who's stuck, and who's not?"

"One set of black boots is just like another. Did you think the mice could see people's faces?"

Gwen sighed and pushed her food away. "Do they hear human speech well enough for you to interpret it?"

Pouncer jumped off of Ysabel's lap, freeing her to stand. "Mice hear high-pitched sounds better than low ones. They can't make out male voices very well, so I can't either." She resumed preparing chocolate, whipping it so hard the drink splattered everywhere.

"Watch it!" Jenna blotted the chocolate off of her sleeve with a towel.

"Wait. Something's happening." Ysabel set down the chocolate pot. "Now the strange spots have vanished, and all of the boots are moving again. But there's only three pairs of boots. The other pair disappeared, like the strange spots."

"What does that mean?" Gwen asked. "When will someone come back to tell us what's happening?"

Kay turned from the window. "Kron just appeared outside. Charles and Dorian are with him."

"And my father?" Ysabel asked.

"He's not there."

Everyone exchanged curious glances, then rushed to the kitchen door. Jenna used her longer legs to get outside first. Kron looked exhausted, as if both he and his satchel were deflated. Charles had his hands clasped together as if he held something in them, and Dorian stared around him with a dazed expression.

Jenna held out her hand in case any of the men needed support. "By All Four, what happened?"

"He somehow knew we were coming," Kron replied. "He had time traps guarding all the entrances. My wards protected me, but I didn't think Charles and Dorian would need their own artifacts. Thank the Four all the traps did was suspend them in time."

"We couldn't move, but we could see and hear everything," Charles said.

Gwen shuddered and clenched her scarred hand. "Just like my experience with Sal-thaath."

"I think he may have made the traps and given them to the Honored Lathatilltin," Kron said. "They were more difficult to disarm than I expected. By the time I freed Charles and Dorian, the Honored Lathatilltin disappeared through a portal that closed behind him."

"Were you able to track where it led?" Lex asked.

Kron shook his head. "He could be anywhere in Challen, or even the Dead Land."

Jenna wished she could thrash the deathbushes again. This trip had been a waste of time. Perhaps they'd trimmed the deathbushes down for now, but the plants would grow back very quickly, perhaps within a couple of days. She couldn't destroy them with Chaos Season magic; if anything, they seemed to make Chaos Season worse. Now Ysabel's father had access to Sal-thaath's magic and had used it to escape? What could possibly be worse?

Charles approached her and opened his hands. "Jenna, are these seeds from the deathbush?"

Once glance was enough to confirm it. After her experience with them in the atrium, she'd remember those seeds for a thousand lifetimes. "Where did you find them?"

"They were in Lathatilltin's private study." Charles didn't bother with the Selathen title. "We searched his apartment after Kron freed us. They were in a tall vase. I took all of them, but how many were there to begin with?" He shrugged.

"By All Four, Papa plans to plant more of those frozen plants?" Ysabel asked. "Weren't they dreadful enough in our front yard?"

"If he grows enough of them, will they spawn a Chaos Season?" Kay asked. "That's a bitter harvest."

"I should take this news to the king," Lex said. "We must prepare ourselves for a plant invasion."

Jenna didn't like the sound of that at all. She beckoned to Charles. "Before we go home, we should make the soil out front as ...unfertile as possible, to prevent more deathbushes from growing."

He frowned. "That's against everything Summer wants us to do."

"So is this plant."

Charles let out a deliberate sigh. "I don't suppose there's any food, is there? I didn't work any magic over there, but I'm still hungry."

"There's flatcakes, cheese, and chocolate." Ysabel swept her hand back toward the kitchen. "We cooked them ourselves."

Jenna waited for Dorian to make a snide insult, but he said nothing. He still seemed distracted, as if his mind was off somewhere in the clouds.

Gwen approached him and asked softly, "Avi, are you all right? Do you need my assistance?"

He started, then stared down at her and shook his head. "No, child." He sounded so calm and polite his insult barely registered.

With a raised eyebrow, Gwen silently inquired what Jenna, Ysabel, and Kay thought of Dorian's behavior. They all responded with shrugs.

There must have been more to those time traps than Kron said. Maybe Charles knows what happened to Dorian. They were both stuck in them.

After a quick meal, Jenna led Charles to the front lawn of Ysabel's house. Fog hung in the air, making it difficult to judge how quickly the deathbushes were recovering. Mindful of how she'd nearly gotten trapped, Jenna kept one foot on the stone walk as she crouched and rubbed soil between her fingers. Still too many nutrients in it for her comfort. How could she drain them? If she force-grew plants to use them, the deathbushes might use the new plants as fertilizer—or grow back on their own.

"Charles, what happened while you and Dorian were trapped?" she asked. "You said you couldn't move, but you could still see and hear everything."

"Nothing worth mentioning. Ysabel's father kept praising his time goddess and her son. He said they were more powerful than the Four and could turn back time to revive the dead."

Jenna stared at Charles' face, shrouded by fog. "Do you think she could do that?" It would be very awkward to have her absent husband return. She'd already had her marriage tattoo altered, though Dorian hadn't…. She dropped the soil. "What about Dorian? What if Salth could bring Margaret back to life for him?"

Charles laughed. "Of course she can't do that. Margaret's soul is safe with the Four. They wouldn't let Salth bring her back in the wrong season." As he watched her, his expression became more worried and uncertain. "They wouldn't, would They?"

"Do you think Dorian is desperate enough to believe Salth?"

"He could be." Charles raked his fingers through the dirt. "But he's served the Four as long as any of us. He knows Them. He's loyal to Them. He has to be."

Something stirred in the ground beneath Jenna's hands. "Charles! You're supposed to be hurting the soil, not making it better!"

"Well, I've never had to do that before!" he answered, sounding as peevish as his six decades warranted.

A familiar-looking sprout popped out next to them. Jenna reached for it before it could poke out thorns. "Help me pull!"

Charles put his hands on either side of the sprout, loosening the root. Despite Jenna taking care to pull slowly and steadily, the root still broke before she dragged all of it out. She glared at the white strands and coiled them into a ball. She hesitated to grab it, remembering what had happened the last time. "Let's get this inside before it wraps around me again."

"What do you mean?"

Wishing she could recall her words, Jenna sprinted back through the house and into the kitchen. By the time she reached the stove, tendrils poked out between her fingers. Her sister Avatars glanced at her, then sprang into action. Gwen and Ysabel used long forks to scrape the young deathbush off of Jenna, and Kay opened the stove door so they could fling plant pieces into the fire. She poked at it with another fork, protecting her hands with a towel, until the deathbush was no more than smoke and ashes.

Charles nodded at them. "Better salt the yard."

"I already tried that. It doesn't work on these plants."

He frowned. "By All Four, these plants are obviously magical, but they're not invincible. Find their weakness, Jenna. We're counting on you."

Since Sophia wasn't here, Jenna thrust out her bosom and put on her best smile. "Aren't you going to help me? You're the current Avi Summer, after all. It's your responsibility."

He shook his head. "I've been Avi long enough. I'm ready to retire to my family's vineyard. This is your task, young Ava."

Before she could protest, Charles turned to Kron and said, "I think it's time we head home. We have much to talk about. Where's this portal of yours?"

"I'll make another one inside the house," Kron replied. "We've already attracted enough attention."

Kron used the doorway between the kitchen and the dining room for his latest portal, which led them back to the Summer Study. Jenna trudged through with her head down. It seemed less and less likely she and her quartet would ever tame Chaos Season successfully.

* * *

"It seems our enemy has recruited an army of her own," Lex said later that evening.

Instead of meeting again in the uncomfortable map room, all of the Season Avatars, plus Lex and Kron, had gathered in the Summer Parlor. To keep the room cool in the summer, it had no direct sun exposure and was shaded by oaks next to the house. Small tables throughout the room held trays for ice sculptures. Dorian had created prancing horses, while most of Kay's looked more like blocks with a few odd lumps and edges. They wouldn't last the night, but they did provide relief from the heat. Jenna sat next to one of Kay's blocks and wished she dared relax enough to sleep. Couldn't they wait until morning for this meeting? Maybe then her head wouldn't feel like molasses in Snowmoon.

"We don't know the Selathens are actually assembling into an army," Gwen said to Lex. "So far, it seems that it's just a few discontents who are helping Salth."

"It doesn't matter if they have one man or ten thousand on their side. We must be prepared to engage with them." He stalked angrily back and forth, as if trying to find a battle plan hidden among paintings and vases of preserved flowers.

Kay looked up from her workbasket of rags and sewing supplies. Setting aside the dress that she planned to rework into a child's garment for the poor, she said in a quiet voice, "Begging your pardon,

Your Royal Highness, but the men aren't the real problem. I'm more concerned about the way deathbushes make Chaos Season worse."

"That's my point, Ava." She flinched as he shook a finger at her. "The Selathens have seeds of those strange plants. I'm sure they mean to turn them into a weapon."

Freeze it, did Lex always have to think like a War Avatar? Jenna had to admit he was right about the deathbushes, though. Even without their connection to Chaos Season, they still stole the life from other plants and threatened humans and creatures with their poisonous thorns. She couldn't find a single use for them. She needed to banish them from Challen.

A chunk of ice dropped off the sculpture. Jenna touched it to her forehead and neck. "Let's figure out how to destroy the deathbushes, then."

"Burn them," Ysabel suggested.

"These plants have long roots that can survive fire. They'll just re-sprout. Besides, fire has its own dangers. Do you really want to risk setting your family house on fire?"

Ysabel glumly shook her head.

"We could send burrowing animals to gnaw through the roots," Sophia said. "If they chew them up thoroughly enough, they won't grow back."

Charles nodded, his face for once intent on the conversation. "All we have to do is find them."

Kron turned away from a cabinet of specimens. "I used to specialize in creating magical finders. If I can attune one to the deathbushes, then the Ava Falls can track them down."

"Ysabel needs to stay with her quartet. We don't know when the next Chaos Season will happen, but the next quartet is responsible for taming it. Humm." Sophia glanced at her husband. "Dear, are you thinking what I'm thinking?"

"I never know what you're thinking."

She continued, "You and I would make the perfect team to handle the deathbushes."

"What!" He blinked at her. "What do you mean? I thought I was supposed to stay here and help Jenna study the deathbushes."

"She has the Summer Archives and the atrium. She can handle it on her own."

Jenna swelled with pride at Sophia's praise.

Sophia patted her husband's hand. "It would be nice to do something that's just the two of us, don't you think?"

"Then I should stay at the One Oak and help the girls manage it," Dorian said.

Gwen stiffened at his words.

"What about me?" Lex asked. "As general, I can oversee—"

Sophia dismissed him with a hand wave. "We can manage ourselves, Your Royal Highness." She turned to Kron. "Could you tell us more about these finders?"

As Kron explained how they worked, Dorian slipped out of the room. Lex, frowning, stalked out a few moments later. Jenna hesitated, wondering if she was being disloyal to the Season Avatars, before following him.

Although candles burned in the Summer Study, Lex retreated down the hall toward the stairs. Jenna hurried to catch up to him. "Your Royal Highness—" it was safer to use his title where servants might overhear— "is something the matter?"

He turned, glanced at her, and looked around as if he also worried about eavesdroppers. "Ava, how exactly is one supposed to command your troops?"

She blinked. "You mean, our quartets? Usually, the Ava or Avi Spring makes the final decisions, but everyone else has a say."

"So…Lady Io Havil is your leader? And the older three Season Avatars have no leader?"

She nodded.

"What about Kron? How does he fit into your magic system?"

That was harder to explain, especially since he didn't belong. "Gwen and I met him after a lecture he gave at the University. He claims he was our first teacher in magic, but instead of being reborn the way we are, he came forward in time inside a magic water clock."

Lex nodded. "I remember reading about the pre-Annexation find, but Court duties kept me away from the lecture."

Jenna wondered if they would have become reacquainted then. Probably not, as Gwen would have ignored Lex in favor of Kron. "Kron doesn't serve the Four the way we do, and he claims his magic is his own, not a gift from a god. Nonetheless, he supports the Four and is Salth's enemy. Or she's his enemy, I'm not sure. He's our ally, just as you are."

Lex scowled again and ascended a couple of steps. "Do you consider him your primary ally?"

"By All Four, Lex, what do you mean?"

He stared down at her. "I have far more leadership experience than Kron or Lady lo Havil. Why don't you and the other Avatars listen to me?"

He thinks he should be in charge? Gwen would have a fit—or give him a fit. "Gwen has more experience than you realize," she said, her loyalty automatically going to her Ava Spring. "Lifetimes of it."

Lex's eyes darkened, not with anger, but with another emotion she wasn't sure of. "Jenna, I had hoped…I had thought…we were allies."

"Of course we are!" She smiled, hoping to appease him. "But Gwen's my Ava Spring. She'll always come first for me."

He gave her an odd look. "Are you both…Fallswomen, then?"

I wish. Jenna herself ultimately planned to follow the traditional route with another marriage, but she wouldn't turn down a tryst of any type along the way. Gwen, on the other hand, had always preferred one lifetime partner of the opposite sex. Jenna was disqualified in this life, perhaps for all their future lives too.

"Gwen has always believed that as a Spring Avatar, she can't honor Fall in that way," Jenna replied to Lex.

He narrowed his eyes. "And you?"

By All Four, why did his question make her feel like they were warring with each other? *It doesn't have to be this way.* She still gulped as she stared up at him. He'd stepped in to save her earlier that day. At the very least, she owed him honesty. If she trusted him with her secrets, maybe he would do the same with his.

"Summer is like Fall, more accepting of those who don't always fit in the normal order of things."

Lex raised an eyebrow. "I will admit we took affairs out of their proper order, but that doesn't seem like reason to consider yourself a Fallswoman."

"I've only been with men in this life," Jenna said quickly. "And I do want to remarry." She lowered her eyelashes and peeked out from under them, shifting to show off her cleavage.

His gaze dropped exactly where she wanted it to go and lingered there appreciatively. "My first wife died over a decade ago of illness. We were back in Fip at the time, where we have no healing Avatars."

"Did you love her?" Maybe he still did.

"Not at first. It took time for us to become accustomed to each other. Lady Io Havil reminds me of her. Both she and Quilla are very proper noblewomen, but Quilla never hated me the way the Spring Avatar does. Since then, I've have women pursue me for my magic or rank or both. Very few of them, if any, were interested in Lex, not the War Avatar or the king's brother."

He took a step down toward her. "Jenna, I thought perhaps you were the exception. But if there's even the slightest suspicion…" Lex sighed. "I suppose it doesn't matter. Eagle's Talons, the longer I stay here, the more I wonder why War wants me to. I still don't see how this alliance between different types of Avatars can work. I must commune with Him tonight." He stared at her intently, enough to make her warm in ways that had nothing to do with the weather. He nodded his head at her. "Good night, Ava."

He ascended the stairs rapidly and turned toward his quarters. Jenna watched his muscles flowing beneath his clothes. She wished she dared follow him and show him he was the man she wanted most. It wasn't his fault Jenna couldn't have Gwen, after all.

Was he beginning to have feelings for her the way she did for him? Did she have a chance with him? If only she could forget about Gwen. Loving one felt like a betrayal of the other.

CHAPTER NINETEEN

Jacob's Journal

As Jenna rose the next morning, she didn't need weather magic to tell her today would be hot enough to roast corncobs while they were still on the stalk. Her nightgown, damp with sweat, clung to her. A maid had left a tray with covered dishes on the table next to her fireplace. Bread, cheese, a couple of boiled eggs, and a pot of chocolate—everything at the same temperature. Why had food been left at all? Normally she would have breakfast downstairs with the other Avatars. She devoured her meal, then summoned Clover to help her wash and dress—and maybe share the latest news.

"Are the other Avatars in my quartet up yet?" she asked. She hoped Gwen wouldn't insist on them practicing linking today. Lex dominated her thoughts, and she didn't want to share him with the others.

"I'm afraid I don't know, Ava."

"Well, what about the older Season Avatars?"

Clover held out a lightweight morning dress for Jenna's inspection. "The older Ava Fall has the whole house turned upside down. Apparently she and her husband have to go on a journey." She glanced up at Jenna. "Is the Ava Spring forcing them to leave?"

"No, nothing like that. They're helping us destroy some nasty weeds invading the country."

"That's all? They'll be back?"

"They'll return when all the deathbushes are gone," Jenna said. She wondered how many seasons that would take.

Clover's worried expression eased a little, but she fussed with the buttons on Jenna's dress longer than necessary. "It's just that the Ava Spring seemed a bit upset herself," she said as she assisted Jenna into her dress. "She didn't finish her breakfast, and she cancelled her daily visit to Midpoint. Said she still wanted her mare, though."

A sick feeling rose in Jenna's own stomach. Maybe she should have demanded something else to eat. "And no one knows what upset her?"

Clover shook her head, somehow managing to continue doing up the buttons.

"Do you know if Gwen already went out?" Gwen was a much better rider than Jenna, so she'd never catch her. Best to find out what had happened so she could figure out how to soothe Gwen's temper.

"She's probably long gone by now, Ava."

Thank the Four for small mercies. "Then let me visit my son. Better yet, have him brought down here. It's too hot for an infant in the nursery."

Thinking of Robbie should have made her breasts swell with milk, but they felt empty. When Callie brought him down, Jenna tried to nurse him, but he refused. "He must know I've lost my milk." She clutched him close to her anyway, no matter how he squirmed.

"Perhaps it's for the best, Ava," Callie said. "I can feed him, but only you can provide plant magic to Challen."

That wasn't a consolation. Jenna held her son for several more minutes until his fussing reached a critical pitch, then handed him back. If Gwen was here and in a better mood, she could ask her to restore her milk. Perhaps Jenna should talk to Ysabel or Kay instead. They would know what was bothering Gwen.

"Thank you," she said to the servants. "That will be all."

She gave Robbie a kiss for luck before leaving.

Kay accosted Jenna before she could go downstairs to the main floor. "I'm sorry, but I can't make it cooler. This is appropriate for the season, and we're due for a storm in the next couple of days."

Seeing Kay look as fresh as spring when sweat was already beading on Jenna's scalp made her more irritated. "Oh, By All Four, Kay, this is my season. I know what to expect." She wiped her forehead. "Is the heat getting to Gwen too?"

Kay looked down. "I hear it was a book."

"A book?" *By All Four Gods and Goddesses, it can't be that one…*

"Someone left an old journal in the breakfast nook, right where Gwen normally sits. She couldn't help but page through it. Suddenly, she gasped and started to choke." Kay shook her head. "Before I could do anything, she coughed out a piece of sausage. She said something, but I couldn't make out the words. Then she flushed and ran out of the room."

"The journal. Whose was it? Where is it?"

"It's probably still in the nook. I think the first name started with 'J,' like your name, but the last name ended with 'th'…"

"By All Four!" Jenna turned and ran out of the room, cutting through the central atrium. The door to the seed vault hung open, but she had no time to close it. Charles was probably looking for supplies for his trip. He could take care of it later.

In the breakfast nook, the maids had already cleared the dirty dishes and the food from the sideboard. However, they'd left the journal out. Jenna recognized it immediately; it was the one she'd tried to hide. Worse yet, a silver fork held the book open at a page near the end. Jenna didn't need to read it to recall the words: *I've killed her. By All Four Gods and Goddesses, I killed Glory. How could I have been so selfish as to hurt the most important person in my life?*

"Freeze you!" she yelled at the book. She ripped out the accusing page and threw it into the fireplace, even though no fire burned. She wanted to send the journal after it, but lifetimes of memories held her back. Someday she might need to reference the earlier parts of Jacob's career, when he'd dealt with various blights and funguses. Besides, what was the point of destroying the book now that Gwen had discovered her secret? The only thing Jenna could do now was follow Gwen and beg forgiveness.

She hurried to the stable and asked a groom to saddle a horse for her. The man wasn't much older than her, but he looked her up and down as if more interested in her riding ability than her curves. "Have you ever ridden before, Ava?"

"Does it matter? Just mount me on a horse and send me after Gwen!"

"But Ava, you're not dressed for hard riding. You'd have to get a riding skirt, and then we'd have to find you a gentle mare or gelding while we teach you how to balance yourself and handle the reins...."

"Freeze it." At this rate, Gwen could ride across the Salt Waters into Fip before Jenna was ready. "I'll just walk. Which way did the Spring Avatar go?"

"Into the forest, Ava."

The forest surrounding the One Oak wasn't the largest in Challen, but it was still big enough to hide a single Avatar. However, Jenna's affinity with plants might help her find Gwen.

She set out from the stable and studied the plants alongside the diverging paths. Off to the right, a thistle held long dark hairs that could have come from a horse's tail. Crushed leaves gave off green scent. Nodding grimly to herself, Jenna hiked after Gwen, the lover she'd betrayed. Maybe Gwen would turn around and come back along this path, or maybe she would follow another trail back to the One Oak. Maybe she was sick enough of her duties to flee Challen. It didn't matter where she had gone as long as Jenna found her.

Jenna hadn't expected to be hiking outdoors. Although her feet were still callused from years of working barefoot on the farm, her slippers soon bore stains and rips. She paused to take them off and carry them. Whenever trees or shrubs closed in on her, she carefully worked her way through the branches so the lace on her dress wouldn't get caught. Kay had made her realize how much human effort was behind her glorious new wardrobe.

By midday, the birds and other creatures were silent in the heat streaming through the leaves. Jenna hoped she'd find a stream or pond to drink from. She stopped in a small clearing to search for water-loving plants when she heard a horse trotting her way. Panic made her dive off the path. She needed to explain herself to Gwen, but no words had come to her during the journey.

Gwen rode into the clearing. In a pale yellow gown and a hat still balanced on her head, she looked far cooler than Jenna felt. Her face twisted into something red and ugly. "You! Of all the frozen people I could have met out here, it had to be you." She halted her horse and tried to turn the mare in another direction.

Jenna crept toward her, twigs caught in her dress. "Please, Gwen, at least let me say I'm sorry."

"That doesn't change anything."

"It was another life for both of us! We're better off forgetting about it!"

Gwen curled her lip. "I wish it had stayed forgotten. I was better off when that memory was walled away, even if some of my healing knowledge was behind that barrier."

"You...you remember that moment?"

"Which one?" Never had blue eyes been so cold and cruel. "The one where I found you and the governess in our own bed, or the one where I slipped off the stair and felt myself falling?"

"It shouldn't have happened that way." Jenna came forward, ready to throw herself under the horse's hooves if necessary to appease Gwen. "That last part was an accident, a complete accident. You shouldn't have died." Her voice cracked on the last word.

"Even I can't heal myself of a broken neck, Jenna."

She winced. Decades and another life later, she could still remember scrambling out of the bed and running naked after Gwen—or

Glory, as she'd been named in that life. Glory had been downstairs attending a ball packed with nobles, so she shouldn't have come up upstairs for any reason, even if she'd been suspicious of Mara. Because of the ball, she'd been wearing a saffron dress with a long train. The bustle holding it up had broken as she'd fled, and the heavy silk had tangled and tripped her. A sickening snap, and both of them lost everything at once.

"If it helps at all, I grieved for your every heartbeat afterward," Jenna said.

Gwen sniffed. "And how many others consoled you?"

"That doesn't matter. None of them really mattered. My soul may belong to Summer, but the rest of me belongs to you. It always has."

"You say that every lifetime, but you always share yourself with someone else. Or several someones. By All Four Gods and Goddesses, Jenna Dorshay t'Reve, why?"

Jenna wasn't sure herself. Sometimes Gwen became so serious, so caught up in their Avatar work, that she neglected the physical part of their relationship. Then Jenna would notice someone with an inviting smile, or an attractive figure, and she couldn't help flirting with him or her. Sometimes Gwen would notice and become possessive of Jenna, allowing both of them to share passion. But more often the flirtation would become a real attraction and give Jenna a chance to relieve her frustration. It never was as good as it was with Gwen, since the link between them quadrupled their pleasure, but it would be enough to content her for a while. But if Gwen didn't understand that after all of their lives together, Jenna couldn't explain it. So she shrugged and said, "Because I'm a Summer."

"And yet none of the other Summer Avatars behave like you do."

"How can you be sure of that? They're from different generations."

"It would still be somewhere in their journals, or in another Avatar's." Gwen sighed and blew a lock of golden hair out of her face. "By All Four, sometimes I wish They'd switch up our quartets from life to life. I'd rather be paired with a different Summer Avatar this time."

The words couldn't have been more lethal. Jenna's heart seized up for an instant, but then stubbornly continued. Not be paired together! As far back as Jenna could remember, Gwen had been there, her name, gender, and face different, but her spirit still the same bright inspiration Jenna relied on. Gwen was as much a part of Jenna as her plant magic; working with a strange Spring Avatar would surely make all her magic go awry.

"Gwendolyn." Desperate, Jenna knelt in the dirt. "Don't renounce me, even if I deserve it. I'd rather lose my magic than lose you."

"I don't have any choice, do I?" Gwen stared down at her. "I had a dream last night, a dream that felt like a memory. I was between lives, pleading with the Four Gods and Goddesses to break up our quartet. They refused, and the Goddess of Spring said we four made the best team." She frowned, the closest she ever came to disagreeing with the Four. "Then I said, 'At least make sure Jenna and I can't get married next time.'"

Her dream explained why they were both women this time instead of one man and one woman, the way they normally incarnated. But By the Four, Gwen's words were more cursed than the pottery shard she bore under her skin. They stabbed Jenna with a wound she knew she'd bear for all her lifetimes.

Maybe that's why she's so reluctant to marry this time. Deep down, she must know we belong together and doesn't want to be with anyone else. Unlike Jenna, who'd thrown herself at Lex as soon as she learned she couldn't marry Gwen this in this life.

Maybe Gwen was right. Maybe Jenna did flirt—and more—too much with others. Maybe they would be better suited to other partners instead of each other. But the thought of not being with Gwen in some fashion made Jenna ache inside.

"At least we still have the link," Jenna said.

Gwen made a sour expression. "Unfortunately, we do."

She pulled her mare away from browsing on wild grass and urged the animal into a trot, heading straight toward Jenna. Jenna froze, expecting to be run down. At the last heartbeat, instinct made her dodge to the side. Gwen continued toward the One Oak without speaking or looking back.

CHAPTER TWENTY

A Picnic

Jenna pulled leaves off of her gown as she watched Gwen depart. What was she supposed to do now? Would Gwen ever be willing to link with her, especially when Ysabel and Kay found out what Jenna had done? They might also blame her for Gwen's last death, and she'd be excluded from the group, only tolerated when her magic was needed to help tame a Chaos Season. That would hurt too, though not as much as Gwen's anger did. What could she do to atone?

Jenna followed the path away from the house for a while, wishing there was some wondrous plant she could give Gwen that would earn her forgiveness. Even a flower made out of gems wouldn't be enough. Finding nothing that could help her, but unwilling to return to the One Oak, she circled around until she came to the Chikasi River, then followed it toward her tree. At least it needed her like no other creature did. Even her own baby had others to tend to him now. When he was old enough to understand what she'd done, he'd reject her too.

Her oak seedling seemed to be doing well. It hadn't grown taller since her last visit, but its branches were longer and its leaves greener. Jenna pressed herself against its trunk, half-wishing she could step inside it and disappear. The God of Summer could do that, but she wasn't as powerful as Him. Instead, as she fed her tree more magic to help it grow, she whispered her story to it.

"I've known Gwen for hundreds of years and several lives," she told it. "We never agree, but we're supposed to be opposites. We Avatars work better as a team when we can each share something different. We've had more arguments over the years than you have leaves, but we've always managed to make up and go on working together and loving each other. Until now." Her breath caught. "Maybe centuries from now, when our memories of this life are fragmented and overshadowed by newer ones, we'll go back to what we once were. But how can I endure until then?"

Hunger finally forced her to return to the house. As she took a wandering path through the oaks, a black-and-white animal made her pause. It wasn't a skunk as she'd first thought, but Pouncer, Ysabel's anilink. She froze, not certain she wanted to face another Avatar. Ysabel appeared before Jenna could escape. The smell of meat and bread overpowered the scents of the woods, making Jenna's stomach growl.

"I thought you'd be hungry." Ysabel held out a basket for Jenna's inspection. "There's meat pies, and a couple of berry ones. I brought a jug of chocolate too, but it might be cold by now."

"That's better in this heat." Jenna wondered if Ysabel was trying to tame her with food, as if she was a wild animal. She supposed she ought to be grateful anyone cared enough to feed her. Maybe Ysabel didn't know yet what she'd done as Jacob.

"Is there a good spot to sit nearby?" Ysabel asked. "Or do you want to go to the gazebo?"

"I prefer the company of trees right now." Seeing Ysabel's hurt expression, Jenna added, "I mean, as far as plants go. You and your anilink are welcome anytime." She pointed to an ancient oak with a huge protruding root. "That looks like a perfect spot to sit."

Ysabel still looked uncertain, but Jenna sat on the root and patted the spot next to her. The root warmed under her touch, as if she'd bonded with this tree in another life and it still remembered her. Pouncer circled at her feet, waiting for scraps. Ysabel shooed him away long enough to shake out a blanket and settle it over part of the root and the ground. Finches, woodpeckers, and flickers peeked out of nearby trees, watching her. She took out two pies for herself, then passed the basket to Jenna. "You can have the rest."

Suddenly ravenous, Jenna tore into the hand-sized pastries. She ate four in the time Ysabel finished hers. While Jenna searched the basket for another pie, Ysabel opened the jug of chocolate. Pounce sniffed at it, but she raised her finger and said, "You can't have everything, you walking stomach. Some foods aren't good for cats."

Jenna pulled out a couple of plain, chipped mugs and smiled at them. "This looks more like what we used back on the farm than something I'd expect to be drinking out of at the One Oak."

"Even Avatars aren't allowed to bring the finest china into the woods for a picnic," Ysabel said. "The housekeeper actually scolded me when I tried taking cups from the table. You should have seen her face when she remembered I'm one of the Avatars. You'd have thought I was going to send fleas or rats after her."

Jenna's smile disappeared. "Rats. In my last life, I was descended from a family of ratcatchers. That's where 'Raddesdeath' came from."

"Pouncer, leave the birds alone." Ysabel glared at her cat as he chased a flock of finches away. "Why would Summer send you into a family like that? They don't sound like they do anything with plants."

"You'd be surprised. I worked with a lot of herbs, learning about their healing and poisonous properties, before I became an Avatar." She turned away, facing the tree. "Maybe I should have stayed a ratcatcher."

Ysabel tapped her to take the cups. "By All Four, why would you say that?" She looked astonished. Maybe she didn't know, but she would soon through the link.

"Don't you know what Jacob Raddesdeath did? He killed Glory, the Ava Spring!"

The jug of chocolate slipped out of Ysabel's hand, splashing liquid on the root and some grass next to it.

"What? How? Are you sure?" She frowned as she blotted chocolate from her dress with the blanket. "I don't remember it that way. She fell down the stairs and broke her neck."

"Yes, well…that was after she caught me—I mean, Jacob—in bed. With someone else."

"Oh. Oh!" Ysabel shook her head sadly. "Yes, I remember now. How could I have forgotten? It was quite the scandal, especially since our replacements were barely into their teens. I swear you and Gwen always cross each other in every life. I don't understand why the Four keep putting you two together—or why you two marry each other in every life."

"Except this one," Jenna said. "I don't think Gwen will even want to link with me after this."

Ysabel shrugged. "We all have to link if we're going to tame Chaos Season."

"And—you don't mind that?"

Ysabel leaned over and picked up the shards of the jug. "I hope this pottery isn't as dangerous as the shards from Kron's water clock. I don't want to give that nasty Sal-thaath a chance to enter Challen."

Jenna grabbed Ysabel's arm, half-hoping the link would form between them without Gwen. "Tell me true, Ysabel, do you hate me? Do you think I'm not worthy to be an Avatar?"

"That's up to the Four to decide, isn't it? There are some Avatars I don't like very much, but I don't hate you, or Gwen, or Kay." Now Ysabel glanced at her for a heartbeat. "But I do think you could not provoke Gwen as much as you normally do."

"She needs provoking, otherwise she'd never do anything fun. Spring should make people happy, not worry that they're shirking their chores—"

Pouncer sprang up and hissed at nothing Jenna could see. Fur rose along his spine. Had he sensed a fox, or something far more dangerous?

A bell rang, sending deep notes to penetrate the trees. All the birds flew off. The bell rang four times, paused, then pealed another quartet of notes. Jenna had only needed one note to know what was happening.

"A Chaos Season." Jenna jumped up. "They never come at good times, do they?"

"Where do you think this one is?"

Jenna grabbed the basket, then decided it would slow her down and set it next to the tree. She could come get it later. "More importantly, who's going to handle it, us or them?"

"We have to," Ysabel said as she scrambled back along the trail. "The older Avatars can't link."

"Shouldn't we go straight to my sapling?" Jenna asked. "We have to meet there anyway."

"First we have to figure out where in Challen the storm is!"

Freeze it, Ysabel was right. It had been too long since Jenna had properly tamed a Chaos Season. "Then this way is shorter." Jenna wove her way around the oak. Pouncer ran ahead of her on a path too narrow for people. She followed it anyway, brushing each plant with an apology for disturbing it. "What makes you think we'll be able to link?"

Ysabel didn't reply, but as she caught up to Jenna, she gave her an odd glance, as if to say they had no choice. Jenna knew that facing the magical weather storm would be nothing next to the emotional storm the four of them would create in their link.

CHAPTER TWENTY-ONE

Peaches in Chaos

Gwen paced back and forth in the map room when Jenna and Ysabel arrived, out of breath. Kay huddled in the center of the map, eyes closed and hands outstretched as if she could touch the Chaos Season from here. For once, the presence of Dorian standing in a corner, arms crossed and glaring at his successor, didn't seem to bother her. Sophia and Charles nodded at Jenna and Ysabel but didn't speak. They appeared willing to let the other Avatars handle this Chaos Season.

"Where is it?" Jenna asked as soon as she caught her breath. "How big is it?"

"Kay's still determining that," Gwen replied. "Maybe Pouncer can help. The rest of us should prepare ourselves while we wait."

She clapped her hands, and several maids came forward, led by the butler. Some carried serving trays of food and drink, while others bore cloaks and boots. Jenna found more room for cold chicken and cheese, then washed them down with cream-topped chocolate. As soon as she was done, two maids assisted her with dressing. She accepted the cloak but refused the boots. "If it's not close by, do I need the boots? I can ground myself better if I touch soil."

"How do you know it won't come here?" Dorian asked. "If Kay loses control—"

Gwen rounded on him and said, "She won't if you stop telling her she will. Kay, have you located it yet?"

She didn't respond, so Gwen went over to her and tapped her shoulder. "Kay?"

She jumped, then shivered as if she'd been shoved into a snow-bank. "South of Wistica, near the Salt Waters."

"Is it close to a town or city?"

Kay frowned. "I don't know."

Gwen sighed. "We'll find out when we link. Are we ready?" She looked at Kay and Ysabel, but barely glanced at Jenna.

So that was how it was going to be. Well, she might not have been born a noble, but Avatars had their pride too. Jenna straightened her shoulders and loudly announced, "I'm ready."

"Ysabel? Kay?"

Jenna wondered if Gwen had ignored her. Well, she wouldn't be able to do that when they needed her tree to help extend their link. In the meantime, Jenna marched out of the room without waiting for the others. They could catch up with her.

She was halfway to her tree before she remembered she hadn't even had a chance to check on Robbie. What a poor mama she was turning out to be. *We had better do a good job of taming this Chaos Season. The Four know I'm not good for anything else.*

A stray thought danced through her mind that she didn't belong with this quartet anymore, that she should leave them and let them find a different Summer Avatar. "Ha!" She shook her head to clear the madness. There were no other Summer Avatars her age; she'd seen her birth record in the Hall of Records, and the page was blank except for her name. No, they were all bound to each other for this lifetime. Only once they were all dead could the Four even think about rear-ranging the quartets, and Jenna had no intention of dying for a long time.

She hoped her sister Avatars could prevent that.

As Jenna reached her tree, the sky started to cloud over. Summer warmth faded so quickly Jenna searched around her for other signs of Chaos Season. The leaves on the trees stayed green, and snow didn't fall. Nonetheless, she pulled her cloak around her for protection—though she did remove her boots—and laid a hand on her oak. *You've done very well for yourself in such a short time,* she told it. *Now you need to strengthen your roots and help us reach deep across Challen to tame Chaos Season. Are you ready?*

The tree's branches rustled with eagerness.

Gwen, Ysabel, and Kay appeared, followed by the three older Avatars. "Now remember, Gwen," Sophia said, "Kay needs to tame the weather before you let Jenna and Ysabel restore the plants and animals. Of course, if they're in danger, you can save them, because we can't help them if they die."

Gwen nodded, smiled, and said, "Yes, Sophia," so politely Jenna was certain she really meant, "I already know this, Sophia."

As the other girls drew closer, they moved into their traditional positions. Ysabel stood on Jenna's left. She helped her cat climb up to perch on her shoulder, with Pouncer leaning against her head and resting his front paws on her ear and temple. Kay drew next to Ysabel, facing Jenna. Despite her running to Jenna's tree, Kay still had pale cheeks, as if neither sun nor blood could touch them. She twisted her head around, searching everywhere for something no one else could see.

"I was wearing an outfit similar to this in my nightmares," she said.

Jenna supposed dreaming about dying—especially in circumstances that might leave a soul trapped and unable to be reborn—would make anyone nervous. Kay couldn't afford distraction now. None of them could. "Well, what could happen here on the Avatars' estate, with the rest of us to help you?" she asked.

"That didn't help Margaret," Kay said.

Gwen paused before taking her place between Jenna and Ysabel. "All of the cursed shards are accounted for, Kay. They can't harm you or anyone else."

Jenna glanced at Gwen's violet bracelet, secretly glad she didn't have to hold that hand. Ysabel would grasp Gwen's wrist instead.

Gwen took a deep breath. "In the names of the Four Gods and Goddesses of Challen, let us restore the seasons to their proper order, along with the plants and animals of our beloved land." She raised her hand into the air. "For the Goddess of Spring!"

Jenna copied her gesture. "The God of Summer!"

"The Goddess of Fall!"

"And the God of Winter!" Kay's voice, though soft, was still firm.

They lowered their hands, then spread their arms out so they could link. Jenna leaned backward against her tree, making contact with her head and one foot. She offered her hands to Gwen and Kay. Kay took one without hesitation, but Gwen took a deep breath before linking with Jenna.

You're still mad at me, aren't you? Jenna winced as she realized Ysabel and Kay were already linked with them. Details of their quarrels past and present leaked out.

That doesn't matter. Gwen pictured an orchard covered in ice. *We have work to do. Let's hunt down the Chaos Season and undo it.*

Currents of unease ran through the entire group. Jenna did her best to ignore them. She sent her thoughts into her tree and down into its root system. From there, she searched to the southeast for a disturbance of hot and cold, excessive digging as animals sought shelter, or other signs of Chaos Season. Through the link, she could feel Kay's mind riding the wind as she outpaced Jenna. The distraction made her fall farther behind, but she continued her quest in case she found something Kay would overlook.

Here, Kay said. *It seems to be a small one.*

Jenna let Gwen bring her back fully into the link. An orchard of peach trees drooped with ripening fruit now coated in ice. Dead honeybees lay scattered over snow. A farming family attempted to drive a cow and a few goats into their barn, but the cow wouldn't move. It stood in place, mooing.

Her calf is missing, Ysabel reported. *I'll send it toward her.*

Jenna didn't bother responding. Her task—restoring the orchard—was obvious. As Kay pulled magic from the air to melt the ice and snow, Jenna moved from tree to tree, fruit to fruit, making sure the peaches didn't die. A few had, so she let them fall where animals could eat them. She encouraged the rest to keep growing. While Kay removed ice on the outside, Jenna urged the trees to thaw any parts of themselves that had frozen.

I found the calf, Ysabel said. *But it's freezing, poor thing. I need more magic to help it recover from snowsickness—and worms.*

Gwen shunted more magic to her, draining so much from Jenna she lost contact with the tree she was working on.

Watch it! she sent. *The rest of us need magic too.*

You and Kay have already taken care of most of this Chaos Season, Gwen said. *Now Ysabel needs a turn.*

No, I'm not done. Look at all this fruit I have to protect. Jenna pictured the orchard. Half of it had been restored to the proper season, but half of it was still covered in frost. An extra-heavy branch broke off and took several smaller branches with it. *See?*

Plants are hardier than animals, Ysabel said. *The trees can wait longer than this calf.* She showed them an animal covered in snow, too cold to call out for help.

Kay immediately warmed the area around the calf while Ysabel tended it. Jenna returned her attention to the trees, but with more magic going to Ysabel than to her, she couldn't work as quickly. If it was just one animal, then it shouldn't take Ysabel long to heal it and make sure its owners found it. Jenna worked her way through several trees, depleting her magic without receiving more from Kay. As she neared the farmhouse, she spotted a small vegetable garden that had been frosted over.

Look at this, she told the others. *This is where the farmers grow the food they'll need during the winter. I have to save these plants so they don't starve. Give me more magic, now.*

Magic trickled to her, but not as much as she needed. Ysabel still received the bulk of the magic Kay extracted from the weather.

By All Four, what are you doing with that? Jenna immersed herself back into the link to check. *Songbirds? You're healing songbirds?*

They're important too. Ysabel sounded indignant. *They eat the pests that eat your precious plants.*

She was right, but that didn't mean the birds were more important than the orchard or the vegetable garden. *You don't need all that magic for them. Let me have some.* Jenna directed her attention at Gwen. *Gwen, share the magic equally. It's not fair otherwise.*

There isn't much magic I can give anyone. Kay, shouldn't there be more magic in this Chaos Season?

Kay was silent for a few minutes before saying, *Something else is taking magic from this Chaos Season. It's leaving me with less energy to restore summer.*

Well, where is it going?

I can't trace it. It disappears to my senses.

That's impossible! Jenna said.

We've already been through so many impossible things to get to the One Oak. Gwen sighed. *What's one more abnormality?*

Jenna almost felt pity for Gwen and Kay. Something wasn't right with this Chaos Season. But if they didn't fix it, people would starve, and she couldn't let that happen. The God of Summer would be disappointed in her. So she pulled again at the link, trying to pry more magic from Gwen.

Jenna Dorshay t'Reve, stop it! Gwen pulled back. *There's nothing more to give you.*

Well, take it from Ysabel then. She has plenty.

I do not. There are more animals in jeopardy here than you realize. They need my help more than these people do.

Under Ysabel's thoughts was the memory of The Four's Chals, money given to people of Challen when the Season Avatars couldn't restore their property. A donation from the Avatars' coffers would help this family buy supplies for the winter if their peach harvest or personal garden suffered losses, but chals were of no use to wild plant or animals that could only be helped by magic. Jenna knew what Ysabel intended with her words, but the attitude behind them irritated her. When she was growing up, she'd been able to use her talents to keep her family from going hungry, but she knew how thin the margin between feast and famine could be.

The Four's Chals don't solve everything, Jenna snapped. *How will we find these people again to give them the chals? What if they have nowhere to spend them? You may know animals, Ysabel, but you don't know farmers.*

Ysabel drew back from the link as if that had been a deadly insult. By the Four, if Jenna wanted to hurt her feelings, she could do a better job of it—

FREEZE IT! Gwen shouted. *Everyone stop arguing!*

The link was silent for a few heartbeats before Kay whispered, *Gwen, weather....*

Chaos Season returned, this time flipping the season from the end of the year to the beginning. The snow and ice melted. The peaches seemed to melt too as they shrank back toward being flowers again.

Jenna pounced on them. *By All Four, no. Spring is over. If you return to blossoms, you won't have time to grow properly before the frost returns.* She pulled on whatever magic she could gather to force-grow the fruit to its proper stage. At the same time, Ysabel demanded more magic of her own as a goat bit the human driving it into the barn. Gwen exerted her own magic to heal the wound....

Faster than Jenna thought possible, the Chaos Season ended as summer weather snapped back into place. Kay moaned. A sensation of lightheadedness was their only warning as her mind disappeared from the link.

"Kay!" Gwen cried out loud as she shook herself free of Ysabel and Jenna.

"No, wait!" Just for an instant, Jenna thought she saw a familiar but ugly sprout pop out of the ground in the middle of the orchard. But before she could investigate, the link was gone, along with her vision of the peach farm.

Gwen sprang forward toward Kay, who had slumped to the ground.

"By All Four, is she—" Ysabel didn't finish her sentence.

Gwen touched Kay's temple as though she was made of glass. If Kay had been pale before, now she looked as if she'd been coated with a layer of frost. Jenna's heart thumped. Kay couldn't possibly be dead, could she? The dreams Salth had sent her couldn't be real; they were just lies to scare her. Maybe she had let them scare her to death. By All Four, that small Chaos Season couldn't have killed Kay. She'd handled much stronger ones in their previous lives.

As Jenna muttered a prayer to the Four Gods and Goddesses for Kay, Gwen announced, "She's not dead. She fainted." She placed a hand on Kay's forehead and frowned. "But that shouldn't have happened."

"Do you need more magic?" Jenna asked. She'd manage to find extra magic to give Gwen from somewhere.

Gwen shook her head. At the same time, Kay stirred. "What happened?" she whispered.

"I'm not sure. It's as if the magic holding our link in place just disappeared. It must have been pulled out through you."

Kay groaned. "I knew it. I've lost any weather skills I ever had. I'm not fit to be an Ava Win."

"By All Four, that's not true, and you know it." Gwen offered Kay a hand up before Jenna could. "Maybe it was just a long way for us to reach for our first attempt at taming Chaos Season. Let's go back to the One Oak. It's near dinner time, and we'll all feel better after we eat." She managed a faint grin. "Though I don't feel up to dressing for it."

She and Kay headed back to the house, with Sophia helping to support Kay. Dorian struck off on his own. Charles joined Jenna, with Ysabel and Pouncer bringing up the rear.

"What happened?" Charles asked. "I sensed a little through my own tree, but I couldn't tell what went wrong at the end."

It had gone wrong from the start, with the other three denying Jenna the magic she needed to do her duty. Despite that, she didn't want to share their private issues with anyone else, not even another Avatar. Jenna shrugged. "We weren't prepared for Chaos to return after it should have been tamed."

Charles detoured around a stump. "Maybe Dorian's right. Maybe Kay is too weak. She refused to perform weather magic for several years, didn't she?"

"She'll make that up in due time." Jenna remembered another reason why Kay wasn't to blame. "Besides, I was sure I saw a deathbush sprout in that orchard, right at the end."

Charles sighed. "By All Four, how will we ever get rid of them?"

He veered off to one of the greenhouses, leaving Jenna alone with Ysabel and Pouncer. After Ysabel had been so supportive earlier, her current silence felt like an accusation. "I really didn't have enough magic for the orchard," Jenna muttered.

"And I didn't have enough magic for all of the animals either. I hope Chaos Season stopped after we left." Ysabel chewed her lip. "I'll send a pigeon in the morning to find out."

Jenna nodded. She'd expected her first Chaos Season to be a triumph, an easy demonstration of her skill. But just as the current Avatars were in no hurry to return to their own estates, Chaos Season wasn't going to yield to her.

I can't tame it on my own. I need all three of them, Kay and Ysabel and Gwen. Especially Gwen. She was still angry with me, and that affected our link.

Jenna had already apologized for her crimes. What could she do to convince Gwen to forgive her?

CHAPTER TWENTY-TWO

The Uses of Chocolate

All seven Avatars, plus Kron and Lex, were present for dinner. It was an informal affair, even though the cooks outdid themselves with chilled summer soups, a quartet of ducks, an individual loaf of bread for each Avatar, peas garnished with mint, and berry tarts. Everyone spent more time eating than speaking. Jenna was glad when she could withdraw. Instead of joining the others in the informal parlor where Ysabel played the pianoforte, she climbed all the way up to the nursery.

"Thank the Four you came," the nurse said, an edge in her normally calm voice. "He's been fussy all day."

"Poor thing missed his mama," Jenna said, reaching for him.

Robbie quieted as she sang him a song about all the flowers in the garden and rocked him by the window, watching the sunset. He fell asleep in her arms, but despite the nurse's warning that she would spoil him, Jenna continued to hold him. She ought to go to bed herself, but it was too peaceful up here away from the other Avatars. She might encounter Gwen if she returned to her suite too soon.

When steps sounded on the stair, Jenna assumed it was Clover searching for her. The masculine scents of spruce and smoke surprised her. She turned to see Lex stooping as he entered the nursery.

"Eagle's Talons, why is the ceiling so low?" he complained. "If I stand up, I might break the roof."

Jenna suppressed a smile. Even she had to duck when she retrieved items from the corners of the room. "Forgive me if I don't rise and curtsey, Your Highness," she said. "My arms are full at the moment."

"No need to be so formal. All I want to do is see my son." He approached her and peered at their sleeping child for several heartbeats. "I thought he'd be bigger by now. Is he healthy? The Ava Spring hasn't found any problems, has she?"

Jenna sighed. "No, he's fine." She started to lower Robbie into his crib. He stirred as if he was going to wake up, so she continued to hold him.

Lex extended his arms. "May I hold him?"

Maybe he's becoming more attached to his son after all. "Of course. Mind Robbie's head, though. He still can't hold it up on his own."

She showed Lex how to cradle an infant. The War Avatar was surprisingly gentle as he handled his son. Jenna watched them and wondered how often Lex would find time for Robbie as the boy grew up. What was she going to tell him when he asked who his father was? She hadn't thought that far ahead that day under the rosebush.

When Lex set Robbie down a few minutes later, he turned to Jenna and said, "I heard there was another Chaos Season today. Were you able to tame it successfully?"

How had he heard about that but not about her quarrel with Gwen? "We were managing it until the end. Then…we fell apart over how to share the magic."

"Ah. It must be hard working with so many other Avatars." Lex strolled over to the shelves of toys, smiling as he found a set of tin soldiers. He set them up on the floor, red-coated soldiers attacking blue. "You have a general, but secretly, all of you must consider yourself equal to her."

"Equal in magic, certainly," Jenna said. "Of course, we aren't all born noble. Some of us can practice our magic better as farmers.

Gwen leads us because her Goddess is first among the Four, not because she's noble."

"Interesting. And yet you must disagree with her from time to time."

Jenna's cheeks grew warm. "It wasn't her fault. It was mine."

Lex looked up from the toy soldiers. The air was so still Jenna fancied she could hear clouds rumbling overhead.

Meeting her gaze, he said, "So I've heard."

He knew she'd been Jacob, then. Jenna dug her nails into her palms. "That was another life," she said desperately. "By All Four Gods and Goddesses, can't I start over, try to do better by those I love?"

"You're Summer's Avatar," Lex said gently. "He shelters those who are different. Gods sometimes put Their Avatars into difficult positions; I should know." A vein in his throat throbbed in time with his heart. "Jenna, when we lay together last summer, I thought there would be nothing more between us. I didn't expect you to come to the One Oak for several years yet, certainly not with our son. Then War directed me to stay in Challen this year and ally myself with your quartet. I thought Gwen would be the most appropriate match for me, but your beauty, charm, and warrior spirit draw me. I wish there could be more between us, but as a Fip, I need a loyal wife I can trust." He spread his hands. "Perhaps there can be no alliance between our gods, at least not the way I originally pictured it."

O Four, hard enough to hear she'd come so close to a union with Lex and lost it for crimes from a previous life, but now she'd failed the Four too? She was a failure, a worthless Avatar. She didn't deserve Gwen or Lex or anyone. If only she could run away from the One Oak. She should crawl back to Bull Rock. Her parents could always use more help on the farm, and she deserved all the disgrace her neighbors would heap on her.

"Jenna, don't cry." Lex brushed her cheek with a callused finger. "It will work out."

She shook her head, afraid to speak. It couldn't work out. There was no one to replace her as Summer Avatar.

He leaned down to kiss her, a quick taste of his breath on her lips. She wrapped herself around him and opened her mouth to his. He pulled her closer. They kissed fiercely, as if they knew they would both lose this battle. Jenna hoped the moment would never end, but all too soon he pulled away from her and hurried downstairs.

Jenna sobbed into one of Robbie's extra blankets, then lay there in the dark until she fell asleep.

* * *

The next morning dawned cloudy, with the promise of a thunderstorm before noon. Jenna hoped it would rain all day. She sipped her morning cup of chocolate as she stared out the window, searching for signs of Chaos Season. The Four knew she and the other Avatars needed time to regroup. Maybe they should find the peach orchard they'd worked on yesterday and find out how much damage still had to be cleaned up. Or she could perform some more tests on deathbush seeds—assuming she could prevent them from sprouting and overtaking the One Oak. It would be a wonder if she could perform at least one of her tasks without causing more problems than she solved.

Jenna checked the sky again. A thunderstorm would mean lightning and possible tree damage. Maybe she ought to check on her tree before the storm started. It was unlikely such a small tree would be hit by lightning, but she could protect it further by setting up a lightning rod. And if she was going to walk about with a lightning rod in the middle of a storm, the best protection she could find would be Kay.

"I'll take breakfast downstairs," she told Clover. "I need to speak to Kay." *I'm sure Gwen wants to avoid me as much as I do her.*

Jenna peeked around the corner before entering the breakfast nook. The Four were with her; Kay sat by herself with a bowl of porridge and an equal-sized bowl of berries. Jenna helped herself to the same but also took some toast and slathered it with butter and honey.

"Is it a natural storm, or is Chaos Season involved?" she said, gesturing toward the window.

Kay scraped her porridge bowl clean. "It started as a natural storm, but yesterday's Chaos Season will make it stronger."

"When will it start?"

"In another hour."

"Think we have time to set up a lightning rod near my tree before then?"

Kay mixed cream into her berries. "That depends on how soon we leave. I can hold the storm back for a short while, but we should let it happen as the God of Winter wills. It's not good to interfere with the weather all of the time."

Jenna nodded. She summoned the butler and, between bites of her meal, asked him to have a lightning rod brought out from the stable so it would be ready when they were.

The lightning rod featured an arrowhead at one tip. Underneath it was a blue glass globe the size of her hand. A long copper wire ran to the ground rod. Jenna studied the lightning rod, trying to figure out how she would fasten it to her tree. Maybe she could force-grow a branch to hold it in place. If Kron were available, he could manage it with ease, but Jenna didn't think they had time to find him. The clouds were already getting darker.

"We should hurry," Kay said. She left without taking the shawl the maid offered her.

Jenna followed Kay. The lightning rod and cable were heavier than she expected. The ground rod dragged after her, catching on tufts of grass until she picked it up. Juggling the entire assembly made it hard to see where she was going.

"Kay, I need some help," she called.

Kay came back to take the ground rod. She led the way, not speaking until Jenna's tree came into sight. "I'm sorry for yesterday," she finally said.

"It wasn't your fault. It was mine. Well, Gwen's too." As soon as Jenna said that, she regretted it. It wasn't loyal to blame Gwen for problems she had caused. "But she was upset because of something that happened between us in a previous life."

Kay rolled her eyes. "Many previous lives, Jenna. But last time was the worst. It was quite…shocking, how we had to retire early as Avatars." She looked away. "It's almost enough to make me understand what Dorian is going through. It's no wonder he's impatient when I'm so horrible with my weather magic."

"I swear by the Four you do better when he's not around."

Even though they were alone, Kay lowered her voice. "Well, he does upset me."

"On purpose, I bet."

As they approached Jenna's oak, she examined it. While still not fully grown, the top branch was at least thirty feet off the ground. The grass surrounding the tree had been torn up. What had done it? It was too early for squirrels to be burying acorns.

"How are you going to get the lightning rod up to the top of the tree?" Kay asked.

The grass would have to wait. "You don't think the Summer Avatar can climb her own tree?"

"But how are you going to keep the lightning rod in place without nails?"

"I'll find a way." Jenna looked up at the sky, gauging how long she had until the rain started. "Just keep it from raining until I'm done, please."

Kay nodded, then backed off a few paces and closed her eyes. The wind picked up, but it calmed when she held out her hands to it.

Jenna removed her boots, tucked the lighting rod under her arm, and scrambled up. Her tree bent under her weight, but she sent strength into it until it steadied. She halted before the branches grew too thin to hold her even with magic.

The lightning rod proved as difficult to mount as Kay had predicted. Jenna wrapped the chain around the rod's base, but it wouldn't stay upright. She didn't want to splice open the tree to clamp the rod, as that would send the lightning's power into the tree and possibly kill it. Finally, she found a tight spot in the fork of a branch and wedged the lightning rod into it. Jenna worked her way back down. She still needed to dig a hole for the ground rod. Next time she would ask the butler for tools and a laborer too, not just the lightning rod.

"How much time do I have, Kay?" she called.

Kay didn't answer, but strain showed in her face. The air cooled enough to make Jenna's skin prickle.

"I'll be right back." She picked up her skirts and ran for the forest. There had to be some strong branches there. She didn't get far before a colorful blanket caught her eye. Ysabel must have left it there yesterday when they'd rushed to fight Chaos Season. *Might as well bring it in before it's ruined.* Maybe the picnic basket was still there, along with something she could use to dig.

The basket was there, along with shards of the empty cup. The blanket bore brown spots where the pot of chocolate had spilled. Jenna didn't have time to fold the blanket, so she flung it over her shoulders. The grass shoots underneath the stained blanket had wilted. That was odd. They hadn't been deprived of sunlight for that long. Curious, she brushed her fingertips against the grass, sampling both healthy and ailing plants. Something inside the sick ones interfered with their growth. She touched the tree, but it didn't seem affected.

Odd, very odd. She spotted a stick that would suit her purpose, so she grabbed that along with the picnic basket. Lugging them both back to her tree cost her more time. Kay swayed back and forth as if she was charming the storm into obedience. Jenna didn't dare distract her, so she plunged her stick into the loose soil and worked it until she made a hole wide and deep enough for the ground bar. Flickers of lightning danced in the cloud above. Even with Kay close by, she had to be careful.

Jenna nudged the ground rod closer to her with the stick, but she didn't have enough control to push the rod into the hole. For that, she had to handle the rod herself. It took only a few heartbeats to push it into place and sweep dirt over it with her foot. As she did so, she kicked up a deathbush seed.

By All Four, what's that doing here? She grabbed it before it could sprout and dropped it into the basket.

"Kay? Kay?" She edged closer to here. "I'm done. We can go back to the One Oak."

She didn't respond.

"Kay?" What would happen if she shook her?

"Dorian's really driving this storm into a frenzy," Kay said without opening her eyes. "I wonder why."

"It doesn't matter. Let's go back. The plants need to be watered more than I do."

"Should I defy him? Or let him think he's stronger than me?"

"Which way will keep me dry?"

With a groan, Kay opened her eyes and spread out her arms. Rain fell on either side of them, but not on top of them.

Jenna had done enough running for one morning, especially with her extra burdens. They walked back slowly, as Kay kept looking around.

"It's been so long since I let myself experience a storm," she said. "I might stay out here and prove to myself it won't kill me, but I won't be climbing any trees this time."

Jenna wondered if she or another Avatar from their quartet should keep Kay company, just in case something happened. Gwen would be the best choice, as she could lend Kay additional magic or heal her if necessary. But after last night, Gwen probably wouldn't want to see Jenna. *It's for Kay's sake, for all our sakes,* she reminded herself.

"Enjoy your magic," she told Kay. "Just don't bring on your season in the middle of mine."

Kay's eyes widened.

"It was only a jest," Jenna said.

The rain came down more strongly as soon as she entered the One Oak. The light inside was so dim the hallway sconces had been lit. Jenna searched the common rooms for Gwen before finding her in the Spring Study, reading an old journal with a mug of chocolate and a pastry by her side.

Gwen glanced up, then covered the front of her journal. "What do you want?"

"I…I just thought you should know Kay's out in the storm."

Gwen peered out the window, but it was so gray outside Jenna doubted she could see anything. "I suppose that's good. She needs the practice."

"I thought one of us—well, you—should be with her, in case something happens."

She sighed. "I've seen more hospitable Chaos Seasons, but I suppose you're right. Are you coming too?"

Jenna stared at the chocolate, remembering what she'd observed in the woods: plants wilting in the presence of chocolate. "Actually, there's something I need to do in the atrium. Don't get too wet."

"Jenna Dorshay t'Reve!"

She bolted, stopping in the dining room for her own pastry and to ask a maid to bring the strongest pot of chocolate the cook could prepare to the atrium. While she waited for it, she cleared a space and set the largest metal bucket she could find on one of the tables. On one side, she placed a jar of lamp oil; on the other, a candle and a lucifer. If this experiment grew out of her control, she needed to destroy it quickly.

A knock sounded on the door, and the maid entered, balancing a pot and a porcelain cup on a silver tray. "It's very hot, Ava," she said.

A rag was still wrapped around the pot handle. "You should let it cool before drinking it. Are you sure you don't want cream with it?"

"No, thank you. This isn't for drinking." Before the maid could say anything, Jenna added, "That will be all." It would be safer to have no one else around when she tried this.

She placed the deathbush seed in the center of the bucket. Some rain must have moistened it, for the shell was cracked, exposing green. She eyed it, waiting to see if the seed sprouted. The chocolate was still too hot for the test she wanted to run, though that gave her another idea. She stepped out to the hallway, summoned the maid back, and asked her for boiling water. Boiling water would be easier to prepare in large amounts than chocolate, so it would make a better weapon against the deathbushes—assuming it killed them. Or assuming the chocolate did, for that matter.

The deathbush seed cracked open further, exposing the sprout. It wouldn't stay so small and vulnerable for long. *Hurry with that water,* Jenna silently urged the maid.

By the time she returned with another towel-wrapped carafe, the sprout had a taproot as long as Jenna's thumb and its first set of real leaves. "By All Four, how are you growing so quickly?" she asked it. "You're not even in soil and had only a sprinkle of water." The deathbush's growth served as further confirmation magic was involved.

The deathbush's stem turned upward toward her.

"Oh, no, you don't." She picked up the boiling water first and drizzled a stream directly on the little deathbush. Any normal plant would be cooked. The plant drooped and curled up on itself. Then, after a few heartbeats, its shoots turned a darker green. The root branched, absorbing more water. Frowning, Jenna touched the carafe and quickly pulled her finger away. Yes, the water was hot. It should have killed the deathbush. If this plant could survive boiling water, vinegar, and salt, chocolate should have no effect on it—unless her hunch was right and that something in chocolate could kill plants. Of course, the chocolate might help it grow faster too...

Jenna hesitated for a few moments, then grabbed the chocolate and poured some into the bucket. If this didn't work, she'd pour oil into the bucket and set it on fire.

The deathbush stretched its root toward the chocolate and absorbed it eagerly. She had been wrong. Jenna reached for the oil so she could drench the plant in it. Instead of becoming greener and longer, the deathbush sprout turned yellowish. She stared at it for several heart-beats, expecting it to continue growing. After a while, she prodded it. It wasn't completely dead, but it had lost a lot of vitality. In this weak-ened state, it was vulnerable to her magic. One burst killed the deathbush.

"Thanks be to the Four." She picked up the deathbush seedling. It had sprouted less than an hour ago, but it was already longer than her hand. She should burn it just to make sure it didn't come back to life…

A sudden pain stabbed her in the belly. She dropped the seedling, fearful it was causing this despite being dead. The pain didn't go away. She folded over herself, placing her hands over her belly. Maybe this was her moonflow returning, but it usually wasn't this in-tense. Wasn't it supposed to be better after having a child?

"Gwen? Gwen, where are you?" she called. She should summon the maid to fetch Gwen. The atrium suddenly seemed too big and too isolated from the rest of the house. If she screamed, no one would hear her.

Spring Summer Fall Winter, help me…

"Jenna!" A breathless voice called her from a distance. Kay? What was she doing in the house? "Jenna? Where are you?"

Her throat went dry, but she managed to croak out, "Here."

"Jenna?" The door to the atrium opened. "Jenna? Are you in here? You'd better come quick. I think something's wrong with your tree."

CHAPTER TWENTY-THREE

Deathbush Against Oak

My tree! Sometimes, if there was a strong bond between a Summer Avatar and her tree, or the Fall Avatar with her anilink, an injury to one could cause physical distress to the other. Jenna hadn't realized her bond with the oak sapling had already reached that point. Under other circumstances, she would be proud to have accomplished that, but not when it was hurting her.

"What's wrong?" she said between stabs of pain. "Where's Gwen?" She might need Gwen's help to make it to her tree.

"She's out there by your tree. I think she's trying to protect it."

"From what?"

"A strange plant. I think it's one of your deathbushes."

"A deathbush? Here, by my tree?" Indignation drove Jenna to a standing position. "Not if I can do something about it!" Thank the Four she had a weapon. She clutched the table as she rose to her feet. "We need Ysabel. Her anilink too." The chocolate should help, but Jenna wanted as much magic as possible available to her in case her tree was threatened.

"I'll go find her," Kay said.

Before she could dart off, Jenna added, "And ask the cooks to make more chocolate. We need to bring it with us."

"By the Eagle," Lex said from the doorway, "I knew your magic requires you to eat and drink constantly, but I didn't think you needed to do it in the middle of Chaos Season."

It depended on how big the Chaos Season was, but Jenna didn't have the strength to tell him that. "Help me," she whispered.

"Ava?" He glanced around to see if Kay was present. "Jenna? What happened?"

"My tree. I must get to my tree. With this." She grabbed the flask of chocolate.

He stepped forward. "You look pale. You should rest."

She shook her head.

"Then let me help you." Before she could respond, he gathered her up, lifting her as if she was as light as Kay. Jenna put one arm around his neck to balance herself and clutched the chocolate with the other. The smell of his aftershave and the drink blended well together.

Jenna guided him to the riverbank where her tree waited. He carried her across muddy paths the entire way, breathing heavily but his strength never flagging. She wondered if his great stamina was part of his war magic. Then she saw her tree, and everything else receded from her mind.

A deathbush had sprouted next to her oak. It already had climbed halfway up the trunk, twining around her tree as if it meant to seduce it. Thorns pierced the tree's bark. Were they meant to damage the tree or steal nutrients from it? The leaves on the lowest branches had yellowed, so Jenna suspected the deathbush was draining her tree—and draining her.

Gwen paced back and forth, studying the deathbush and the lightning rod. She looked up, and a curious expression came over her face as she veered toward them. "Jenna, are you all right?"

For a heartbeat, Jenna wondered if Gwen herself had planted the deathbush seed. But no, no matter how mad Gwen was at her, she'd never physically harmed her. She wouldn't do anything that would interfere with their ability to tame Chaos Season either.

Someone planted that seed here, not a squirrel. That's why the grass was torn up earlier. Who had done it? Maybe Ysabel's father had snuck onto the One Oak. He would target his daughter, however, and even if he wanted to harm Jenna's tree, how could he pick it out from all the other oaks? It had to be another Avatar. Was it Charles, secretly hiding a desire to hold on to his power the way Dorian wanted to continue being the Winter Avatar?

"Jenna?" Gwen came up to her and reached out with her good hand. "Are you all right? Is the deathbush affecting you?"

"She seemed weak and in pain when I found her," Lex said.

At that, her temper rose. She bit it off before she took it out on him. "Let me down." She tapped the jug of chocolate. "I have a new weapon that will teach this deathbush not to attack my tree."

"Chocolate?" Gwen raised her eyebrows. "By All Four, what are you planning to do, drown it? Why not throw the plant into the Chikasi?"

"Chocolate can poison deathbushes." As Lex set her down, she struggled to maintain her balance. Chocolate sloshed out of the jug. "Here. I'll show you."

Gwen grasped her hand. A flood of well-being drove the cramps away and made her legs feel stronger. Jenna nodded thanks but kept her gaze focused on the plant. Step by step, she advanced on it, carafe held ready to pour the chocolate on the deathbush roots. She hoped it would be enough—and that it wouldn't bother her oak. The other tree hadn't appeared damaged, but she hadn't examined it closely.

The deathbush unwrapped a branch from the oak's tree trunk and sent it questing toward her. Maybe she shouldn't have announced what she planned to do—

Lex darted in front of her and hacked the branch off with his magic battleaxe. As soon as he was out of her way, she rushed forward, and dumped the chocolate right on top of the deathbush's roots. The plant writhed. Part of its stem yellowed, but the rest of it was still active. The chocolate did work, but as Jenna had feared, it wasn't strong enough. She grasped the deathbush, avoiding the thorns. In its weakened state, it was unable to resist her magic. It released her tree, turned brown, and drooped. Her own breathing came easier. Instead of resting, she clawed the dead deathbush out of the ground until she was sure she'd ripped up the entire root system. Thank the Four it hadn't tangled with her oak's. Then her energy gave out again, and she felt herself losing her balance.

Lex grabbed her, amusement in his brown eyes. "Remind me never to get you mad at me, Ava." Even though he used her formal title, his voice held an intimate tone. In other circumstances, she would have continued the flirtation. For now, all she could think of was her poor tree. She laid her hands on it and gave it what magic she could spare. One branch would never sprout leaves again, but the rest of the tree was undamaged or would heal.

It should never have been attacked in the first place. Could her tree show her who had planted the deathbush seed? She pressed her hands harder against the rough bark. All she could gleam from the tree's senses were light, moisture, and nutrient levels. Except…there had been heavy vibrations in the earth surrounding the tree just before dawn, heavier than Jenna's steps. A man, perhaps. After the vibrations ceased, the light levels changed as clouds blocked the sun and brought more moisture into the air.

Light and moisture…weather. Something the Avi Winter could change. Maybe he was using the storm to remove his tracks and water the deathbush seed. It all fit, although Jenna didn't understand why Dorian would attack her tree. What had she done to him? Kay had always been the one to bear the brunt of his anger because she was destined to replace him. Jenna's tree couldn't hurt him—but it would help her quartet tame Chaos Season and prove that he was no longer needed.

She removed her hands from her tree. She was wrong. She had to be wrong. Avatars might not get along with each other or resist letting their season end, but they weren't supposed to harm each other. And going against the Four's will by preventing other Avatars from taming Chaos Season had to be a crime so severe his soul would be frozen forever after death, never being reborn. Would the Four really punish one of Their own like that?

"You look pale," Gwen said. "I hope you saved some chocolate for us."

"That doesn't matter," she said. "Dorian planted that deathbush seed next to my tree. He's not going to give up his season, Gwen, and he'll make sure we can't tame Chaos Season by ourselves."

CHAPTER TWENTY-FOUR

A Trap in a Tree

"I don't believe it," Sophia said for the twentieth time that hour. Her plate lay clean before her. Neither she nor her husband had even bothered to touch the soup or chicken the cook had prepared for lunch. Their empty plates made Jenna feel guilty as she took another slice of bread, as if she should fast too. But she would need all the energy she could find to deal with the rest of the deathbushes—and Dorian. So she kept chewing, though everything tasted bitter to her.

Jenna swallowed, then pushed the dried deathbush remains toward Sophia. "Do you really believe a seed found its way next to my tree all by itself? Especially when Kay and I went out there before the storm and noticed how broken-up the ground was?"

"Where would he have gotten the seed?" Sophia said.

"There's a store of them in the atrium," Charles said. "He could have taken one from there." He peered at Jenna. "Do you have a count of how many there were?"

"It should be on the paper I stored them in," she said.

"And you had written the name on there too, correct? Then anyone could have found them," Sophia said.

"But who else here knows how quickly the deathbush grows, or how it seems to cause a Chaos Season wherever it sprouts?" Gwen asked. "Who else knows which sapling out there is Jenna's? Only the Avatars do."

"And Kron," Sophia said. Her gaze flickered toward Lex, but she didn't add him. One couldn't accuse the Avatar of War of a crime when he was the king's brother. Jenna knew he had to be innocent. He hadn't known where her tree was, and he'd fought against the deathbushes with her.

That left Sophia and Charles as possible suspects, despite their upcoming trip to find and destroy deathbushes all over Challen. Charles obviously knew the most about plants, and he was the one Jenna would replace. However, he seemed indifferent to his magic, more interested in retiring to his family home and raising grapes. Jenna didn't know Sophia well enough to guess how she felt about being ousted. With Margaret gone, Sophia did the most to hold her quartet together. Maybe she wasn't willing to give up her power either. Dorian was still the most likely one to have planted the deathbush seed, but Jenna couldn't rule anyone else out without more proof.

"We can't condemn our Avi Win on the basis of what a tree sensed," Sophia said.

"Now, now, Dear, trees know more than you give them credit for." Charles didn't bother straightening up as he spoke.

"Ysabel, was Pouncer outside this morning?" Gwen asked. "His senses are sharper than an oak's. Maybe he can identify who planted that seed."

Ysabel shook her head. "It was raining pretty hard earlier. Pouncer stayed inside, curled up on my bed. He wouldn't be able to learn anything now. The rain would have washed away a person's scent."

More reason to believe the Avi Win was behind this. He would be clever enough to hide the evidence. If only they could figure out a way to trap him.

Jenna hesitatingly slid her hand next to Gwen's, hoping the Ava Spring would take the hint and link with her. She ignored it.

Frustrated, Jenna asked, "So, what do we do now? Set a watch on my tree all day and night?"

"What about Pouncer?" Ysabel reached for her cat, but he bounded over to Gwen, demanding she pet him. "Is he in danger too? I maintain a mental link with him, but it's impossible to keep a cat under physical watch."

Gwen stroked Pouncer absent-mindedly as she studied Kay. "Kay, you haven't said anything about Dorian. You've worked with him the most. What do you think?"

She stared down at her plate.

"Kay?"

"At least he hasn't appeared in my dreams," she said, so softly Jenna had to strain to hear her.

Jenna exchanged looks with Gwen and Ysabel. The older Avatars didn't know about Kay's nightmares of her death—and fate worse than death.

Gwen scratched Pouncer behind the ear for several heartbeats. No one else spoke or pretended to eat. Finally, Gwen rose and brushed black cat hair off of her dress. "Sophia's right. We can't prove Dorian committed such a blasphemous deed on what little Jenna has told us."

Here was further proof Gwen was nursing the grudge about her last death. Jenna couldn't decide if she wanted to shake some sense into Gwen or plead for forgiveness again.

"I'd really like to know more about how my favorite drink can kill the nastiest plant we've ever seen. And what about the magic in the deathbush itself? We should study that too." Gwen swept toward the door. "Jenna, Ysabel, Kay, let's find Kron and ask him to portal us to Tradetown again. This time we'll destroy the menace there for once and for all."

It was a good idea, though Jenna didn't like the idea of leaving her tree unattended while Dorian was at the One Oak. Maybe Lex would guard her tree personally if she asked him nicely. As she left, she hoped Dorian never thought of threatening her own son with his magic. Maybe Robbie would be safer coming with her.

Gwen led all of them to Ysabel's side of the house and into the Fall Study. Preserved animal skins and trays of pinned butterflies gave Jenna the feeling they were being watched.

"Ysabel, ask Pouncer to wait outside and keep watch for anyone," Gwen said. "I mean anyone from the lowest scullery maid to Kron and the Avatar of War. If there are any other creatures you can use, have them stand sentry too."

"Why? What's going on?"

Gwen waited until the door was closed and Ysabel nodded to her before extending her hands and inviting a link. She continued, *We will go to one of the deathbushes, but not the ones in Tradetown. We'll go to that peach orchard near Wistica. Let's see if Dorian follows us there.*

What if we trigger a Chaos Season and make matters worse? Kay asked.

That's why all four of us need to be on hand to deal with it.

Jenna twitched at the thought of taming a Chaos Season so far from her tree. It could be done, but it would be more difficult for her. *I still don't like the idea of leaving my tree alone for so long. I wish I had some way to protect it. I could surround it with other thorny plants, but that wouldn't keep Charles out and just create problems for us when we have to work there. If only I could hang a bell on it that would ring when someone else approaches my tree.*

Kron could create something like that, Ysabel said. *He just needs something to work with.*

The lightning rod! Jenna smiled grimly. *The perfect trap for a weather Avatar.*

Gwen broke the link. "Let's find Kron and ask him to help us."

* * *

Kron, who'd taken over an old carriage house as his workshop, wasn't pleased with their idea at first. He set aside the clock he was taking apart to glare at them, softening only when he faced Ysabel.

"We need all twelve of you to face Salth and Sal-thaath. It's bad enough that five of the Avatars are dead. I thought perhaps the Four would send them to be reborn and we would just have to wait for them to grow up. But if there are divisions and jealousies among you, time might not solve that problem." He sighed. "Dorian—was he Domina, by any chance? She was difficult to work with."

Jenna exchanged looks with the other Avatars. "We usually have some idea who was who, but only for a few generations back," she replied. "We don't have a lot of records from your time, and none of us can read them anymore. Even our memories from so long ago are unclear."

"I suppose it's not important who he was as long as we can persuade him Salth is the true enemy of us all," Kron said. "All of you need to work together to confront her and end Chaos Season."

Gwen crossed her arms. "I suppose then Dorian would complain we would lack purpose if there's no Chaos Season. I for one would be happy to see it gone. There's no end to sick or injured people who need healing."

Jenna, along with Ysabel, nodded agreement. Plants and animals always needed them. She was relieved when Kay added, "If the Four wish us to end Chaos Season, I'll do my best to help."

"At this point, we don't know for certain that Dorian planted that deathbush seed next to Jenna's tree," Gwen said. "Until we prove it one way or another, we can't trust him."

Kron leaned forward. "But what will you do if he is behind it?"

Gwen looked away. "That may also depend on Charles and Sophia. At best, they will all agree to step down and let us take our place. If he won't leave quietly…." She shrugged. "We might have to turn our magic on him. Hopefully not Charles and Sophia too."

"It sounds as if we could lose all three of them." He frowned. "I don't like this."

"Neither do we, but what else can we do?"

"Let him continue to use his power as before. That's what this is all about, correct?" He sighed, suddenly looking older. "Some things never change."

"But…but…" Kay fiddled with her fingers for a few heartbeats before continuing, "Our weather magics interfere with each other."

"It's not just that," Gwen said. "He's been cruel to Kay all along. I won't stand for someone treating one of my sister Avatars that way."

Kron shook his head. "I hope the Four didn't make a mistake in choosing Domina."

Kay paled so much Jenna wondered if she was going to faint. Gwen put her hand behind Kay's back as if to steady her.

"The Four don't make mistakes," Kay said. "They can't."

"They're not what you think they are, Kay." He stared at her for a few heartbeats, as if he was trying to send her a silent message. He finally sighed. "Well, I hope They had a reason for choosing Domina, I mean, Dorian. He must be part of Their plan." He gestured at the clock face. "Just as this circle would be incomplete if you cut out a wedge, so you're incomplete without the other Avatars. I wish you'd accept that so we can figure out a plan for facing Salth."

"We don't have to confront her now, Kron." Gwen laid her hand with the shard on his workbench, close to him. Was that meant as a subtle threat? "We have another, more urgent problem."

Jenna saw her chance. "The deathbushes. We need to destroy them, but they use magic to help them grow, so physically killing them brings about small Chaos Seasons. I have a poison that's safe for humans but not deathbushes. But we need to portal to every known deathbush to give it to them."

"Do we need to give it the plants ourselves?" Ysabel asked. "Or could anyone do it, if they knew how?"

"We should still be on hand to manage any possible Chaos Season," Gwen said firmly.

"Then we have to travel away from the One Oak. My tree will be in danger." Jenna lowered her gaze and fluttered her eyelashes, but

Kron didn't seem moved. By the Four, he must be the world's most faithful man. Ysabel ought to be the one flirting with him if they were going to persuade him to help them, but she stood close to the door, studying everything else in the workshop except the man who'd traveled through time for her.

Jenna grabbed Ysabel's hand and tugged her forward. Turning her face so Kron wouldn't see, Jenna smiled and batted her eyelashes again so Ysabel would get the hint. She raised her eyebrow questioningly, and Jenna nodded. Ysabel grimaced for a heartbeat, then smoothed her expression into something more welcoming as she stepped forward.

"Please, Kron," she said, "my sister Avatars need help, and you're the only one who can give it to them."

He studied her for a few long heartbeats that seemed to stretch into forever. Finally, he sighed. "If you ask, Dearest, how can I refuse?"

Jenna repressed a smile.

Kron rummaged through a couple of chests, selecting items that made no sense to Jenna: a child's broken rattle, the clock hands, a pair of small black buttons, and a larger pair of white ones. He turned to her and said, "I need thread from your dress."

"Thread? This dress?"

"Any one you've worn, but this one is most convenient. It doesn't have to be much."

Kay knelt and fingered the stitching of Jenna's hem. She pulled a length from the back and silently handed it to Kron.

"Better make sure Dorian's not at the tree right now," he said. "If he sees me working, he might get suspicious."

"What if he sees your artifact?" Gwen asked.

"He won't. I'll meet you in the Summer Study. Since I already used that door as a portal to Tradetown, it'll be easier to use it again."

"But we're not going to Tradetown this time," Gwen said. "There's another deathbush we want to take care of first."

Kron spoke angrily in the ancient language only he understood. Jenna wondered what type of curse he was using. He switched back to Challen and said, "Have any of you ever been there before?"

"Only in thought when we tamed Chaos Season yesterday."

"That may not be enough," he said with a frown. "I need a picture to focus on, otherwise I don't know where to direct the portal."

"I'll sketch the orchard," Gwen told him.

After he left, she turned to Jenna, Ysabel, and Kay and said, "We should be ready in case we need to handle another Chaos Season. I recommend getting something to eat and bundling up in our Chaos Season clothes. Try to remember as much as you can about that peach orchard. All the details have to be right for Kron to create a portal."

They hurried to get ready. Ysabel had the cooks prepare a picnic basket similar to the one she'd shared with Jenna, only with much more food. "Have them make up another one with chocolate," Jenna said when Ysabel returned to the study.

"Won't that be heavy?" Kay asked.

"What do they make chocolate from?" Gwen didn't look up from her sketchpad. "It's not like beer or wine, sold in barrels, is it?"

Ysabel smiled. "No. At home, we bought it as a powder that the cook adds to milk and boiling water and whips with an egg wheel. I'm sure they do the same here."

Gwen switched colored pencils. "Then let's just bring the powder and let Kay add the water. I hope the deathbushes don't want milk and sugar with their chocolate. I see no reason to give it to them."

"The day plants ask for that is the day I turn them over to Ysabel," Jenna said. "Cause then they're no longer true plants."

Gwen smiled for a heartbeat before returning to her sketch.

Kron returned before she was done. He gave Jenna half of the rattle. She shook it, but it remained silent. "I don't think Robbie would like this," she said as she offered it back to him. "All he can do is chew on it."

"It's not for Robbie, it's for you."

She raised an eyebrow. "I'm too old for rattles. Wait, does this have something to do with my tree?"

"Yes. It's the alarm. When anyone other than you comes within touching distance of the tree, the lightning rod will shake the other half of the rattle. That will make your half sound out."

"Does that mean we won't be able to get close to the tree either?" Gwen said. "That could be inconvenient during a Chaos Season."

"I can disable it when we return. But first, where are we going? Do you have a picture for me that I can focus on?"

"In a heartbeat. I have to finish this part…here." Gwen turned her sketchbook to face them. "Will this do, Kron?"

Her trees showed good attention to detail in the placement of the branches. Kron shook his head. "Trees? Only the God of Summer knows how many there are in Challen. That's hardly specific enough. We might arrive somewhere else on this estate, or at the border with Selath, or anywhere in between."

Jenna suppressed a laugh. Did Kron really have such trouble telling peach trees from oaks?

"Was there a building close by?" he asked. "I do best portaling to structures instead of natural landmarks."

"There was a farmhouse with a garden," Jenna replied.

Gwen closed her eyes and massaged her temples. "I remember seeing it, but I can't recall exact details."

"Would linking with me help?" As Gwen opened her eyes to stare at Jenna, Jenna continued, "Or Ysabel and Kay too? They might have noticed something I missed."

Ysabel had gone off to fetch chocolate. Kay shook her head. "Sorry, I don't think I can help. I was too busy dealing with the weather."

"As you're supposed to," Gwen said.

"I remember inspecting the vegetables, so I might have noticed other details about the house." Jenna confronted Gwen with her own gaze. "If you're willing to link with me, that is."

Gwen regarded her for a few heartbeats, her blue eyes as cool as lakes, before reaching over and touching Jenna's wrist. Jenna struggled to bring up the memory of the house, not just the garden. There were red checkered curtains in the window. The house itself was a two-story cream stucco with dark brown trim on the windowsills and door. Gwen released Jenna and sketched furiously for a few moments, long enough for Ysabel to return lugging another basket with her cat peeking out of it.

"I have about five pounds' worth of chocolate," Ysabel said, showing her a couple of tins. "And a tin opener. I hope that's enough."

"Maybe we could portal to Wistica afterward and purchase more," Jenna said.

"Will this one do?" Gwen asked Kron as she showed him her new drawing.

He studied it for a while before replying, "I can try it. Are we ready?"

Gwen draped her cloak loosely about her. "Go ahead."

Kron traced the door frame, starting from the bottom and working his way up, over, and back down to the floor. Then he swung the door open to reveal the farmhouse. He stepped through, and Jenna and the others followed.

It looked as if the farmers had been busy cleaning up the damage from Chaos Season. A pile of broken branches had been stacked near the house for firewood. The smell of preserves wafted out of the house, making Jenna wonder if the farmer's wife would give them a jar or two for their help. A couple of children, their backs to the Avatars, squabbled as they weeded the vegetable garden. Another girl carrying two buckets of water approached the house. She shrieked, splashing water. "Ma! Pa! Strangers!"

Gwen stepped forward. "Have no fear, child. We're the new Season Avatars. We tamed the Chaos Season here yesterday, and we're here to help you with any problems left over from the storm."

The girl glared at Gwen. "That's not possible. My Pa says the Avatars live a long way from here, in the center of the country. It would take—" she scrunched up her face—"a long time for anyone to travel from there to here."

"Not so long when you have a friend with magic of his own." Gwen moved to a grassy patch before bending on one knee and extending her hand to the girl. "I'm Lady Gwendolyn lo Havil, the Spring Avatar. Was anyone hurt yesterday? No? Well, may I touch you anyway and make sure there's nothing you need me to heal?"

"My tooth?" The girl wiggled a loose tooth.

Gwen smiled. "That will come out when the Goddess of Spring decides it's ready." She turned back to Jenna and the other Avatars. "I'll check the rest of the family. You can spread out and examine the farm. Call me if you need me."

"I'll send Pouncer for you," Ysabel replied.

Kron took the basket from her, and they walked into the orchard. Jenna stopped at each tree to touch it. Most of them hadn't been severely damaged. For those that had lost branches, she sped up regrowth where it was possible and healed over other wounds. "Ysabel, this tree has pests," she said. "Can you kill them before they spread?"

She nodded and set a mole back on the ground, away from Pouncer, before coming over to the diseased tree. "I can't reach the infected area," she said. "Kron, could you give me a boost?"

"Of course, Dearest." He cupped his hands to make a step for her. Jenna wondered when Ysabel had started warming to him. It seemed a bit sudden after her earlier reluctance.

Obviously I can't instruct anyone in the ways of love. She glanced at Kay, who was observing the clouds. "Have you heard anything from your intended lately?" she asked.

"Jon? When he got my first letter he was upset. He didn't understand why I wouldn't tell anyone, even him, that I was the next Ava Win. Then he thought he wasn't good enough for me anymore, that I would want to marry a nobleman now. I wrote back and told him that didn't matter to me. I want someone who loves the Four and is a hard worker. But he still doesn't think an Avatar can marry a locomotive driver. So he's taken his savings that were meant for our home and gone to the University in Wistica."

"What's he going to study?"

"He wants to be a surveyor, someone who finds coal for the loco-motives—"

"Wait! What's that?"

At the edge of the orchard, two figures attacked a familiar-looking plant with shovels. The deathbush was already taller than Jenna.

"Ysabel!" Jenna called. "Bring the chocolate!"

One of the men lunged forward, but the deathbush flung out a branch, blocking his blow and slapping his arm. He cried out and stag-gered away.

"We need Gwen," Jenna told Kay. She nodded and ran back to Ysabel.

Jenna picked up her skirt and ran forward. "Get back! That plant is dangerous!"

The second man was a year or two younger than Jenna, with youth-pox blemishing his forehead. He stared at Jenna as if she were one of the Four. In other circumstances she might have flirted with him in spite of the youthpox. Now, however, she had to take care of the deathbush before the young farmer was poisoned too.

"Stand back!" she told him again.

"By All Four, who are you? Where did you come from?"

"I'm the Ava Summer. The other Avatars are here too. The Ava Spring will help your father." She hoped Gwen would get there in time. "Let me handle the deathbush. Haven't you heard of them?"

"How would I have heard of them?" He dropped his shovel, grabbed his father, and dragged him away from the plant.

Jenna was saved from talking about the other deathbush sightings as Ysabel, Kay, and Kron appeared. Gwen ran, passing them. She headed straight to the poisoned man and laid both hands on his arm. Jenna hoped the shard wouldn't cause any problems.

She ran toward Ysabel to take the basket herself. One of the tins was open, and some of the chocolate had left a trail in the dirt. She hoped the chocolate didn't poison peach trees, but the deathbush was far away from them. As she approached the deathbush with the tin, it whipped its branches at her as if it knew what she meant to do.

"Enough of that!" she snapped at it. "I'm the Ava Summer, and I'm sick of you and all the other deathbushes!"

A flock of songbirds descended on the deathbush. Some perched momentarily on the branches, nimbly avoiding the thorns. Others plucked off leaves and taunted the plant with their prizes. Humming-birds darted around at speeds impossible for the branches to match. A pair of branches collided, but unfortunately they didn't poison each other.

With the birds distracting the deathbush, Jenna was able to duck under the branches. How much powder did she need? Jenna poured out a generous handful close to the main stem of the deathbush. Nothing happened.

"Kay, I need rain!" Jenna hoped her voice carried past the plant.

She mixed the chocolate powder into the loose dirt, then crawled backwards away from the deathbush. A couple of branches dropped low to block her, but she kicked them and kept going. Another branch snarled in her hair, forcing her to stop and untangle herself. Long hair was pretty, but sometimes it was impractical for an Avatar, even if she wore it up.

Rain spattered her as soon she was clear of the plant. The chocolate couldn't work quickly enough for her. Jenna grabbed the closest branch and blasted it with all of her magic. Her power splintered the branch but left the rest of the tree intact. She reached for another branch. The tree writhed, eluding her grasp. Suddenly, all of its branches hung limp. Leaves yellowed even as she grabbed two branches and sent death into the tree. She didn't let go until the entire plant had turned brown.

She wiped her hands and turned to the youth. "Burn it. Dig out the roots and burn them too. Don't let a single seed escape."

He nodded with a dazed look on his face. Had Gwen saved his father? Before she could ask, the temperature dropped. The rain turned to hail.

"You don't need to freeze the deathbush, Kay," she said. "I took care of it."

"I didn't change the weather. It's Chaos Season again."

Jenna sighed. "Where's Gwen?"

"Here." She strode forward, reaching out to them. "Let's tame this before it gets out of control."

Pouncer yowled.

Jenna, Kay, and Ysabel quickly linked with Gwen. Kay directed her magic at the cold front generated by the deathbush. Uncertainty colored her thoughts as she said to them, *This cold front is bigger than it should be.*

She directed their attention higher up into the clouds. They were dark as far as Kay could sense—and that was over the entire country of Challen.

By All Four, is Chaos Season really that widespread? Gwen asked.

I'm afraid so, Kay replied. *I sense snow in the north and along the Selathen border and water storms by the coasts. The center of the country is heating up so quickly it's lowering the level of the Chikasi River.*

This isn't the best place to tame the weather, then. We need to return to the One Oak.

A rattling sound diverted Jenna's attention from the link. She looked around, trying to figure out what was making the sound. She heard it again, close by but from below. Her sash! She'd tied Kron's rattle onto the sash of her dress.

Someone's near my tree! she told the others. *We have to go there now!*

Gwen dropped the link. Kron was standing a short distance away, talking to the farmers. "No, I'm not a new type of Avatar. My magic doesn't come from the Four or any other god. I was born with it."

"So were the Avatars," the older man said. He still looked pale under his tan, but otherwise he seemed fully recovered from the deathbush attack.

"It's not the same thing. The Four gifted it to them. I should know—"

"Kron, how quickly can you take us home?" Gwen asked. "Could you open a portal to Jenna's tree instead of the study this time?"

"Why the rush? Are you done here? I thought the weather seemed a bit strange a few heartbeats ago."

"There are weather problems all over—" Kay said.

"And my tree is under attack!" Jenna said.

Kron pulled a bundle of sticks out of his satchel. They were hollow and strung together on a rope. He stood one stick on end and used the rest of the sticks to trace a doorway in the air. Jenna' tree, complete with the lightning rod and alarm system, was visible on the other side.

So was Lex.

CHAPTER TWENTY-FIVE

Jenna's Loyalty

Jenna's heart froze. Had Lex been sent here to sabotage the Season Avatars? By All Four, why? Even if he didn't care for her after all, even if he sought revenge on Gwen for rejecting him, he knew how important the Season Avatars were for Challen. He couldn't condemn the entire country to Chaos Season, could he?

Lex shifted into a guard stance, a long and narrow sword in his grip. Dorian was visible behind him.

"By All Four, which one attempted to sabotage Jenna's tree?" Gwen whispered.

"You don't have to lower your voice," Kron said. "They can't hear us when we're on this side of the portal."

"Then let's watch them for a few heartbeats first." A hard expression came over Gwen's face. "Maybe we'll learn what we need to know that way."

"We can't hear them," Kay said.

"I can fix that." Kron took a pen and a pot of ink out of his satchel and carefully inked some ancient characters on one of his sticks. He stared at them bemusedly as he wiped the pen nib on his jacket. "Sorry. I forgot to use the modern language, but it should still work."

"—Can't believe you'd defend the lightskirt." Dorian sneered at Lex. "You must have lifted her skirts—along with half of the men in that small town she came from."

"That's not true!"

Jenna dashed toward the portal, but Gwen held up a hand to block her. "Not yet," she said.

Jenna wondered what she was thinking. Perhaps Gwen thought Dorian was right. Yes, Jenna had flirted with and kissed half the young men in Bull Rock, but she'd rejected most of them after that. There had been only two she'd wanted to plow her field, but once she saw Lex, they both withered in comparison. She could show this to Gwen with her memories if they linked. Would that redeem her character to Gwen—or to Lex?

Lex didn't respond to either of Dorian's accusations. "Jenna is the Avatar of Summer, chosen by the God of Summer." He held his blade in a guard position. "You would be wise to speak of her with more respect."

"Or what? You'll run me through with that sword?" Dorian laughed so bitterly he couldn't have shown more grief if he'd wept. "By the Four, do it then! Send me to my loving Margaret! There's nothing else for me here."

"You can't win this battle," Lex said with supernatural calm. "I advise you to retreat and seek other ground."

Dorian paced back and front of the Avatar of War, fingers twitching as if he itched to throw lightning at Lex. Would he dare? Jenna's heart raced. She wished she could hurl her own weapons at Dorian. She'd even sacrifice her own oak to save Lex.

Gwen and Kron grabbed her arms. "You'll only make things worse if you charge in now," Gwen murmured into one ear.

"Yes," Kron said. "Let him realize how foolish he's being and slink off like a lizard when the sun goes down. Maybe this is just all words. Maybe this doesn't even have anything to do with whoever planted that deathbush."

"That's easy for you to say!" Jenna struggled in the dual grip. If only one person held her, she might have been able to break free, but both Gwen and Kron were stronger than she would have guessed. She glared at him. "You wouldn't be saying that if he was threatening Ysabel!"

"I would worry about her," Kron said quickly, "but I know the four of you have strong magic. She would find some way to protect herself."

"Against the weather? What would she do, summon furry creatures to keep her warm? Even Lex's sword wouldn't shield him against lightning!"

"Jenna." Ysabel leaned forward. "That's not important right now."

"Chaos Season is," Kay said. "We should be taming it."

Gwen studied the scene in front of them. "You're right, Kay. People could be dying while we're waiting for Lex and Dorian to finish their—quarrel. We may as well pass through—"

Dorian halted and raised his hands.

"By the Eagle, Avatar, I order you to leave!" Lex said. "There's nothing for you to do here. Attacking the royal family is treason, even for you."

"Then get out of the way, Royal Avatar. Better yet, take that lightning rod and Kron's ridiculous fripperies off of Jenna's tree. If I can stop the girls from becoming full Avatars, Salth will revive Margaret. The Honored Lathatilltin promised me she would."

Kay gasped, covering her hands with her mouth.

"Now," Gwen said grimly, crossing through the portal.

Jenna pushed past Gwen. As fast as she ran, lightning was faster. Bolts flew from Dorian's fingertips to the tree she'd nurtured. Jenna screamed. But instead of scorching her tree, the lightning arced to the lightning rod and passed into the ground, leaving a burnt smell in its wake.

Thank the Four... Jenna's legs quivered from the remnant of her terror. Dorian raised his hands again...

"Stop!" Kay shouted. Her hair, too short for braids or chignons, stood on end as a ball of lightning hovered above her hand.

Dorian laughed. "Foolish girl, do you think you're a match for me?"

She faced him. "I know my magic works better when you're not around to interfere."

Keeping her gaze on both of them, Jenna took a couple of side steps toward her tree, both to check on it and to be ready to tap into it. A dark shadow flickered over the ground as it headed toward the One Oak. Pouncer. Ysabel must have sent him to fetch Sophia and Charles. Jenna wondered if that was a wise decision. The three older Avatars could no longer link with each other, but if they chose to stand together, they would be formidable foes.

Since when does Avatar oppose Avatar, or one quartet another quartet? she cried out to herself. *We should be facing Chaos Season now instead of warring with each other. By the Four, I hope Lex's magic didn't cause this.*

"Dorian," Gwen said, "We feel Chaos Season active in many places around Challen. Stop interfering with us and our magic so we can tame it. We won't ask you again."

"I should hope not. You won't have reason to."

Dorian raised his hands again. Jenna tensed, expecting another bolt of lightning aimed at her tree—or even them. Instead, the sky above them grew darker as clouds formed. The air dried out, making plants thirsty. Jenna reached out for her tree and caressed its bark reassuringly. The gesture didn't make her feel any calmer, though.

Gwen, Ysabel, and Kay approached her and stretched their arms out to link. Before they could, Jenna glanced upward. A crow glided over them before settling in her tree. Brighteyes, Sophia's anilink. Sophia and Charles hurried after him. They hadn't bothered with their Chaos Season cloaks. That was probably a mistake.

Sophia halted several feet from Dorian and huffed for a couple of heartbeats. "By All Four, what's going on? You're staring at Dorian as if he caused a hurricane."

"We fear he's trying to do exactly that, Ava," Kron said.

"We caught him trying to sabotage my tree—twice!" Jenna wrapped an arm around her tree's trunk. "First he planted deathbushes next to it, then he shot lightning at it! If I hadn't protected it earlier with a lightning rod, he would have burnt it up!"

"What?" Sophia's whole face was circles, from her shocked eyes to her open mouth. "I know you haven't seen Dorian at his best, but he wouldn't do that."

Gwen raised her head. "We saw him do it. The four of us, Kron, and the War Avatar."

"Then there must be some misunderstanding."

"Of course there is." Dorian shook his head. "It was simply a test of your magic. If I had meant to destroy your tree, why use lightning when the lightning rod was already in place?"

What he said made sense, but Jenna didn't trust it. Lightning bolts were never friendly.

Gwen planted her hands on her hips. "You weren't testing us, you were trying to prevent us from taming Chaos Season."

"We heard you," Kay whispered, her face pale. "And why."

Dorian turned to face the rest of his quartet. "Charles, Sophia, we've been together hundreds of years. Will you stand by me now, for Margaret's sake?"

"How could we not?" Charles smiled and held out his hand as if welcoming Dorian back into their group.

"Then help me drive off these interlopers so Margaret can live again."

Charles and Sophia stared at him for a couple of heartbeats, and Charles let his hand drop. The wind picked up, hard enough to shake the branches of Jenna's tree. Jenna reached out for the other members of her quartet before Dorian could blow them away. The four of them held on to each other's arms to avoid being pulled into the link.

"By All Four Gods and Goddess, Dorian, are you mad?" Sophia asked. "They're not interlopers. They're the next group of Avatars, and they have just as much right to be here as we do, perhaps more so."

"We can't do our job properly anymore," Charles held his jacket close about him. "You know that."

Dorian looked smug. "But I can reach across Challen on my own."

"How?" Gwen asked.

"Those new plants contain weather magic, and they've seeded all over Challen. Tapping into them extends my power."

"Fool!" Charles said. "Those plants are dangerous and must be destroyed before they trigger a country-wide Chaos Season."

Dorian's smile deepened. "They already have."

Gwen shook her cursed hand at Dorian. "We've been talking long enough. Let's link and tame the Chaos Season!"

"We need to kill the deathbushes first," Jenna said. "Otherwise, they'll bring Chaos Season back when we think we're done."

The wind whipped up another level, shaking Jenna's tree and ripping the lightning rod off. "What makes you think I'll ever let you upstarts tame Chaos Season?"

"Dorian gran Garnell!" Sophia put a hand over her heart. "You can't interfere with them! That's going against everything we're sworn before the Four to do! What would Margaret say?"

The wind ebbed for a heartbeat, long enough to give Jenna hope that Dorian would see reason. Then he screamed, "It's never enough! Winter chose me first. Why do I have to share my power with other Avatars? Why do you always hold me back? If you won't let me trade these girls to Salth for Margaret, I'll trade you instead, freeze it!"

Sophia and Charles studied each other, identical stricken expressions on their faces. Then they turned to Dorian, chanting in unison. "By Spring, Summer, Fall, and Winter, the Four Gods and Goddesses of Challen, we, Charles and Sophia vin Estcher, eject you from our quartet of Avatars. May we never link again, never share thoughts or magic with you, in this life or in any life to come. May the Four Themselves pass judgment on you."

While their last words rang in the air, they turned their backs on him.

Stunned, Jenna gripped Gwen's arm even tighter as they all pushed cloth aside to link. This was another first in the history of the Season Avatars. Every quartet had its share of troubles. Sometimes Avatars would isolate themselves from their companions for a while, or sometimes groups would break up once they'd passed their duties to the next generation of Avatars. But never before had a quartet of Avatars denounced one of their own.

Is that even possible? Kay asked. *How will their quartet function if they don't have a Winter Avatar in their next life? Would the God of Winter take his gift from Dorian and give it to someone else?*

No one knew.

They broke their link to see how Dorian reacted. He stared at Charles' and Sophia's backs, his hand raised as if he meant to throw something at them. "Sophia? Charles? You can't turn away from me. The Four put us together many lives ago. You're my last link to Margaret, closer than our children. You can't leave me too."

They didn't respond.

"Say something! Anything!" He circled around to face them, but they turned away from him again.

"You can't ignore me forever." He lowered his voice. "I can make you pay attention to me—"

"Dorian gran Garnell, that's enough." Gwen dropped contact with Jenna and Ysabel to stride forward. Maybe she was strong enough to handle him on her own, but she should have the support of her Avatars. Jenna followed her, running her hand along a tree branch until it rose out of her reach. Ysabel took a position on the other side of Gwen. Face still pale, Kay hesitated before edging in front of everyone else, ready to match her magic against Dorian's.

Gwen glanced at each of them, giving them slight nods, before glaring at Dorian. "Take your things from the One Oak and leave. You're no longer welcome here."

"It doesn't matter what you or anyone else says. I'm still an Avatar. See?" He spread out his arms, and the wind picked up, trying to push them backward. Jenna reached out for Gwen to secure her. Kay frowned as she fought back with her own counterwind. "Winter hasn't taken His magic from me."

"Yet. How many heartbeats will it take?"

Instead of answering, Dorian summoned a stronger wind. This one seemed focused on Jenna's tree, shaking it so hard the lightning rod came loose and fell off. Maybe Dorian was gearing up to attack her tree again. If he were any closer, she'd have her tree flail him with its branches. Too bad he'd chosen a spot out in the open. The grass where he stood was too short to do more than tickle his feet.

Jenna retreated just far enough so she could make contact with her oak. Linking with it, she searched for a nearby plant she could use against Dorian. No poison oak or dangerous mushrooms grew nearby. Maybe the other oaks could fling their unripe acorns at him....

Dorian raised his right hand, fingertips glowing with lightning. He pointed threateningly at her tree. However, a flicker of light drew Jenna's attention to his left hand. The one aimed at Gwen.

Jenna released her tree. "Gwen! Watch out!"

She lunged toward Gwen, and then everything happened at once.

Twin bolts streamed from Dorian's hands. Jenna's heart leaped into her mouth. She'd never reach Gwen in time. The lightning bolt headed for Gwen abruptly faded away an instant before it struck her. Already committed to the action, Jenna couldn't stop herself from knocking Gwen to the ground and falling on top of her. A thunderous boom over-head almost drowned out the sound of cracking wood. Leaves brushed against Jenna's back. They were heavy, still attached to their branches.

Lex cried, "Guilty!" and advanced on Dorian with his sword.

"By All Four, Lex, you can't kill him!" Kron said, searching for something in his satchel.

A blanket of fog descended, blinding them all.

CHAPTER TWENTY-SIX

Chaos Season Over Challen

"Get off of me, Jenna! By All Four, how can you be so heavy?"

Gwen's complaints made Jenna smile. At least she didn't sound hurt.

While Kay dispersed the fog, Ysabel and Kron helped pull the branches off of Jenna. She stood up and stopped smiling. Her tree had lost half of its branches on the side facing her. Strips of bark had been blown off and littered the ground. The trunk had split in a vertical groove deep enough for Jenna to insert her finger half way. She checked the other side of the tree for damage, then put her hand on the trunk and checked for damage to the root system. Thank the Four the injuries were confined to one side of the tree. She still had a chance to heal it.

I'm so sorry I stopped protecting you even for a heartbeat, she told her tree. She pressed herself against it, sending all the magic she held into it. If she could force-grow new bark over the groove, it would protect the tree while she encouraged new wood to fill the gap.

Gwen touched her and gave her more energy. *Why did you let go of your tree?*

You were in danger! The memory of Dorian launching his lightning played in the link.

I wasn't really, not with Kay there to take care of the lightning.

Jenna tried to repress her worries over Kay's skill before they seeped into the link. *I was worried about you.*

Silly goose, Gwen said affectionately. *I'm just glad you weren't touching your tree when it was hit.*

I should have been. I could have stopped it from being broken up.

Not likely, Jenna. You would have been hurt by the lightning along with your tree. You can always rear another tree, but we can't add another Summer Avatar to our group.

Thoughts of Dorian sobered them both for a couple of heartbeats. Then Jenna said, *You're the only Spring Avatar I could ever follow.* She tried to put as much feeling behind the thoughts as she could. Not just how much she thought Gwen was a good healer, even with the shard embedded in her hand, or how dedicated she was to her role. After so many lifetimes, it went deeper than that. They were friends who'd weathered countless triumphs and sorrows together. No matter how often the Four reincarnated them into opposite backgrounds, no matter how much they argued with and hurt each other, they belonged together one way or another.

Gwen sighed. *We can talk about that later. But...thank you.* She released Jenna. "First things first. Ysabel, Kay, we need to link and help Jenna heal her tree. Then we tame every trace of Chaos Season we can find."

"What about Dorian?" Kay asked.

Jenna forced herself to stop looking at her wounded tree. Dorian was nowhere to be seen. He must have used the fog as cover to make his way to the One Oak, though she wondered why he would have bothered. Surely Gwen would give him enough time to pack before throwing him out?

Lex jogged back to them, looking grim. "He's gone."

"Gone? He couldn't have left that quickly," Charles said. "He must be gathering his things."

"Would he really do that?" Sophia asked. "Leave so easily, without protest? The servants don't even know yet that we...that we...cast him out."

"I don't think he's anywhere on the estate anymore," Lex said. "I had a strong sense of an enemy just before the fog came, and the enemy presence faded very soon afterward."

"But how could he have left?" Charles said.

Lex stared at Kron with hard eyes. "Kron is the only one of us who can create portals. And he didn't want me to kill Dorian."

"We need twelve Avatars to defeat Salth," Kron said. "We can't kill Dorian, no matter what he does. Salth is far worse than him."

As they continued to argue, Jenna glanced at Gwen. Why waste time talking when her tree was wounded and Chaos Season raged? Gwen nodded as if she knew what Jenna was thinking. Ysabel, her cat Pouncer, and Kay came forward. Pouncer huddled against Ysabel, Ysabel and Kay touched Gwen, and Gwen linked them all to Jenna.

Jenna laid both hands on her tree and channeled magic into it. Dorian's magic lingered in the wound, interfering with her ability to heal it. Even Kay, who could filter the wild magic of Chaos Season into something they could use, wasn't able to remove all of it. Jenna did her best to push it into the outer layer of the bark, where it would do the least damage. She repaired the injured wood and coaxed new branches to sprout from the jagged stumps left behind. Ysabel hummed a lullaby in the background. Jenna thought of her son, comfortable in the nursery. This tree was also like a child of hers, and she hoped someday Robbie would be able to play in its shade. Her tree couldn't experience feelings the way humans or even animals did, but its leaves rustled windlessly in what she hoped was acceptance, maybe even forgiveness.

Time for a break, Gwen said before severing the link.

"But Chaos Season—" Kay started.

"We'll manage it better once we refresh ourselves." Gwen shook out her arms. "Ah, I thought I sensed food."

A pair of maids carried a heavy picnic basket between them. While Gwen thanked them and showed them where to put it, Jenna inspected her tree. A white streak in the bark showed where the lightning bolt had run to earth, and the new branches were only half as big as the ones on the other side of the oak. Not only did it make her tree look strange, but the imbalance might cause her tree to fall over. She defied Gwen long enough to strengthen the root system. Her limbs shook with exhaustion once she stepped away from her oak.

"We'll eat quickly," Gwen said as she handed Jenna a plate loaded with bread, cheese, sliced tomatoes, and cold meat. "The break will give Kron, Lex, Sophia, and Charles time to find and destroy as many death-bushes as they can so the plants don't feed the Chaos Season."

"Does that mean Lex changed his mind about Kron helping Dorian escape?" Jenna asked. "Or are they still searching for him?"

"I'm not sure," Gwen replied. "I know they argued about it for a while before Sophia and Charles reminded them of the deathbushes. I listened to them through Pouncer. He understands human language very well, even for an anilink."

"Pouncer's always been very smart," Ysabel said proudly.

The food did make Jenna feel better, although she wished there had been some chocolate to moisten her mouth and give her more energy. They must have taken all the powder for the deathbushes.

By the time they were done, the sun had come out. Summer heat would soon have them all sweating like farm girls, not glowing like ladies.

Gwen looked at each of them in turn. "Are we ready?"

They all nodded, even Pouncer.

"Good." She gestured at Jenna's oak. "Back to work, Avatars. By the time we're done, let no one doubt we are Avatars indeed."

Jenna raised her shoulders a little higher at the thought.

They returned to the tree, prayed to each of the Four, and linked again. As Jenna sunk her mind deep into the ground, Kay searched the sky for Chaos Season. Anywhere she found weather magic mixing up the seasons, she pulled it in her with her own magic. Gwen caught it and sent most of it on to Jenna and Ysabel while keeping some to heal people hurt in the storms. Jenna and Ysabel did the same for affected plants and animals.

They followed this pattern as they worked their way all over Challen. Tradetown had been suffering a torrential downpour that Kay had to stop. On the other side of the country, in Wistica, high winds and rough water threatened to turn into a hurricane. She turned them back out across the Salt Waters, away from known shipping paths. Further inland, Jenna intervened to make sure the crops didn't ripen too soon. In other areas, where grain, fruits, and vegetables had been blasted with out-of-season chills, she reached back into the plants and forced them to start over. Sometimes she was able to coax them to fertilize themselves, but more often, Ysabel recruited bees to spread pollen. Ysabel was busy herself with keeping animals from molting or growing the wrong type of coat for the season, making sure they didn't migrate at the wrong times, or even attempting to mate.

With Chaos Season affecting the entire country, there was an incredible amount of plants and animals to take care of. Jenna and the other three Avatars managed them all, from the smallest seeds to the tallest trees. All she sensed was plant life—what it was, how many individual plants there were in a particular spot, and what she needed to do for them. Gwen fed magic to her the heartbeat before she needed it. Jenna felt someone tuck a cloak over her shoulders; a few times, broth or water brushed her lips. She could scarcely divert her attention long enough to swallow it. Once or twice she caught plants magically returning to their natural state before she could take care of them herself. Charles must be assisting her with his limited abilities. Dorian would probably complain that wasn't right, but she didn't care. With so many different Chaos Seasons to tame, help was appreciated.

Finally, Kay swept the clouds away from a small town and said wearily, *I can't find any more traces of Chaos Season anywhere in Challen.*

Well done, Kay, Gwen sent to her. *Jenna, Ysabel, are you finished?*

Nearly. Ysabel separated a pair of stags before they could lock horns. *Now I am.*

Jenna inspected a final field of corn and decided she didn't need to do anything, as the ears were at the perfect stage to harvest. If she was there in person, she'd devour half the field without bothering to roast and butter the corn. *So am I. Gwen?*

She sighed. *Healing is never done…but I don't have enough magic left to close a paper cut. We've done our share; now we leave the rest in the Four's hands.* Despite her fatigue, a strand of elation threaded through her thoughts. *We did it. We tamed our first Chaos Season, thank the Four.*

Technically it wasn't their first, as they'd also managed the one on the peach farm. But they hadn't worked as well together, and Jenna didn't even want to think about the reasons why.

We praise Spring, Summer, Fall, and Winter for granting us the means of taming Chaos Season, Kay said. *May the Four watch over us and Challen in all seasons.*

May it be so, they echoed.

Gwen released the link, and they could focus on their surroundings again. A cluster of lanterns glowed nearby, but otherwise it was dark. Not quite; a faint glow appeared in the east. Had they really worked all day and through the night? Jenna opened her mouth but found her tongue too dry to speak clearly.

"Avas?" the butler asked. "Are you finished?"

Jenna nodded before she realized he probably couldn't see her. She tried to step toward the waiting lights and servants, but her legs collapsed under her. All was darkness again.

CHAPTER TWENTY-SEVEN

A Talk with Lex

"This is Mama's tree, Robbie," Jenna said as she placed his hand on the tree trunk. "It's an oak, like the One Oak where we live."

Robbie reached for a twig and attempted to put it in his mouth, but she took it away. "No, Sweetie, you're not a beaver."

It had been two days since Jenna and the others had finished restoring the country after Chaos Season. She was grateful no other storms had occurred in the meantime. They had all needed the chance to rest and replenish their strength. Jenna also needed to give her tree attention and an occasional boost of magic as it continued to heal. The view of the Chikasi River from here soothed her. Why, it was so quiet here she could hear the sound of a horse cantering up to the house....

Jenna sighed. That would be another messenger with damage or death reports from another part of Challen. At least Kron was willing to use his artifact magic to travel and fix damaged buildings. Every time Gwen received more death reports, she retreated to the Spring Study to grieve in private. Jenna wished she would let her offer comfort. Maybe if she'd been born a man in this life Gwen would be willing to cry on her shoulder. She'd have to help Gwen find someone who could hold her and remind her she couldn't keep everyone alive forever, out of season.

Well, if Gwen's not going to let me talk some sense into her, I'm just going to stay here and enjoy the shade with my child.

Robbie started fretting and wouldn't calm down when she let him suckle on her sadly dry breast. The summer heat became uncomfortable, even in the shade. By the time Ysabel and Pouncer approached, Jenna was ready to roll up the blanket and take Robbie in.

"Gwen wants the four of us to meet in her study," Ysabel said when she was close enough to talk to Jenna without raising her voice.

"Another meeting? Here, can you hold Robbie for a heartbeat? Thanks." Jenna shook the blanket out before rolling it up and tucking it under her arm. "Do we really need to go over another report about all our mistakes? It'd be nice to have people grateful to us for a change. We helped a lot of people and plants—and animals, but we always get blamed for not saving everyone and everything."

"Sometimes the Four use Chaos Season to harvest souls." Ysabel's normal smile disappeared. "I suppose it's easier to blame us than the Four."

Jenna sighed. "You're right, but it never gets easier no matter how many lives we lead." She reached for Robbie again, craving to cuddle him. "Let's go see what more bad news Gwen has for us."

She hoped it didn't have anything to do with deathbushes. Charles, Kron, and Sophia had dosed all the plants they could find with chocolate, and Lex had returned to Wistica to claim more cocoa powder for them to keep on reserve. She almost wished the deathbushes were still a threat so he'd have to stay at the One Oak. Even if he didn't love her, maybe she could seduce him into another kiss.

Robbie continued to fuss, so as soon as they reached the house, Jenna kissed him and turned him over to his nurse. Then she descended to the second floor where Gwen waited in the Spring Study. The room smelled of lemons, wax, and Gwen's ever-present violet bracelet. Despite the warm day, a fire burned in the fireplace as Gwen tossed letters into it. Kay sent the heat out of the open window.

"I don't feel right keeping Margaret's personal correspondence," Gwen said at Jenna's inquiring look. "I would pass it to Dorian, but..."

"I don't care if he ever gets one of her letters, or anything else he owns," Kay said with uncharacteristic venom. "He interfered with my magic."

"And a lot of other things."

With Dorian gone, he could no longer deny Gwen or Kay full access to the Spring and Winter Wings of the house. No wonder Gwen felt the need to remove traces of the older Avatars from her study.

Jenna squeezed next to Ysabel on a window seat. "So, did you send Dorian's things to his family's house, or just give them to the poor in Midpoint?"

"I sent them back to his family. There's still no sign of him in Challen."

"Lex isn't going to like that," Jenna said.

Ysabel shifted away from her. "Well, Kron didn't portal Dorian away for safekeeping, even if he says we still need him. I suppose his dream of ending Chaos Season for good is just a dream, never to come true."

"Now is not the season to worry about that." Gwen held up an envelope marked with a red eagle. "A messenger from the king dropped this off only an hour ago. He must have sent her as soon as Lex returned to Wistica." She picked up a gold-trimmed letter opener and slit the envelope. She cleared her throat for effect, then read aloud, "To Lady Gwendolyn lo Havil, Ava Spring; Jenna Dorshay t'Reve, Ava Summer; Ysabel s'Ivena Lathatilltin, Ava Fall; and Kay Seltich, Ava Winter; greetings. Our brother reports that you have demonstrated your skill at taming Chaos Season. We therefore request, desire, and command you—"

"Surely one of those would have been enough," Jenna muttered.

Gwen raised her eyebrow and remained silent until Jenna said, "Sorry."

She continued, "Command you to appear before us in exactly one quarter-moon, the final day of Cornmoon, to swear loyalty to us and be acknowledged as the rightful Season Avatars of Challen."

At last, everyone would acknowledge them as Avatars. It was what Jenna had wanted for so many years, to be seen as someone more than just another farm girl. But now she could only think of Lex. He would be there. He would have to be there. Seeing him was more important than going through a ceremony to make the king feel as if he was in control of the Avatars. She'd been an Avatar all along. But maybe now Lex would see she was truly his equal, worthy of being more than just a tumble behind a barn.

"Will there be a ball afterward?" Jenna asked. That would be the perfect place to battle again with the Avatar of War, especially since she now had a better idea of what to expect and how to handle the men there.

Ysabel's eyes brightened; Kay looked as if she wanted to dive under the furniture and never come out.

"I imagine so." Gwen sighed. "After this, I'll have no excuse to postpone my marriage again."

"But you won't marry William?" Jenna asked.

"No. Which means I have to reconsider all of the candidates my family will surely suggest to me."

"Tell them you'll only marry a summer-born," Jenna said.

She raised an eyebrow. "Why?"

Because only a summer-born would be able to bring out the passion she suppressed. That wasn't something Jenna felt comfortable telling Gwen in front of Ysabel and Kay, no matter how many times the four of them had linked.

"Lathtin always wanted to visit Wistica, but Father didn't want him attending University there," Ysabel said. "I hope we have some time to see the city as well as the palace."

"But we'll have to get formal dresses, won't we?" Kay shook her head. "So many seamstresses will have to work into the night to finish them in time."

"I'll wager the head housekeeper already made arrangements for them as soon as we all returned." Gwen set the king's letter aside. "So, I take it we're ready to be officially recognized as Season Avatars?"

"It still doesn't feel right." Kay wove her fingers together. "I wish we'd found out what happened to Dorian."

"He can't bother us anymore, Kay," Gwen said. "Salth hasn't been sending you nightmares again, has she?"

Some of the worry left Kay's face. "I have been sleeping better," she replied. "But it—it's still coming."

The death she'd foreseen? How could that reach her here?

"Then we'll weather that season when it arrives." Gwen rose. "For now, let's go see about formalwear suitable for Avas."

* * *

Jenna smoothed the silk of her green-and-white gown—more green than white, of course—as Clover finished putting her hair up. She wished the other Avatars were in the same room with her so they could talk as they prepared themselves for the ceremony. Apparently it was an honor for the king to grant each of them use of a different room. Too bad it didn't do anything for her nervousness.

"You'll be fine, Ava." Clover sighed as she pinned a rose over Jenna's ear. "You're used to this sort of thing, aren't you?"

Jenna laughed. "I was born in Bull Rock, remember?"

"But you've been here in other lives, haven't you? Even the One Oak isn't half as grand as the palace—begging your pardon, Ava. It's so kind of the palace servants to let us watch from a hidey-hole. I'm looking forward to the feast afterward."

Jenna's stomach rumbled at the mention of food. She hadn't had to use her plant magic recently, but preparing for a royal ceremony was exhausting in its own way.

"What about Robbie and Callie?" she asked. "Where will they be?"

She'd invited her family to the investiture, but they couldn't be spared from the farm. She'd have to write them later and tell them about it. She'd deliberately excluded her absent husband's relations. They hadn't been fond of her during the brief moons of her marriage, so they didn't need to profit from her now. Robbie was her only family present, and she didn't want him to be neglected.

"I think she was going to sit off to the side, so she can take your son away if he gets overtired."

Hopefully Lex would have a chance to see Robbie again before that happened.

Someone knocked on the door. A male servant announced, "Ten minutes, Ava."

"You'd better join the other Avas, Ava. That sounds strange, doesn't it?" Clover giggled, causing Jenna to join in. By the time someone knocked on the door again, they could barely hear it over the laughter.

Gwen shook her head, making the dyed ostrich feathers in her hair bob. "Jenna Dorshay t'Reve, I should have guessed you wouldn't take this seriously. You never do."

"Well, you always take things too seriously, Lady Gwendolyn lo Havil, so I have to balance you out."

Gwen smiled slightly for a few heartbeats. "Let's go."

Clover helped Jenna by straightening out the train of her gown. Ysabel and Kay were already outside, bedecked in so much finery and jewels they looked lost within it. Jenna wondered if she looked equally strange to them.

A nobleman wearing enough medals to compete with Lex approached Gwen. "Ava, I need you to line up the other Avatars so we can proceed to the main entrance of the formal reception room. You will tell each of them to wait until I cue them—"

"We're right here, able to hear you," Jenna said. "You can address us too."

A pained expression crossed his face for a heartbeat. Then he turned to Gwen again. "Lady lo Havil, will you please explain to the other Season Avatars that they technically aren't ennobled until after the ceremony—"

Gwen crossed her arms. "Lord su Ziggen, we've all been Avatars long before your family invaded Challen with the rest of the Fip army. We are born into different backgrounds to help us develop our magic, not so others can look down on an Avatar born without a prefix to her name."

"But surely they aren't as familiar with the protocol—"

Trumpets announced the king arriving in the formal reception room below.

"Freeze protocol!" Gwen said. "We have to hurry!"

They dashed down a staircase, nearly getting their trains tangled in the confusion. Maids met them by the doorway, hovering like birds as they made last-minute adjustments to their outfits. Gwen fussed with one of her long silk gloves embroidered with violets to match her bracelet, but her personal maid scolded her and tugged the glove back into place. Gwen shrugged and leaned closer to Jenna, Ysabel, and Kay. "Don't worry about the ceremony," she whispered. "We've been through this before, and you'll remember what to do. After taming that Chaos Season, we can do anything."

Musicians began to play a delicate tune with piping flutes. Gwen straightened herself as the doors opened, then paced through them with stately dignity. Jenna tried to copy Gwen's poise as she waited for the music to change. Her cue came as stringed instruments took over the melody. She took a deep breath and entered the room. On each side of the aisle, she could see hundreds of nobles staring at her. *By the Four, what if there's a stain on my dress somewhere, or what if Clover forgot to do up all my buttons and my unmentionables are showing?* Her smile felt frozen in place, but her feet glided forward. Seeing Gwen calmly kneeling in front of the king helped steady

Jenna's nerves. Even better, though, was catching sight of Lex stand-ing behind his brother. His gaze shifted to her, and he smiled slightly, enough to ease her nervousness but not enough to show if his care for her extended to a deeper level. Perhaps he didn't dare display his feel-ings in front of such a large crowd. Or perhaps he still thought she was beneath him.

She looked away and focused on Gwen. When Jenna reached the king, she executed a curtsey, then sank to her knees on a green cush-ion next to Gwen. Sometime during her procession, the music had shifted to a Fall theme. However, she didn't dare glance back to watch Ysabel. Instead, she studied the embroidery on the king's robe and the patterns in the marble floor.

When Kay had made her own way to the front of the room, the mu-sic halted. The king rose. Shuffles from behind Jenna indicated the nobles were paying respect to him too. He raised his hands and spoke: "Nobles of Challen, the Four Gods and Goddesses of Challen have sent us Their Avatars to tame Chaos Season and provide for this coun-try. As each God or Goddess yields to another in the proper season, so does one quartet of Avatars make way for another generation to take on their sacred task. We honor the previous Avatars: Margaret gran Garnell, Ava Spring; Charles vin Estecher, Avi Summer; Sophia vin Estecher, Ava Fall; and Dorian gran Garnell, Avi Winter. Now that the gran Garnells are with the God of Winter, it's up to these four young women to replace the entire quartet."

Does he think both Margaret and Dorian are dead? Jenna won-dered. Maybe Dorian would find peace if his soul had been reunited with his wife's, or maybe he'd been frozen forever for turning on other Avatars. But that could only happen if he really was dead. Jenna wasn't sure.

"Lady Gwendolyn lo Havil, come forward and pledge loyalty to me," the king said.

She rose, took a few steps, then knelt again directly in front of him. It seemed a bit silly to Jenna, but she knew she'd have to do it too if she didn't want to cause problems for the other Avatars.

"I, Gwendolyn lo Havil, Spring Avatar, do pledge before the Four Gods and Goddesses of Challen to serve my country and its ruler all the days of my life," Gwen recited.

When the Fips had first conquered Challen, they had demanded each of the Avatars provide them with tribute or perform a service for them before being recognized. These days, with the staff at the One Oak automatically sending chals to the king at every season change, no valuables changed hands at this ceremony. The only remnant of that part of the ceremony was the king kissing Gwen's cheek as he helped her rise.

"Jenna dor Treve," the king said, looking at her with irritation, "come forward."

By the Four, it would take some time to get used to the new version of her name. Jenna suppressed the urge to hurry as she approached the king. She copied Gwen's motions and pledged herself as before, but her gaze kept straying to Lex's face instead of the king's. Lex's mouth tightened as his brother leaned in, scraping her cheek with his beard.

"So you're the mother of Lex's child," he murmured.

"Your Majesty!" Just in time, she remembered to whisper. The air grew close with the weight of a thousand stares.

He smiled. "I can tell you have a warrior spirit."

Then it was over, and she was able to return to her cushion to wonder what he had meant by that. A noblewoman tugged her train back into place as Ysabel approached the king. Lex refused to look at Jenna for the rest of the ceremony, making her heart sink. By All Four, let him complain to his brother if he was jealous. He was the one who insisted on kissing all the Avatars!

After Kay's turn to be recognized and ennobled, the king announced, "As ruler of Challen, breadbasket of the Fip Empire, I declare the ladies in front of me to be the true Season Avatars of Challen, with all the rights and responsibilities that accompany their positions. Let us celebrate now with a dance!"

The musicians started a waltz. Clover came forward with Robbie in a velvet suit. Jenna cradled her sleepy child for a moment while Clover bustled her train so she could dance.

"Ava, your partner is too young to walk, let alone dance with you." Lex stood at her shoulder. "Allow me to accompany you instead."

She barely had time to hand Robbie back to his nurse before Lex swept her away, pressing her close enough to his body to shock their audience. For Jenna, it was a thrill nearly as powerful as taming Chaos Season.

"Ava—Jenna—perhaps I've misjudged you. You are more loyal than I realized." He looked in her eyes. "If you can give me half the loyalty you show your Ava Spring, I'll be a lucky man indeed."

"I'll give you all that and more," she whispered.

"Then I will wed you," he announced. "Though we must wait until your mourning time for your first husband is done."

Jenna blinked. "Did I hear you properly? Are you asking me to marry you?"

"Isn't that what I just said?"

"Well, a woman prefers a little more wooing before a proposal. I'm not a town you can persuade to surrender without firing a single shot."

His mouth quirked. "Here I thought you were the conqueror of my heart, and I was surrendering to you."

Her own heart soared at his words, but she forced down her excitement and said, "How could a mere farm girl overcome the Avatar of War?"

"With courage and beauty," he replied. "No shield, no wall, can keep you out of my heart. You've undermined all the barriers I thought there were between us. I can't imagine any other woman I'd want at my side."

Jenna wondered if that included Gwen.

Lex smiled at her. "Our marriage will give me an excuse to adopt our son, though to avoid scandal, he won't be able to claim War Blood." His grip on her tightened. "Naturally, all of our other children will be candidates for the next War Avatar."

Did he think she'd be foolish enough to have a child with someone else? She'd learned her lesson: no more affairs. Lex would have to work very hard to keep her satisfied. Hopefully, Gwen would be willing to ensure he was up for the challenge.

"Of course," Jenna agreed. She hoped the Fip God wouldn't claim any of her children. Perhaps He would find a better candidate back in the Fip heartland, especially if her children were raised to worship the Four.

Lex still hadn't proposed properly to her. She met his gaze boldly. "Is that all you want to say to me?"

"No." He grasped her tighter as he whirled her away from the crowded dance floor. Jenna thought she saw Gwen off to the side, arguing with her father and former fiancé. Gwen's Aunt Gabri leaned on a cane next to her. Then Jenna and Lex were past them. He led her out through a pair of glass doors to a small courtyard. A fountain played water music in the center, while the scent of roses grew stronger from the bushes that bordered the edge of the courtyard. She smiled, remembering the afternoon Lex had given her Robbie.

Lex pulled her over to the fountain. In the starlight, his face was shadowed. "Perhaps wooing should not be done with words alone, but with more…delightful weapons."

He kissed her, drawing her into his strong embrace. She opened her lips and pressed herself against him. Would anyone else notice if the rosebushes suddenly intertwined and grew ten feet? If they had more privacy, they could make love in the center of the garden.

Lex pulled away before she could use her magic. "Is that sufficient wooing, or shall we continue?" He smiled. "How will you answer me now, Jenna?"

"Yes, oh yes." She clung to him. "But perhaps we should test that weapon again, to see how strong it is."

Lex chuckled. "We'd best not linger too long here, as much as I would like to. Otherwise, there will be gossip about us. Shall we see what's been laid out on the supper table? I hear it's a spread fit for an Avatar, or several of them."

She agreed, beaming at shocked nobles as Lex took her arm and escorted her to a small room filled with tables of food. Gwen stood there alone, a goblet of wine in her hand and meat scraps for Pouncer in the other.

Jenna made straight for her as Lex ordered a servant to prepare plates of food for them. "Gwen, I'm betrothed!"

"I'm not."

"Oh." Jenna stared at her, trying to gauge her mood. She knew Gwen hadn't been in love with William, but she'd been concerned about breaking the engagement anyway. Some of the tension Gwen always bore was gone. Her shoulders didn't sag under the perpetual burden she carried. "Congratulations, I think?"

"Oh, it is congratulations." Gwen smiled as she fed Ysabel's cat. A collar around his neck twinkled with garnets and rubies. "Aunt Gabri took my side against my father. She said I have a wise old head on my shoulders, and even if I am over-willful, whoever I choose would be suitable and have the Four's blessings, so my father should bless him too. Wasn't that a wonderful thing to say?"

"Especially coming from your aunt." Jenna leaned closer to her. "Only consult your heart too when you choose someone, not just your head."

Gwen sighed. "My heart hasn't found anyone it prefers above all others yet."

That's what happens when you ask for a life in which we can't marry. Jenna checked to make sure they weren't touching. Gwen didn't need to overhear that thought.

Lex approached them and gave a glass of wine to Jenna.

"Congratulations to both of you," Gwen said. "I wish you much happiness, Your Royal Highness."

Lex dipped his head toward her. "Ava, there are many fine young men here who would be overjoyed to meet you."

"I know. How will I ever choose among them?" She suddenly looked up at Jenna and smiled knowingly. "A summerborn. I shall choose a summerborn. You know why, Jenna."

Jenna tried not to choke on her wine. A summerborn man couldn't link with Gwen the way the two of them could, but if he could give her the passion she needed, it might work.

Ysabel entered the supper room, her cheeks flushed. Kron followed her, looking annoyed. "By All Four, I can't believe how many men want to dance with me!" She fanned herself.

"Far too many," Kron muttered.

"Even with Jon next to her, Poor Kay is surrounded by noblemen. I don't know if she's going to faint or freeze them!"

Gwen plucked a pastry off of her plate and handed the rest of her food to one of the servers. "I suppose we'd better rescue her. Perhaps we could all dance a quadrille together."

"I don't know that dance, but I'd like to learn," Kron said to Ysabel.

Jenna hid a smile as she finished her wine. Kron must be worried Ysabel would prefer a younger man over him. Perhaps now that Jenna was settled, she could help her sister Avatars find suitable mates of their own. Summer was the best time to find a new love, but love had to be strong enough to last through all four seasons.

If love is strong enough, it will last. Jenna bit down a pang as Lex offered Gwen his free arm and she accepted. Both of them were honorable, so she also had to be honorable to be worthy of them.
Someday she and Gwen would be ready to love each other again. Until then, she would be happy with Lex.

The group proceeded into the ballroom to meet their future, one Jenna hoped would be full of love, laughter, and magic.

Author's Note

Thanks for reading my work; I hope you enjoyed it. If you did, please consider leaving a review. Reviews help other readers decide if a particular book is for them, and many advertisers require a certain number of positive reviews before accepting a book.

Although the deathbush is not based on a real plant, I drew inspiration for it from Amy Stewart's book *Wicked Plants: The Weed that Killed Lincoln's Mother and Other Botanical Atrocities.* Cocoa beans or pods can harm other plants, according to *The Triumph of Seeds: How Grains, Nuts, Kernels, Pulses and Pips Conquered the Plant Kingdom and Shaped Human History* by Thor Hanson. I have not found any data proving processed cocoa powder would be toxic to other plants, but for the purposes of this story I decided the powder would be effective against a fictitious plant.

Of all the Season Avatars, Jenna has the most interest in sex—and what we would consider the most liberal views on sex. Challen itself is more progressive on social issues than technologically-equivalent Victorian England. Those who for whatever reason do not wish to marry can dedicate themselves to the God of Summer or Goddess of Fall, like Ysabel's mother. Although Jenna might do this, Gwen wouldn't at this point of her life. She believes her duty to produce heirs is more important than her own desires. I've mulled over whether Gwen and Jenna would have a sexual relationship, but they're not ready for one yet. After so many lifetimes as spouses, they need time away from each other. That said, I have plans to continue writing in this world after the Season Avatars series finishes this particular story arc. Anything else I say at this point would be a potential spoiler, so you'll have to wait and see how the characters develop.

As always, thanks go out to my beta reviewers, Bert Hammerstead and Elizabeth Hull, for catching my mistakes and to Maria Zannini of

The Book Diva for creating the cover. I also thank my husband, Eugene, and my son, Alex, for putting up with my constant reading and writing.

There are two more novels planned in this series. As of May 2016, the first draft of Book Four, *Fifth Season,* is complete. I've also started the final book, *Summon the Seasons.* These books will feature Ysabel and Kay respectively. I also eventually plan to publish a short story collection featuring the Season Avatars. Please check my blog or website often to learn when these stories will be ready.

Thanks again for reading!

Best,

Sandra

The Season Avatars

(Names in parentheses are from the Avatars' first lives as shown in *Seasons' Beginnings*.)

Group 1 (Future Avatars)

Gwendolyn lo Havil (Galia)—Spring

Jenna Dorshay t'Reve (Janno)—Summer

Avatar Name: Jenna dor Treve

Ysabel s'Ivena Lathatilltin (Bella)—Fall

Avatar Name: Ysabel ava Sivena

Kay Seltich (Caye)—Winter

Avatar Name: Kay ava Seltich

Group 2 (Current Avatars)

Margaret gran Garnell (Magstrom)—Spring (deceased)

Charles vin Estcher (Carver)—Summer

Sophia vin Estcher (Sylva)—Fall

Dorian gran Garnell (Domina)—Winter

Group 3 (Past Avatars—all deceased)

Tylon fi Vort (Tylan)—Spring

Frederick min Jole (Flilya)—Summer

Helene ava Hartfut (Hala)—Fall

Olivia ava Kalt (Ocul)—Winter

Other Works By the Author

Science Fiction: Catalyst Chronicles Series

Lyon's Legacy
The Mommy Clone
Twinned Universes
Seasonal Stories from the *Sagan*

Non-Fiction

Life at Seventeen Syllables a Day: A Journal in Haiku
SF Women A-Z: A Reader's Guide

Fantasy: Short Stories

The Book of Beasts
Letters to Psyche
Silver Rain

Fantasy: Season Avatars Series

Seasons' Beginnings
Scattered Seasons
Chaos Season
Fifth Season (tentative publication late 2016)
Summon the Seasons (tentative publication 2017)

About the Author

Sandra Ulbrich Almazan started reading at the age of three and only stops when absolutely required to. Although she hasn't been writing quite that long, she did compose a very simple play in German during middle school. Her science fiction novella *Move Over Ms. L.* (an early version of *Lyon's Legacy*) earned an Honorable Mention in the 2001 UPC Science Fiction Awards, and her short story "A Reptile at the Reunion" was published in the anthology *Firestorm of Dragons*. Other works include the science fiction *Catalyst Chronicles* series, the fantasy *Season Avatars* series, *SF Women A-Z: A Reader's Guide,* and several science fiction and fantasy short stories. She is a founding member of Broad Universe, which promotes science fiction, fantasy, and horror written by women. Her undergraduate degree is in molecular biology/English, and she has a Master of Technical and Scientific Communication degree. She currently works for an enzyme company; she's also been a technical writer and a part-time copyeditor for a local newspaper. Some of her other accomplishments are losing on *Jeopardy!* and taking a stuffed orca to three continents. She lives in the Chicago area with her husband, Eugene; and son, Alex. In her rare moments of free time, she enjoys archery, crocheting, listening to classic rock (particularly the Beatles), trooping as a Jawa with the Midwest Garrison of the 501st Legion, and watching improv comedy.

Sandra can be found online at the following links:

website (www.sandraulbrichalmazan.com)
blog (www.ulbrichalmazan.blogspot.com)
Twitter (@ulbrichalmazan)
Facebook (SandraUlbrichAlmazanSffAuthor)

Goodreads (http://www.goodreads.com/author/show/5282664.Sandra_Ulbrich_Almazan).

www.ingramcontent.com/pod-product-compliance
Lightning Source LLC
Chambersburg PA
CBHW070915180626
46817CB00003B/1066